TWICE
AS
Wicked

Wicked Secrets Series

TWICE
AS

Wicked Secrets Series

ELIZABETH
BRIGHT

Entangled Publishing, LLC
2614 South Timberline Road
Suite 105, PMB 159
Fort Collins, CO 80525
rights@entangledpublishing.com

Scandalous is an imprint of Entangled Publishing, LLC.

Edited by Nina Bruhns
Cover design by Erin Dameron-Hill
Cover art from Deposit Photos

Manufactured in the United States of America

First Edition October 2017

SCANDALOUS

For Mom, who inspired my love of reading in general and Jane Austen in particular.

Prologue

1816, Northumberland, England

In their small village just outside of Berwick-upon-Tweed, Adelaide had always been known as the prettier of the Bursnell twins, while Alice was regarded as the smarter—or razor-tongued, as the more uncharitable of her set were wont to say. Which was ridiculous, Alice often thought indignantly but never said out loud, because both sisters were smart.

They were also identical. Same short, slender frame. Same eyes so dark they might as well be black, and same inky hair that framed a startlingly pale face. But—when Alice was honest with herself, which she nearly always was—Adelaide's sweet nature added an extra twinkle to her eyes and a pleasing curve to her lips that threw the balance in her favor.

Everyone loved Adelaide. Alice, most of all.

So, when Adelaide told Alice that she was in a "spot of trouble," Alice had wrapped her arms around her sister, held her tight, and murmured, "Oh, Adelaide. It will all be fine."

And Alice had believed it. As the daughter of Lord

Bursnell, Viscount Westsea, the sweet and lovely Adelaide had a sizable fortune. Most men would thank the stars of heaven for the good fortune of being trapped into marriage with such a charming lady. Surely, the man responsible for the "trouble" would stand up for her.

But no man had appeared to claim the lady, and no amount of threats or entreaties could make the lady name the man.

"You will bring ruin and shame on the family," Lady Westsea had argued. "Think of poor Alice. Who will marry her now? She's twenty!"

That had elicited a low growl from Alice. Adelaide was also twenty, after all, but no one ever feared that *she* would remain unmarried. Which was why the whole matter was so disconcerting. One expected Alice to get into mischief of one sort or another. But Adelaide? It was utterly unthinkable.

"You will never be allowed in society again," Westsea had bellowed.

Adelaide had merely pressed her lips tightly, shaken her head, and clung to the locket around her neck. The locket was identical to the one Alice wore—a two-inch oval of solid silver, engraved with the letter *A* and adorned with a single diamond, their birthstone. Each contained a picture of the other sister. This was their idea of a joke, of course. When they explained why it was so funny to wear a picture of someone who looked exactly like oneself but was most certainly not oneself, all they got was bemused looks.

When Adelaide began increasing, Westsea shipped his daughter to Our Lady of Good Tidings in France, with instructions to give the baby to an orphanage and for Adelaide to join the nunnery. The Bursnell family were members of the Church of England, but when one was ruined, it hardly mattered if one was Catholic.

Neither Adelaide nor the babe had survived the birth.

Lord and Lady Westsea had hidden the breakables—Alice, as the more tempestuous twin, never shied away from a scene—and informed Alice of Adelaide's demise as gently as they could.

Indeed, Alice would have obliged them in creating a scene, as she had a year earlier when her late fiancé had not returned from Waterloo, if only she could summon the requisite amount of passion. But she'd felt...nothing.

She'd wordlessly gotten to her feet, climbed the stairs to her bedroom, and shut the door.

When the door opened one month later, Alice was changed. Into what, she hardly knew, but she was certainly no longer herself. An irrevocable line had been drawn, separating the before from the after.

Before, she was a pair. She had always been a pair, for even longer than she had truly been a person at all. Before, she was a Bursnell Twin. She was Alice, of Alice-and-Adelaide. She had never been Just Alice.

After, she was Just Alice.

Just Alice was an empty shell.

It was Newton's Third Law of Motion: For every action, there is an equal and opposite reaction. Who was she, if not a reaction to Adelaide? She was nothing.

While Alice of Alice-and-Adelaide was high-spirited and energetic and could often be found dragging her sister into one scrape or another, Just Alice spent her time sitting quietly, her eyes tracing words that her mind never bothered to comprehend. Sometimes she remembered to turn the page, other times the book remained suspended, unmoving, for hours on end.

Then one day, Adelaide's effects arrived from across the Channel. Three plain dresses, a handful of letters from Alice, and her silver locket. The dresses were given to a maid, the letters burned, and the locket given to Alice.

Alice trailed her fingertip over the cool metal, tracing the curlicue on the letter *A*. For just a moment, she pretended that she wasn't Alice. She was Adelaide, abandoned to a nunnery, alone except for the nuns and other fallen ladies. How scared she must have been, facing the end of her confinement without her mother or her sister! How often had she opened the locket, seeking solace in the beloved face within?

Alice instinctively flicked the locket open.

And stared.

She stared harder.

Red-gold hair. Piercing blue eyes. A cleft in a strong chin.

It was not her face.

Good lord.

Queasiness shot through her stomach. It was the first thing she had felt in two months. It wasn't pleasant, by any means, but it was something.

She pried the miniature from its casing. It was a simple oil, but surprisingly detailed and lifelike for something so small. The materials were high quality. She turned it over. The initials NE were scratched into the wood. She turned it around again.

Who could it be, but Adelaide's lover?

Alice became aware of a curious sensation traveling through her limbs, filling all the spaces that had been a dark void since her sister's passing. It felt like poison, but Alice cared naught. At least she felt.

She knew he had money.

She knew his initials.

She knew his face.

It wasn't much, but it was enough.

She would find the villain.

And she would destroy him.

Chapter One

He saw her before she saw him.

Standing at the top of the staircase, Lord Nathaniel Eastwood, Viscount Abingdon, had an excellent view of the Duke of Wessex's ballroom and all its occupants—none of whom were half so beguiling as the stranger scowling into her lemonade. A huge crystal chandelier whirled dizzily overhead, casting a kaleidoscope of rainbows over the dark hue of her hair. It was impossible not to notice her. She was wearing a dress of rich red velvet, a vivid contrast to the other young maidens who were clothed in white and pale pastels.

She was, he told himself grimly, exactly the type of woman to put arsenic in one's porridge. It was, unfortunately, a topic with which he was intimately familiar.

And yet, he couldn't tear his eyes away.

Nathaniel hated balls. He hated London, too. Yet here he was, subjected to both horrors at the very same time, an unhappy circumstance he blamed entirely on Wessex. Every season it was the same thing. Wessex would lure Nathaniel from his peaceful estate in Hampshire with the promise of Something Important, which usually turned out to be a scrape involving a woman, who was, more often than not, married. Sometimes it was not even *that* and Wessex was merely bored.

Like this time.

All eyes were on them now. Nathaniel began to sweat. He felt their stares, and while he could not hear their whispers, he could easily imagine what they said. *There is the charming duke and his awkward friend.* Or perhaps they paid him no notice at all. People rarely did when he was standing next to the illustrious Wessex.

Nathaniel glanced at the lady in red. Then he looked away again.

He began to plot his escape. Surely, he could leave after half an hour? That would not be too rude, would it? By that point, Wessex would be occupied with his next victim and would barely notice his presence, anyway. Perhaps he would get a lemonade at the table where the lady in red was standing and then walk the perimeter of the room, saying hello to anyone necessary and leaving the rest alone. Then it would be safe to leave.

He would not dance, of course. Nathaniel never danced.

Again, he looked to the lady in red. Again, he looked away.

"She is something, is she not?" Wessex murmured by his side.

"Who?"

Wessex gave him a speaking glance. It had clearly not escaped his friend's notice just which female had captured Nathaniel's attention. "The lady in red." He eyed the girl speculatively. "A bit sullen, perhaps, but that just adds to her charm. One gets the instinctive feeling that she would not bore a man with chatter of bonnets. If her dance card is not yet full, it will be when I'm through with her." He spoke with the cocky assurance of a man whose advances were never spurned.

"Hmm." Nathaniel grunted noncommittally. Lord Sebastien Sinclair, Duke of Wessex, was a rake. One couldn't expect a rake to ignore a specimen like the lady in red. Why should Nathaniel care if Wessex danced one, three, or twenty dances with the girl? He did not care. But he did want to give his friend a small push down the marble staircase—not enough to kill him, but enough to leave him bruised and unable to dance. Call it an occupational hazard. A rake had to expect the occasional push down a stairway.

Nathaniel was *not* a rake. He was too brusque to be charming and too unfashionable to be dashing. And as he was already in peril of being pushed down any number of staircases, he felt no need to add to the danger with scorned ladies and cuckolded husbands.

Which was why he had no intention of making the acquaintance of the lady in red. She could take her silky hair and her lovely throat and that adorable scowl and go to—

Their eyes met.

Chapter Two

It was him.

Alice was certain of it.

Finding a man based on nothing more than a portrait in a locket, without knowledge of his name, country, or position in life, had proved to be a formidable task, even for one as adept at solving puzzles as she.

It had been a long year, one culminating in several dead ends. But the social season had started, and where else would a rake be during the social season but London? She had been happy to avoid the London season heretofore—first by being affianced, and then by mourning when her fiancé was killed in the final fight with Napoleon—but this year she had been determined to go. For once, her parents were in complete agreement with her scheme, for she, having reached the ripe old age of two and twenty, was in danger of being on the shelf. She was in desperate need of a London season before she expired altogether. So, she had been packed off to London, with her aunt, Lady Beatrice Shaw, serving as her chaperone.

So here she was, in London, and here *he* was, in the very

same ballroom!

Her pulse skittered like a rabbit. She stood frozen, her lemonade halfway to her lips. Every moment of the past year had been dedicated to finding this man, and now that they were face-to-face, she had no idea what to do with him. Did he recognize her, the duplicate of her sister? Oh, surely he did! That intense gaze was too much for a stranger.

Everything about him was too much, actually. He was too tall, his clothes ill-fitting and too large for his body. And that hair! It had grown since he sat for the portrait. Instead of being cropped close to his head, it was unfashionably long, swirling around his face and neck like a lion's mane. In short, he was nothing like the rake she expected.

But he remained Adelaide's seducer and abandoner, and for that he must be punished.

The question remained of how. If only it weren't so hard to think with the spinning chandelier creating a halo of light around his head. He had no right to look so angelic.

She slowly thawed, took a sip of lemonade, and cocked her head to the side to further assess the situation.

Surely, chandeliers were not supposed to spin?

She glanced around. It was clear that the man-lion and his companion had caught the notice of several ladies in attendance. She turned to the lady next to her. "Who is that man?"

"The Duke of Wessex. He is the host, but he has a habit of arriving late to his own parties. I do hope he intends to dance," the lady said.

A duke? Adelaide's seducer was a *duke*? That would make revenge more difficult, but certainly not impossible. A duke could be made to bleed just the same as any other man, she supposed.

"I do love a dark-haired man, don't you? It's so elegant," the lady continued.

Ah. She was referring to his companion, then. "And the other?"

For a moment, the lady looked confused. Then she frowned. "Oh, him. Viscount Abingdon. He never dances, and thank the heavens for that. He is clumsy as an ox."

Excitement rippled through the ballroom like a wave, but no one seemed the least perturbed about the chandelier rippling above his head. They carried on with the dancing and the gossiping without a care in the world. Alice set her drink down and frowned at the ceiling. The chandelier was an elegant monstrosity of at least seven feet, perhaps even eight. It was tiered like a wedding cake, with each tier holding dozens of candles. And it was spinning dizzily on its axis.

And yet...none of the other chandeliers were spinning.

She shifted her gaze between the three chandeliers that graced the ballroom. Was it her imagination, or was this one hanging significantly lower?

It dropped another inch.

She rubbed her eyes and walked closer to the stairs.

Another inch.

"Look out!" she cried, darting up several steps.

The man-lion looked at her curiously and said nothing.

Yet another inch.

Dear God.

She hitched up her dress and barreled up the stairs. If the great oaf would not remove his person from imminent death, then, by God, she would move it for him.

By the time she reached the landing she had built up enough speed to act as a human cannonball. Soft flesh collided with hard muscles, and her whole length from knee to chest pushed against him. He yielded, stumbling backward, taking her with him. The momentum sent them sliding across the slick marble foyer until they stopped in an abrupt tangle of limbs several feet away.

Panting heavily, she took a deep breath and inhaled a lungful of his scent—clean and spicy and male. It did very little to tame her breath or slow her rapid heartbeat. He lay still and silent beneath her, his arms locked about her waist in a rigid vise.

Why, why, *why* wasn't he speaking? Had she knocked him senseless?

"I must say," a smooth voice drawled, "what the devil?"

The face of Duke Wessex hovered above them. Alice tried to push away from the tangle of limbs to stand up, but the arms binding her did not loosen their grip. She might as well be wrapped in steel cords.

"Let go of me at once!" she commanded.

The man-lion stared up at her. He did not speak. Neither did he release her.

A strand of his red-gold mane stuck to her cheek and tickled her nose. She managed to pry one hand free and swatted his hair away from her face. He lifted an eyebrow, and she glared in return. She hated him with the heat of a thousand burning suns—and yet, for the briefest moment, she regretted wearing gloves.

And then everything happened at once.

The chandelier fell like lightning and smashed like a thunderbolt, scattering shards of glass and wax through the air like rain. She felt herself rolled and pinned, shielded from the storm by his broad shoulders and strong back. She gripped the front of his shirt tightly in her fists, tucking herself in closer to him, and buried her face against his chest.

There were screams, and she was aware of men beating out the flames with their coats. And then…nothing. The ballroom went completely silent. She could hear nothing but the viscount's labored breathing.

"For the last time, and now I really must demand an answer, *what the devil?*" Wessex bellowed.

No one had an answer, but everyone had a response. The ballroom was again a bustle of noise and movement. Servants appeared to clean up the fragments of chandelier, and guests elbowed their way to the cloakroom. If the Duke of Wessex's ballroom was to crumble to the ground, they would rather watch it from the outside.

When Alice could see again, she found herself face-to-face with a white cravat.

When she could breathe again, she found her nostrils once more filled with her enemy's male scent—clean soap and balsam. It was rather like being in the Scots pine forest that bordered her parents' estate.

When she could think again, she hoped to God the villain wasn't mortally wounded. He couldn't die. Not yet, not before she had even begun to exact her revenge. Nothing but his long life full of abject misery would sate her.

Also, if he were mortally wounded, she would never get the oaf off her. He must weigh fifteen stone.

"Do get off the poor girl before you suffocate her to death," Wessex said.

The blue eyes above her flashed, and for a moment she was sure he would refuse the command, duke or no. But the arms loosened and he rolled off, allowing her to breathe again.

"Now, then," Wessex murmured. He stretched out his hand.

She took his assistance and allowed him to haul her gracefully to her feet. She smoothed a hand over her hair, determining whether everything was in place. It was not. The braid that had looped around her knot had come quite undone, and the curls that sprang around her face and neck were now flailing madly in all directions.

Bother.

"I know that introducing oneself is not at all the thing,

but we are beyond such conventions at the moment, are we not? I am Lord Sebastien Sinclair, Duke of Wessex. To whom do we owe our deepest gratitude for saving our lives?"

She gave her dress a firm shake to set the shape to rights again and dropped into a curtsy. "Miss Alice Bursnell, Your Grace." She glanced over her shoulder at the man still prostrate on the floor. She expected him to show some surprise at her name. After all, the last person he had seen with this face was called Adelaide, not Alice. But he did not so much as blink.

Was it possible he didn't recognize her? Her already-dark thoughts turned to thunderclouds. Perhaps the man bedded so many women they were all the same to him and he could not distinguish one lady from another, any more than he could fruit flies.

Oh, how she loathed him!

"Miss Bursnell." Duke Wessex bowed. "We thank you." Then he noticed that his friend had not yet risen. "Get up, man. Introductions must be made."

Alice turned to watch as he scrambled to his feet. There was nothing graceful about it. The man was simply enormous. He reminded her of an octopus, long limbs flailing, stuck on its back.

When he was finally upright, Duke Wessex clapped him on the back. "Miss Bursnell, allow me to introduce Lord Nathaniel Eastwood, Viscount Abingdon, whom you so cunningly assailed at the best moment possible."

Nathaniel Eastwood. *NE*.

There was no mistake.

She tried to curtsy but found that her knees refused to cooperate. Bow to her dear sister's seducer? Bow to the man who had ruined Adelaide and deserted her? No, indeed. She simply froze and glared at the man before her.

"Oh, *Alice*!"

She grimaced at the exasperated reproof in her aunt's tone as she bustled to the top of the stairs. Aunt Bea was a very plump woman, and she was breathing hard by the time she reached them. That did not stop her from talking, Alice noted. Nothing ever did.

"Please excuse Alice, Your Grace. Of course, we will make reparations. *Of course.* She didn't mean anything by it. She never does, you know." Aunt Bea fluttered her hands nervously before clasping them together.

Duke Wessex burst into laughter. "Quite all right, ma'am." He studied her carefully, then said, "I believe we have been introduced?"

"Yes, Your Grace. I am Lady Shaw." She curtsied.

"Ah." His expression cleared. "The late Baron Shaw's widow."

"And sister of Viscount Westsea, Your Grace. Miss Bursnell, his daughter, is my niece." She gestured to Alice, who curtsied yet again.

"Begging your pardon, ma'am," Viscount Abingdon interjected. They all turned to look at him. "But *what* didn't she mean?"

Aunt Bea fluttered her hands again and blinked her pale brown eyes rapidly. "My lord?"

"You said Miss Bursnell didn't mean anything by it, that she never does. What didn't she mean?" His smile was pleasant, but Alice detected a threat in that rough voice.

"Why, causing the chandelier to fall, naturally," Aunt Bea said.

Abingdon's smile, Alice noticed, didn't reach his eyes. "Oh? It was Miss Bursnell's doing, then?"

"Well, I didn't see it myself," Aunt Bea admitted. "But it seems the sort of mischief she would find herself in. She is forever having disasters."

"Oh, really, Aunt! I did nothing of the kind," Alice

protested, stamping her foot. Viscount Abingdon gave her a hard look and her insides shivered. She might be hell-bent on revenge, but how was he to know that? Anyway, *her* revenge would be a great deal subtler and more devastating than a falling chandelier. "How would I even accomplish such a thing, I ask you?"

Abingdon said nothing, but Duke Wessex tipped his head back and laughed. "How, indeed? I daresay you could do anything you put your mind to, Miss Bursnell. You did, after all, manage to save our lives quite nicely."

Alice dipped her chin in recognition of the compliment. "Thank you, Your Grace." She directed an icy glance at Lord Abingdon before turning to her aunt. "I must beg that we retire, Aunt. The excitement of the evening has left me quite weak."

Aunt Bea patted her arm reassuringly. "Of course, dear. Here, take my arm."

Alice did her best to appear subdued as they made their way to the ballroom doors, but inside she felt anything but weak.

She felt galvanized.

Yes, indeed. She had found her man.

And now she had a revenge to plan.

Chapter Three

Nathaniel watched Miss Bursnell exit with her aunt. She gave him one last glare over her shoulder as she swept from the room. His cheeks heated. Confound it, why was she looking at him like that? Had he not just saved her from a face full of crystal shards? True, she had tackled him first, and therefore might reasonably claim to have saved his life, but if he hadn't rolled, she would surely be disfigured. Or at least scratched. He hated to think of all that perfect porcelain marred.

Her back was straight as a maypole and there was no sign of droop or weariness in the tilt of her chin or quick step of her foot. Weak, she had claimed? No, she was not that.

"I do believe we shall be seeing more of Miss Bursnell," Wessex remarked. When Nathaniel raised a speculative eyebrow, he added, "Not on my account, I assure you."

Wessex did not intend to seek her out, then? That was unexpected. Miss Bursnell was, after all, female. "What do you mean?"

"Well," Wessex drawled. "We were both standing under that cursed chandelier, you realize."

Nathaniel furrowed his brow.

Wessex sighed. "We were both standing under the chandelier, and yet she only pushed *you* out of the way. Seemed hell-bent on saving you, in fact. I was left to my own devices to escape the danger, which I must say is not the usual treatment of a duke." He flicked a small crystal shard from his shoulder. "What do you make of that?"

Nathaniel watched Miss Bursnell's retreating form with a puzzled frown. If she had created the danger, why had she rescued him? What sort of assassin foiled her own plot? She did not strike him as a stupid woman. "I have absolutely no idea."

But he intended to find out.

Chapter Four

Alice's exploits at the ball made her a celebrity. Callers had been streaming into Aunt Bea's rose-colored drawing room since ten o'clock the next morning, an obscenely early hour according to Aunt Bea.

Alice was tired of the whole thing. If only they would go away and leave her to plot her revenge in peace! But she knew Aunt Bea was delighted with her newfound success. It had been two years since the death of her fiancé at Waterloo and one year since the death of her sister. Those years had been difficult and sad, and Aunt Bea was undoubtedly eager for Alice to set them firmly in the past and move forward with the business of living.

"You have spent so much time mourning the loss of loved ones," her aunt had argued when Alice had tried to escape the drawing room after the first wave of visitors. "It is time to put grieving aside and find a little joy."

Alice vehemently disagreed. Now was not the time for joy. Now was the time for vengeance. She could not simply set aside her grief for her sister, any more than she could set aside her love. They were mingled together, feeding off each other. She could not destroy her grief without first…not exactly *destroying* her love for Adelaide, but certainly diminishing it. As long as Adelaide remained in her daily thoughts, Alice would love her. And she would grieve her.

But she could not bear to disappoint her aunt, so she stayed put in the drawing room. Her current visitors, at least, were all females. They were silly females, to be sure, but at least they were not here to woo her.

"To think *you* saved the *life* of the Duke of Wessex!" Lady Claire Harrison exclaimed with a hand flutter and dreamy sigh. Alice gritted her teeth, but Lady Claire didn't notice. "Did you *actually touch* his person?"

"No, I did not."

The other girls looked at Alice expectantly, waiting for more, but she refused to utter another word, on the grounds that the conversation was rapidly approaching a level of ridiculousness that she refused to be a part of.

"It was Lord Abingdon that Alice *actually touched*," Miss Eliza Benton said, imitating Lady Claire's whispery tone. "I must advise you, Alice, that the next time you are faced with choosing between a viscount and a duke, you should aim for the duke."

The girls tittered, and Alice laughed outright. It was odd to hear such dry wit coming from such an angelic countenance. Miss Eliza Benton was as fair as Alice was dark. Her hair was so pale that it was almost white, her eyes were a lovely shade of aquamarine, and she possessed a dimple in each rosy cheek. She was the sort of woman one might mark as a rival, showing her nothing but friendliness to her face and nothing but judgment to her back.

Alice instantly adored her.

"I was very careless with my heroism," Alice agreed. "I really ought to have requested an introduction first!"

To which Miss Benton threw back her lovely head and laughed.

"Oh, *Alice*," Lady Claire said. "Do not fret, dear. I am *sure* his grace understands that you would have seen to *his* safety first, had you *known* who he was."

Alice hid her smirk behind her teacup. No doubt, Lady Claire would have shoved aside any number of viscounts to save a duke.

"It really is *such* a pity," Lady Claire continued. "Duke Wessex is *so* amusing and *affable*, and Lord Abingdon is... er, *not*."

Lady Claire emphasized nearly every other word, her voice going up and down like a warbler's. It gave Alice a mild bout of seasickness. But, at last, here was her chance to learn more of Viscount Abingdon! If only it did not require encouraging Lady Claire to talk.

"Oh, is he not?" Alice asked, then steadied her nerves against the onslaught.

"No, *indeed*!" Lady Claire exclaimed. "Lord Abingdon is *grouchy* and unbearably *smug*. I am sure he looks down on *us all*. He *never* comes to London, as he prefers his estate in Hampshire, *even* during the season. I daresay he *only* attended last night's ball to *appease* Duke Wessex. They are *good* friends, you know, though *heaven knows* for the life of me I cannot think *why*."

Up, down, *up*, down. Alice took a bracing sip of tea to calm her stomach.

"And he is *not* so *handsome* as Duke Wessex, either," Lady Claire continued, unaware that Alice was close approaching a very bad temper. "It is *truly inelegant* of him to be so *tall*."

"Yes, he really should do something about that," Miss Benton murmured to her teacup.

"And his *hair*!" Lady Claire giggled.

Miss Benton set down her teacup. "I believe he would hide behind that mane of his if he could. He is such a shy, suspicious man."

Before Alice could digest this information, Aunt Bea's butler interrupted.

"Begging your pardon, my lady," Carthright said. "Duke Wessex and Viscount Abingdon are here."

Aunt Bea straightened, her eyes brightening. "Show them in."

Viscount Abingdon entered the drawing room first and immediately found himself confronted with eight pairs of staring female eyes. He took a quick step back, and Alice thought he would have fled if Wessex had not blocked his path.

"Good day, ladies." Wessex bowed. His gaze landed on Miss Benton's golden head. "Ah, Miss Benton. Good day." He turned to the lady of the house. "Ma'am, Lord Abingdon and I have come to offer Miss Bursnell our most sincere thanks for saving our lives last night."

"She was delighted to be of assistance, Your Grace," Aunt Bea said. "Please, do sit down."

Wessex cast his eyes about the room. There were no seats to be had. Alice felt a moment of panic. They could not go! Surely, revenge could not be thwarted by something so trivial as a lack of chairs.

Fortunately, Miss Benton stood. "We really must be going. Thank you for the tea." She sent a look to Lady Claire and the others.

"Oh, *yes*, we *must* be going," Lady Claire said, springing to her feet.

The other girls followed suit.

Miss Benton curtsied to the gentlemen. "Do give my regards to your sister, Lady Freesia," she said to Lord Abingdon, who nodded in return.

The ladies exited. Viscount Abingdon and Duke Wessex sat down.

"May I offer you tea or refreshments?" Aunt Bea asked.

Alice truly loved her aunt, but if she did not cease that ridiculous nervous fluttering, Alice would be forced to bind her hands together with a hair ribbon.

"That would be lovely," Wessex said.

"I will ring for a fresh pot." Aunt Bea summoned the maid. "Now, then. We are so honored by your presence, Your Grace." She glanced at the corner where the other gentleman sat. "And, of course, by yours, as well, Lord Abingdon."

Lord Abingdon inclined his head in acknowledgment but said nothing. He had spoken not a word since his entrance. Miss Benton's words came back to her: *He is such a shy, suspicious man.*

He was even taller than she remembered, and his red-gold hair was tied back in an old-fashioned queue. She dug her fingernails into her palms against the nearly overwhelming urge to undo the ribbon and allow his hair to flow free. It was most unfair that the villain was blessed with a head of hair that any woman would envy. He was ridiculous, she decided. And so was his hair.

The tea arrived. "How do you take your tea, Your Grace?" Alice asked.

"Strong and plain, thank you."

Alice prepared the cup and handed it to Wessex.

"Lord Abingdon? How do you take your tea?"

The man started. "Ah."

Well. That was not very enlightening. Alice crinkled her forehead and waited. Lord Abingdon said nothing. *He looks down on us all*, Lady Claire had said. *He is a shy, suspicious man*, Miss Benton had countered.

Which was it?

A mottled flush formed on his cheeks. Alice cocked her

head to the side and considered. She rephrased the question. "Would you like milk, my lord?" When he nodded, she continued, "Sugar?" He shook his head. "Very well." She made the tea and handed it to him.

Miss Benton had the right of it, then. Viscount Abingdon was painfully shy and likely deeply suspicious to boot. Well, it served him right. If he insisted on gallivanting across England ruining defenseless maidens, he should jolly well suspect that around any corner might lurk a relative seeking revenge.

He was certainly shy and possibly suspicious in *her* company. How, then, was she to exact her revenge? How could she get close enough to ruin him? She must make him trust her, enough that he would let down his guard, let her through the protection that his shy and suspicious nature naturally afforded him.

An idea struck.

Shy or not, the man was a rake. Adelaide's fate had proven that. Therefore, he must get close to the women he seduced. She could use that against him.

As unsettling as it was to her nature, it could work.

Yes. She must make him *love* her.

Chapter Five

While Wessex prattled on to Baroness Shaw and Miss Bursnell, Nathaniel tried to collect himself. He was shaken to his core, but how it had come about, he could hardly say.

Miss Bursnell had simply asked how he took his tea. He had been prepared to answer. He was awkward and shy in company, to be sure, but even he could discuss tea like a proper English gentleman. But then he had looked up at those coal-dark eyes of hers and was assaulted with a sudden, irrefutable knowledge.

She *despised* him.

And he had quite simply lost his words.

Why and wherefore such passionate feelings against him? They had never laid eyes on each other before the evening prior. But hate him she did, that was undeniable. Even given his…unique family situation, he had never before been the recipient of such a hostile look.

Yet, she had done him a kindness in the very same moment. When she realized he had been struck dumb, she had asked him again, but in a way that allowed him to answer without words. She had not laughed, and he hadn't detected even a note of mockery in her tone or eyes. No, just abhorrence.

Why should she be kind when she hated him so?

He did not pretend to understand her.

He watched her from the safety of his rose-colored chair. She, too, sat on a rose settee. Was there a single item in this entire room that wasn't a shade of pink? The mauve carpet, he allowed, had a border of dove gray. And wasn't that a bit of gray trim on that cushion, there? Even so, it was a very pink room. It was a room clearly decorated by a lady who did not have a man's opinion to take into account.

Miss Bursnell, he noted, was not wearing mauve, nor any shade that could remotely be considered pink. She was wearing a dress of dark green, and he was glad of it. Pastels would not suit her, at all. She needed deep colors to bring warmth to that milk-white skin.

She was speaking, he suddenly realized, and looking at him. He ought to pay attention to her words, instead of admiring her complexion. If she asked him a question, he would not be able to answer. Although perhaps, given his response to the tea, she would expect that of him.

"I do so hope it will be fine tomorrow," Miss Bursnell said. "I am so very tired of all this rain. If I don't take some exercise out of doors soon, I shall scream."

"Oh, *Alice*," the baroness murmured reproachfully. "Do not exaggerate. Ladies do not scream."

Miss Bursnell bit her lip, lowering her gaze to the teacup on her lap. The girl was undeniably high-spirited. He doubted that Lady Shaw had meant to hurt her feelings—she seemed genuinely fond of her niece—but he couldn't help flinching on Miss Bursnell's behalf. He knew what it was to feel as if one never quite fit.

The next instant, she raised her head and he felt his soul

reeling back from the angry flash in her eyes. Deuce take it, he hadn't even spoken! Why did she sit and glare at him so?

Wessex, oblivious as always, looked toward the window. "I see the clouds clearing even as we speak. Tomorrow promises the return of the sun, mark my words. Perhaps you would care to join us for a morning ride tomorrow, Miss Bursnell?"

Us?

Nathaniel choked on his tea. He greatly valued his morning rides. They provided solitude at best and, at worst, an amusing conversation with Wessex. He had no intention of spending it in the company of Miss Bursnell. She might not threaten the same sort of danger as the simpering young misses who entered the marriage mart every year, but he was not safe from her. No, indeed, he was not.

And yet he could not very well abandon her to the charms of Duke Wessex, either.

It was a quandary, to be sure.

Baroness Shaw delicately cleared her throat. Wessex looked at her and immediately understood the problem. "I will send word to your friends, Lady Claire and Miss Benton, to join us. Lady Claire's mother will chaperone, I'm certain."

Nathaniel was in an agony of suspense. Would Miss Bursnell say yes? Would she say no?

"Thank you, Your Grace," she said. "A ride sounds absolutely lovely."

And then she turned to Nathaniel and did the very last thing he expected. She smiled.

Damnation! What did she mean by *that*?

Chapter Six

The moment Nathaniel stepped from the dowager baroness's home and onto the walking path he felt lighter. It was a relief to be free of Miss Bursnell's violent stares. They made his stomach shake and filled his mouth with sand. But now he was out in the brisk air, and Wessex was right. The sky was slowly turning from gray to blue, and the steady downpour had become a half-hearted drizzle.

It meant they could ride tomorrow morn.

"You are welcome," Wessex said suddenly.

Nathaniel shot him a baleful look. "And for what do I owe you thanks, pray tell?"

Wessex's gray eyes widened. "Why, for arranging the pleasure of Miss Bursnell's company, naturally." He grinned and slapped Nathaniel on the arm. "Do *not* try to say it won't be a pleasure. You could not keep your eyes off her. Any fool could see you are infatuated with the gel. And I, my friend, am no fool."

Nathaniel frowned as they walked. "I do not trust her, Wessex."

"As you trust no one, that is of little consequence." Wessex waved his walking cane dismissively.

"That is not true," Nathaniel protested. "I trust *you*."

"Just another example of your poor judgment. I am not to be trusted, I assure you. I can give you a long list of women who will verify that."

Nathaniel just laughed. Wessex might be a skirt chaser, but once his good opinion and friendship were earned, his loyalty was unwavering. They had been instant chums at Oxford. When Wessex had inherited his title at nineteen, he'd become quite maudlin for a period, mourning the death of his beloved father. When a classmate had said that Wessex should be a good deal more cheerful now that he was a duke, Nathaniel had given him a sound thrashing for his heartless comment. Nathaniel did not take familial deaths lightly.

Wessex had returned the favor the following year, when Nathaniel was accused of cheating on an exam. The duke defended him, and the professor, deciding that he would rather not make such a powerful enemy, allowed he was mistaken. A professor *could* be mistaken, now and again. A duke could not.

Even now, several years later, the memory rankled. Nathaniel had *not* cheated.

"And is Miss Eliza Benton on that list of women?" he teased.

Wessex grimaced. "Yes, indeed, although I am sure I don't know why. She has never willingly spent more than five minutes at a time in my company. Whenever I enter a room, she is sure to leave it."

Nathaniel arched an eyebrow. "And yet, you will invite her to ride with us tomorrow. Interesting."

"I couldn't resist, dear fellow. I simply could not resist."

Wessex looked so remorseful that Nathaniel was almost inclined to believe his friend might actually harbor feelings for the girl. He shook the thought away. Wessex didn't have feelings—not of *that* particular nature, anyway.

"Tell me, then," Nathaniel said. "If you invited Miss Bursnell on my behalf, and Miss Benton for your own interests, then what, pray tell, is the purpose of Lady Claire?"

Wessex gave a weed a vicious whack with his cane. "Isn't it obvious, dear fellow? Can you imagine a ride with Miss Benton's cruel wit and Miss Bursnell's remarkable ability to topple a man? We need a buffer. Miss Bursnell and Miss Benton are both quite terrifying."

Nathaniel would have laughed if it weren't so very true. Miss Bursnell *was* terrifying—and fascinating, in the manner of a praying mantis.

He must take great care not to lose his head tomorrow.

Chapter Seven

"Do you *think*, Miss Bursnell, that my horse is too *tall* for a *lady*?" Lady Claire clutched the sleeve of Miss Bursnell's deep-blue riding habit. "Surely, they have something smaller. If I fell from such a height, I would break my ankle, and then what? I would be in need of rescue, and the day would be spoiled."

It was the next morning, and the small riding party had gathered in front of the stables at Wessex's London townhouse, close to the park.

Lady Claire's horse, Nathaniel noted, was only slightly taller than a large pony.

Miss Bursnell closed her eyes briefly before answering. Unless he was very much mistaken, she was counting to ten. "The horse is just the right size," she said. "She is barely five hands. Anything smaller and your feet would drag in the dirt."

"You are a horsewoman, Miss Bursnell?" Wessex asked.

"I enjoy the animals a great deal, Your Grace." She gave her dappled gray a firm pat on the neck. "But my father once told me that anyone who called himself a horseman was sure to be thrown that very day. I think I shall try to avoid that particular fate."

Miss Benton joined them with a large bay. "Oh, I do hope that means you intend to go faster than a walk. I am desperate for exercise."

"Indeed, I do." Miss Bursnell smiled. "I—"

"Oh, but I do think a *walk* in Hyde Park would be *just* the thing," Lady Claire interrupted. "Surely, it is *not safe* for us to go at a *faster* pace. It is so *crowded* today."

Miss Benton gave Lady Claire a haughty look. "I will gallop."

"Surely not." Lady Claire looked appalled.

Miss Benton did not budge. "Surely, I will."

"Surely not."

Nathaniel, seeing no end to the argument, decided it would be best to leave the ladies to their disagreement and go see about his mount. To his surprise, Miss Bursnell followed him. He could feel her eyes on him as he took the reins from the groom.

Why did she not speak? Was she trying to drive him mad?

"Good morning, Lord Abingdon," she said finally. "It's a lovely day for a ride, is it not? I daresay the rain was afraid to show its face after the duke promised it to be fair."

Nathaniel was halfway up to the saddle when she spoke. His left foot was in the stirrup, bearing nearly all his body weight, one hand at the horse's neck with the reins, and the other on the back of the saddle. He froze where he was, neither on the ground nor fully mounted, and stared down the other side of the horse at Miss Bursnell.

And said nothing.

She raised both eyebrows. "My lord?" she said uncertainly.

He felt such a fool, dangling from the saddle by one leg, but he couldn't muster words for the life of him. Her loathing had surprised him yesterday, and now he felt it again, even as she stood there uttering banal pleasantries. Her words were gentle, her lips smiled, but oh, her eyes! How they said everything her words did not!

What he had done to deserve such animosity?

So, he stayed mute, standing on one stirrup, hovering above the saddle, his right leg not yet swung over to the other side, staring down at her with what he imagined was a very stupid expression on his face.

She stared back at him assessingly. Finally, she broke her gaze. "I believe I shall go assist Duke Wessex in settling the disagreement between my friends," she murmured. "Excuse me."

Nathaniel was flooded with relief. She had again spared him the seemingly impossible task of speaking in her presence.

It was at that exact moment he felt himself no longer supported. He slid to the ground in a heap, still holding the saddle in his hands. He stared up at the sky. How was it that he was here, on his back in the dirt, instead of in the saddle where he belonged? He seriously regretted his decision to get out of bed that morning.

He felt himself relieved of the saddle's weight a moment later. Miss Bursnell's white face and black hair gazed down at him, aghast.

"Lord Abingdon," she said gravely. "Are you unharmed?"

"Quite," he said as haughtily as possible, given that once *again* he was prostrate at the woman's feet. No matter. At least he had recovered his voice.

She set the saddle down and offered him her hand. When he hesitated, she said, "I am strong enough, my lord. I won't let you fall."

Still he hesitated, staring into her black eyes, and considered her offer.

He could not. No, he could not.

"Miss Bursnell, please go away."

She set her lips in a thin line and dropped her hand to her side. "Very well, my lord. I withdraw my offer." She turned her back to him and immediately engrossed herself with combing her fingers through the horse's mane.

He bit back a growl. He had angered her by refusing her help. But why the devil had she offered to begin with? Could she not see how that would simply humiliate him further? A man's pride could only take so much.

Still, he had been abominably rude. One did not tell ladies to go away.

He gathered himself to his feet, dusted himself off, and turned to her. Her back was still to him, but he could see her shoulders shaking. Dear God, had he made her *cry* with his rudeness?

He cleared his throat. Miss Bursnell seemed not to have heard. Her shoulders still shook.

"Ahem," he said, and cleared his throat again. She did not turn. He gingerly laid a gloved hand on her shoulder. Even with the riding habit, he could feel the shape of her bones and muscles, soft and round, yet firm and strong. She was small, but she was not fragile.

She turned with a start. Her face was dry. Her eyes were not red, but sparkling. Miss Bursnell wasn't crying, at all. She was laughing.

At *him*.

"Excuse me," he said stiffly. He took a quick step back. "Carry on with your mirth, by all means."

And so she did!

His face heated as waves of rollicking giggles bubbled out of her. If she had been Wessex, he would have joined in. But Miss Bursnell wasn't Wessex. She was a harpy sent to destroy him. Or at the very least, embarrass him. While a tease from

Wessex could be considered all in good fun, he did not feel the same way with Miss Bursnell laughing at him.

He swiftly turned away from her and picked up the saddle. He brushed it off and examined it carefully. The girth had given out. That was why the whole saddle had slid off with his weight.

"Abingdon! What sort of blasted trouble have you gotten yourself into now?" Wessex demanded, striding over. Then he noticed the lady. "Begging your pardon, Miss Bursnell. I certainly wouldn't have used such language if I had known a lady was present."

Miss Bursnell merely waved her hand. She was still laughing too hard to respond.

"I require a new saddle," Nathaniel said. He showed Wessex the damage.

The duke's smile was immediately replaced with a frown. They locked eyes. Wessex opened his mouth to speak, but Nathaniel shook his head, nodding in the direction of Miss Bursnell.

Wessex understood. He turned to a groom. "You there! We require a new saddle before our ride."

"Yes, Your Grace." The groom bowed and ran off toward the stable.

Nathaniel followed him, setting his mouth in a grim line. If someone had planned to do away with him today, he—or she—was in for a disappointment. "Thank you. But I prefer to choose my own."

Chapter Eight

What had *that* been all about?

Alice rode beside Eliza. Behind them was Lady Claire, at a very sedate walk. Ahead of her were Viscount Abingdon and Duke Wessex. She watched the viscount thoughtfully. Again, she asked herself, what was that all about? Why had Abingdon been so upset by the damaged saddle?

Leathers sometimes wore out from use, as everyone knew. And while it was grossly irresponsible for the groom not to have examined them before tacking up the horse, it had looked like just that—an irresponsible accident. She'd given the girth one sharp glance when Lord Abingdon showed it to Duke Wessex, and it didn't appear to her to be a clean cut. It had simply looked worn through.

But if it was an accident, why had they acted so strange? The duke had looked so very serious when he saw the rip. Did he suspect foul play?

More important, was there any way to use the incident to her advantage?

Wessex and Abingdon drew their mounts to a stop. "We

have come to a split in the path," Wessex said. "Ladies, the choice is yours."

"*Shall* we continue the path?" Lady Claire said behind them. "If we *turn*, the path is not so full of *friends*. We shall be quite *alone* with our little *party*."

Alice gazed wistfully at the turn. If they stayed on their current path, they would continue at this abominable speed, or perhaps even slower, as they would be obliged to stop every three steps to greet acquaintances. If they turned, however, they might be able to trot a pace, or perhaps even canter.

As if reading her mind, Miss Benton grinned. "Then, by all means, let us turn at once."

"Oh, *Eliza*, you don't *truly* mean to *gallop*, do you?" Lady Claire protested. "You *can't*! Galloping is *forbidden* in the park."

"Then perhaps you should keep quiet so we are not caught."

Seeing a return to the earlier argument, Alice rolled her eyes heavenward and gritted her teeth. It was the first sunny day in a fortnight of rain. Likely, it would be followed by *another* fortnight of rain. This was not how she wished to spend her morning exercise.

She signaled her horse to the turn and urged it to a trot, and then a canter, which was an easier gait to ride when one was inhibited by a sidesaddle. The trot, though slower, was much rougher on a body.

For a moment, she simply enjoyed the sharp wind on her face and the easy rocking of her mount. Then she pulled to a gentle stop and sighed. If she were at home, she would have spent the morning galloping the fields of Colworth, her family estates—astride if there was no one to see her. But she was not at Colworth, she was in London, and her friends were waiting for her, likely still arguing.

She heard hoofbeats approaching and turned around.

Lord Abingdon drew up next to her and stopped.

"Lord Abingdon," she murmured. "I suppose you were sent to reprimand me?"

"Not at all. Lady Claire was sure your horse had run away with you and that you were in need of assistance."

"Ah." Alice grimaced. Lady Claire had perhaps dissolved in hysterics. She seemed the type. "I *do* hope she did not *swoon*."

Lord Abingdon's mouth twitched, but if he noticed her imitation of Lady Claire's whine, he did not say so. "She did not swoon. Although she did say this was what came of ladies riding tall horses." His lips twitched again.

Alice stared at him. Was he trying not to laugh? No, Lord Abingdon was devoid of humor. He could barely string a sentence together. How such a dull man had seduced her sister was beyond her comprehension. Although, to be sure, Adelaide preferred moody heroes to humor, so perhaps Lord Abingdon had suited her quite well.

Alice sighed. She did not want to go back, but neither could she stay here with him, unchaperoned as she was. "Shall we join our friends?"

"By all means." He turned his chestnut around, and Alice followed.

When they approached their friends, Eliza saw them and smiled. "See now, she has returned, and all in one piece."

"*Alice!*" Lady Claire shrieked. The shrill tone nearly drove Alice to turn back once again, this time at a gallop, forbidden or no. "You *poor* thing!"

Alice hid her chuckle behind a gloved hand. "Yes, I feel quite faint from my adventure. The beast just ran away with me!"

Lord Abingdon coughed in his hand. "Did it, indeed?" His voice was low so only she could hear. "How frightening. You must be an excellent horsewoman, Miss Bursnell, for you looked remarkably in control."

Alice arched an eyebrow. "Did I? Thank you, my lord. That is a very kind compliment."

They stared at each other.

He really was a most insufferable creature.

Even if his eyes were very, very blue.

Chapter Nine

Nathaniel was uncertain about the girth. Had it been cut intentionally? Or had it merely worn through? Yesterday after their ride, he had examined it closely, as had Wessex, and neither was sure. If it had been intentional, it was certainly well done and looked like an accident. It was not a clean break, the hallmark of foul play.

Perhaps the damage was just a coincidence.

Nathaniel was even more uncertain as to the validity of coincidences, particularly when the coincidence involved his life. Since the age of sixteen, he'd had more than a dozen narrow escapes. Surely, he could not be as accident-prone as all that.

And once again, Miss Bursnell had been present at the mishap. He was even more mistrustful of Miss Bursnell than he was of coincidences and broken girths. He was certain she despised him, but the whys and wherefores of the matter remained a mystery.

It bothered him. Dash it all, it bothered him.

He was quite aware that women did not like him. His

suspicious nature turned them away. He was not charming, he was not effusive with compliments, and his tall frame was not at all the thing. He had no style, thanks to his habit of wearing clothing too large—the better to disguise the location of his vital organs should someone be attempting to seek them out with a bullet.

He had once been a favorite with the mamas—having both a title and wealth. But even if a mama could convince her daughter to have him, he could never quite rid his mind of suspicion toward the girl, no matter how meek and biddable she seemed. After several years, even the most ardent social climbing mamas had given up, until women as a whole rarely looked his way. So, he was used to women not thinking of him, either good or ill.

But Miss Bursnell was not indifferent to him, unlike all other ladies. Her soul was burning in response to his—and not the romantic sort of burning, either. This was the fire-and-brimstone sort of burning. The only safe thing to do was flee. Which he had, as soon as their ride had concluded.

His Aunt Lydia, the Dowager Marchioness Breesfield, was in London as the sponsor of his younger sister, Freesia. She'd taken on the role that would normally fall to their mother, while Lady Wintham cared for Mama. The Dowager Marchioness and Freesia were staying in St. James's Square.

He needed safe harbor. And perhaps a second opinion.

And so, the next morning, there he went.

He found his aunt in her square, pleasingly appointed sitting room overlooking St. James's Street. She was slim and tall, like all the members of the Eastwood family. Her hair, in the family shade of red-gold, was elegantly coiffed despite the early hour and unexpected visit. But there were threads of silver near her face. Time was continuing its relentless march, whether he wished it to or no.

"Aunt Lydia!" He strode across the room and would

have kissed her cheek if he hadn't been waylaid by a ball of nervous energy throwing herself in his arms.

"Nate! Oh, Nate!" Freesia kissed his cheek emphatically. "I did not know you were in London! Did you know, Aunt Lydia? I am so glad you have come, Nate. I have been introduced to the queen! I did *not* trip on my curtsy, as Aunt Lydia was afraid I would do. Will you be at my coming out on Friday? Oh, say you will! I am dreadfully afraid I will not dance every dance. I could not bear to be a failure."

"There, now." Aunt Lydia sighed, but smiled fondly at his sister. "You have asked two questions, and not paused even once for an answer. Give the man some room to speak, my dear."

Nathaniel chuckled and held Freesia by the shoulders. "Have you grown? How is it possible? I just saw you a month ago."

A smile burst on her face. "It is the Eastwood way. I shall be as tall as Papa before I am done!"

Nathaniel smiled back. His sister was certainly an Eastwood, although she wore it rather better than he, in his opinion. Her height looked elegant on her, and the copper locks more graceful than wild. Her blue eyes were several shades darker than his, more sapphire than aquamarine. Freesia would, in his estimation, be a smashing success on the marriage mart.

"Sit down, Nathaniel," Aunt Lydia commanded. "And tell us what brings you to see us at this ungodly hour."

"I intend to leave London." He looked at his aunt rather than his sister. He did not wish to see her disappointment.

His aunt gazed steadily back at him. "I see."

"Nate!" Freesia was appalled. "The season has not even truly begun! You cannot leave. Aunt Lydia, do make him be reasonable."

Aunt Lydia lifted her lorgnette to her eyes and peered

at him. "I was told that you nearly met your death by falling chandelier. It was the very day we arrived in London."

"Oh, surely, you don't think—" Freesia broke off, flustered. "He never would. Never."

Nathaniel regarded her kindly. Naturally, she would not wish to believe their own brother had attempted fratricide. He didn't much like the thought himself and avoided it whenever possible.

The marchioness tapped her lorgnette against her palm and considered the options. "You cannot leave London, Nathaniel," she said finally. "You must not seek refuge at Haverly Place. He will expect that. If there has been another attempt on your life, whoever caused it, you are safest here, surrounded by your family and friends. There is no one back at Haverly to protect you."

Haverly was the family estate in Hampshire, now deserted save for the servants.

"Nate does not need protection from our brother," Freesia muttered.

"Perhaps not," Aunt Lydia conceded. "But the fact remains that the elder sons in the Eastwood family generally do not live long enough to inherit the title, and second sons always seem to be nearby during the unfortunate accidents. Nathaniel does well to be on his guard."

"Oh, really, Aunt!" Freesia protested. "I suppose you also believe Grandfather poisoned Great Uncle Philip? I don't recall a deathbed confession."

"I don't recall a firm denial, either," Aunt Lydia retorted.

"Undoubtedly, he did not wish to point the finger at Uncle Philip's wife. A wife is much more likely to poison one's porridge, if you ask *me*," Freesia said.

"If it is Nick—and I am not saying it is," Nathaniel added hastily before Freesia could defend him once more, "he may very well have an accomplice."

"Oh?" The marchioness peered at him through her lorgnette. "Anyone in particular?"

Nathaniel hesitated. One did not simply slander a lady, no matter how deep one's feelings of foreboding. "Perhaps I am being overly distrustful. It may all be a coincidence."

Aunt Lydia tapped her foot impatiently. "*What* was a coincidence?"

"There was a particular lady present, both at the ball when the chandelier fell and yesterday, when the girth of my saddle broke." He flushed slightly, the embarrassment of both moments still vivid in his mind. "I do not see how she could accomplish either task, mind you. I only note that she was there. Both times."

"It may be a coincidence, but it *is* a suspicious coincidence," Aunt Lydia agreed. "Who is the lady in question? Come now, out with it."

Nathaniel surrendered. "Miss Alice Bursnell."

The marchioness dropped her lorgnette in surprise. "Viscount Westsea's daughter? Surely not."

Now it was Nathaniel's turn to be surprised. "You know the lady?"

Aunt Lydia gave a slow shake of her head. "I have not been introduced to Miss Bursnell, but I know the name. The Bursnells are a good family. There are two of them, are there not?"

Nathaniel wrinkled his brow. "Two what?"

"Daughters." Aunt Lydia looked at the ceiling, searching her memory. "Yes, I believe Lady Westsea was also blessed with twins."

"If Miss Bursnell has a twin sister, she has never mentioned her in my presence." He frowned. One might say this was yet another coincidence.

"And Miss Bursnell is the reason you wish to flee London?" Aunt Lydia asked. When he nodded, she smiled a slow, feline smile. "My dear boy, have you never heard the saying, keep your friends close and your enemies closer?"

He shuddered. He preferred his own strategy of running away as quickly and as far as possible. It had always worked for him in the past, after all.

But he was no coward. And besides, Freesia would have his head if he left the city before her coming out ball. It was his duty as her brother to attend.

Therefore, there was no choice. He would stay in London.

Even if it meant his demise.

Chapter Ten

Things were going rather well, Alice decided. She had not seen Lord Abingdon since their ride last week, but she had a thick stack of calling cards and invitations. Surely, one of those invitations would afford her the opportunity to meet with him again.

Revenge would soon be hers.

The thought was enough to put her in a cheerful mood, despite the gray skies and intermittent drizzle. She would not allow the weather to deter her from taking in the sights of London. She had always loved history. As a child, she would beg for more lessons even after suffering through French, philosophy, and literature.

She would spend the day at Westminster Abbey, soaking up the architecture and antiquity.

She donned her new pair of Nankeen half boots—much to her aunt's consternation. They were the latest thing, and therefore Aunt Bea heartily disapproved. Aunt Bea would go to her grave believing that a lady's foot belonged in a satin slipper, and if the satin slipper could not withstand the weather, then neither could the lady.

If Mary, Alice's maid, agreed with Aunt Bea about what constituted proper activities for a lady on a rainy day—and Alice suspected she very much did—she did not say. Mary did, however, sigh deeply for every wrong turn Alice led them down, and say in tones of infinite patience, "This way, my lady."

Finally, the western towers loomed above her in all their gray, austere glory. Alice tipped her umbrella back and gazed up, mesmerized. Oh, the creations of man! Stone by stone, day after day, unrelenting labor, and, lo! A masterpiece was born.

"Can you imagine, Mary? Once all these stones were buried in the earth. And now they are...*this*!" She gestured with one arm toward the abbey.

Mary sniffed. "It is raining on your face, my lady."

Alice sighed. One could not expect pragmatic Mary to exalt in the wonders of mankind's creation.

"Seven hundred years, and it's not yet finished," a voice said behind them. "Perhaps it never will be. Every monarch wishes to leave his mark."

It was a voice that was fast becoming familiar to her. A soft, deep voice, like a velvety growl.

What astounding luck!

She turned and curtsied. "Lord Abingdon. What are you doing here?"

"I come here on occasion to ponder deep questions." He said it lightly, as a joke, but it seemed to her he was telling the truth.

"Pray, do not let us interrupt your solitude," she said, smiling. She headed toward the entrance. It was better not to act too eager with a man so shy. She did not want to risk frightening him off. It was a miracle he had managed to untie his tongue to speak to her at all.

"May I accompany you inside? I am familiar with the abbey and would gladly offer you my knowledge."

"Thank you. That would be delightful." She bit her lip against the temptation to crow. Things could not have gone better if she had planned them herself. Fate had delivered him straight into her clutches. It was a sign from heaven.

He offered his arm, and she took it. She could feel his muscles through his coat. She had thought him rather too thin for his height, but lean did not mean weak, she realized now. Suddenly, she remembered that she had been wrapped in those arms after the chandelier fell. Her face felt hot against the cool air, and she lowered her head to hide her flush.

No, he wasn't weak.

He glanced at the muddy hem of her skirt. "I hope your walk was not too uncomfortable. London can be very dirty."

She gathered herself and said, "I don't mind, although I daresay it took rather longer than it ought. I am horrible with direction. If Mary had not been with me, I would be halfway to France by now, and only stopped because of the Channel."

He chuckled. "It is challenging to get one's bearings when you can barely see the sky for the buildings. Shall we begin with the tomb of Edward the Confessor?"

"If you please, my lord."

They entered the chapel. The shrine was a tall pillared square of marble, flanked on either end by a large candle.

"Perhaps you know that King Edward built the abbey as penance for missing a pilgrimage to Rome," Lord Abingdon said, watching as she examined the mosaic. "His shrine is considered the center of Westminster Abbey."

"Considered?" Alice frowned. "Is it not the actual center, then?"

"I very much doubt it, with all the additions and changes through the years, but it is called the center, and it is surely the *heart* of the abbey."

"Ah." She turned her attention to the inscription and read aloud, translating from Latin as she went. "Edward, hero and saint, preeminent in all the praises of his virtues. Dying in 1065, he ascends above the heavens. Lift up your hearts. John Feckenham, Abbot." She gave a small nod of satisfaction. "How lovely."

"Shall I tell you what it said before the shrine was despoiled in 1540?"

She glanced up in surprise. "Please do."

He quoted formally, "In the thousandth year of the Lord, with the seventieth and twice hundredth with the tenth more or less complete this work was made, which Peter the Roman citizen brought to completion." Here, Lord Abingdon paused, straightened, and placed one hand dramatically over his heart. His voice became a haughty whine. "O man, if you wish to know the cause, the king was Henry, the friend of the present saint."

Alice gave an unladylike snort. "Humph! Wasn't that just like a man, making it all about himself?" She glanced quickly around. Would she be struck down by lightning?

But no heavenly censure occurred. Henry III was, after all, a very distant king.

"I daresay that is the theme of all places of worship," the viscount said drily.

She let out a hoot of startled laughter. Had the man just made a joke? She had not expected him to have a sense of humor, much less a ready wit. "Oh, my. You should not say such things." She laughed again. "Even if it is true."

He clasped his hands behind his back and rocked on his heels. She feigned interest in a stained glass window while she observed her nemesis. It was curious. Up close, he was ridiculously handsome, but not in the style Adelaide had always preferred. He was hardly the dandy of her sister's dreams. His coat never fit as it ought, his hair was too long to be fashionable, and anyone with eyes could see he did not care about the knot of his cravat.

Her gaze caught on the objectionable cloth, held there by a strange longing to smooth and straighten and…and…

Oh, heavens. She tossed the feeling aside. It was nothing more than the innate desire of all women to tidy up the messiness of men. She most certainly did *not* wish to touch the gentleman's cheek or take the measure of his square jaw with her fingers.

No, she most certainly did not.

Chapter Eleven

Miss Bursnell had laughed at his joke.

To Nathaniel's recollection, it was the first time anyone other than Wessex had ever laughed at his joke. No one ever thought him amusing. Least of all ladies.

He wished to repeat the experience, to say something clever and have her respond with that spontaneous mirth, but his tongue suddenly swelled to twice its normal size and his brain filled with cotton.

She was watching him, he realized, likely wondering why he had not spoken a single word in the last five minutes.

The back of his neck prickled with sweat. He should say something. But what? He looked at the lady. She looked back steadily.

Dear God. Say something.

He offered his arm again, rather desperately throwing himself on the mercy of convention. "Shall we continue to the coronation chair?"

"By all means." She took his arm and they set off, her

maid following several steps behind.

"I come here, sometimes, to think," he said as they entered the throne room.

"Do you?" The heels of her boots clicked pleasantly against the floor as they walked. "I have always wanted to see the Stone of Scone."

"It is a good story," he said, though admittedly, it did hit a bit close to home for his comfort.

"Tell it to me."

He looked at her, startled. "Surely, you already know it?"

"I wish to hear it from you." Her eyes did not move from his face. "We all have our own way of telling a story, do we not, Lord Abingdon? What you say, what you do not say, these things are more about *you* than about the story itself. That is what is interesting to me."

He regarded her with narrowed eyes. "Miss Bursnell, I do believe you are a bluestocking!"

She laughed. "Perhaps I am, my lord."

"Very well. I will tell you the story." He paused, circling his thoughts. "Once upon a time, as the saying goes, two brothers were born to Isaac. They were born mere seconds apart, with the younger grasping the heel of the elder. The elder was called Esau, and the younger was Jacob. Esau, as the elder, was entitled to the birthright and blessing."

He could feel her eyes on him, but he kept his own firmly on the throne before him.

"Esau did not value his birthright, and Jacob valued it, perhaps, too much," Nathaniel continued. "Esau traded his birthright to Jacob for a bowl of beans. Jacob then tricked Isaac into giving him the blessing, as well, and Esau begged for a lesser blessing. And so things continued. Neither behaved well, and they tormented each other. Jacob was loved, and Esau was less loved. It made him bitter, and he attempted to murder his brother. Jacob escaped and fled. He stopped at night and lay down, taking a rock for a pillow. That night he had a vision from God, wherein He promised to bless him and his descendants." Nathaniel paused and gestured to the coronation chair. "The rock he used for a pillow is the Stone of Scone."

Miss Bursnell breathed in a slow, deep breath. "Fascinating."

He arched an eyebrow. "Was my way of telling the tale interesting to you?" he teased.

"Oh, yes." She twirled the tip of her umbrella against the marble floor. "If I had told the story, you would have heard how Edward the First brought the stone to Westminster Abbey as a spoil of war. I would have laid out all the theories. Is it the Stone of Scone that lies beneath the chair before us, or is it not? Where lies the true Stone, if not in King Edward's Chair? Undoubtedly you would realize from *my* telling of the story that I enjoy a good mystery, and revel in the pursuit of solving a puzzle."

A feeling of unease settled in his stomach.

"But you chose to tell me of Jacob and Esau. What, I wonder, is the significance of that story to you?" She regarded him carefully. "Do you have a brother, by any chance, Lord Abingdon?"

His teasing smirk was instantly replaced with a scowl. Fiend take it, she was a clever one!

"I do have a brother. Nicholas," he said shortly. "My twin, in fact. I am the eldest by a mere twelve minutes. Further than that, I do not care to discuss him with you."

For a split second, she appeared shocked. "Ah! I see."

"No. You do *not* see." He hoped to God his tone conveyed that the subject was closed. He must pay more attention and learn to imitate Wessex, if he continued to be around the lady. Wessex was a master of the haughty setdown.

She turned her head away, freeing him from her piercing

gaze. "Very well. I do *not* see."

But he was horribly afraid that she did see. That he had *allowed* her to see.

Neither behaved well, and they tormented each other, he had said. That was not Biblical. It was his own confession of guilt.

He was afraid she saw through to his very soul.

Chapter Twelve

Alice was rocked to her core. Her world—well, her world as she had understood it for the past fortnight, anyway—had just been thrown into a whirlwind.

Walking home from Westminster Abbey with Mary after Lord Abingdon had made an abrupt and precipitous departure from their company—for which Alice was singularly glad, for she had suddenly become as tongue-tied as the viscount—she was tripping over so many cobblestones in her inattention that Mary was forced to take her arm so she didn't land on her nose, or worse.

Merciful heavens.

Lord Abingdon was not Adelaide's seducer.

From their first meeting, Alice had pondered the mystery of how, exactly, Adelaide had allowed herself to be seduced by a man so clearly not to her usual taste. Adelaide swooned for smooth, brooding, mysterious heroes, and saw nothing romantic about a sense of humor.

Lord Abingdon, however, was bashful and enchantingly bumbling, and yet undeniably in possession of a sly wit. He was, in short, as far from the dashing hero of Adelaide's dreams as he could be.

Now the missing puzzle piece clicked into place. He had a brother. A twin! Likely, the brother was charming and suave, and everything Lord Abingdon was not. Wasn't that how it always went?

And he also had the same initials from the locket—NE, for Nicholas Eastwood, *not* Nathaniel.

Alice did not like to be wrong. On the List of Things Alice Bursnell Very Much Detests, being wrong fell below death of a loved one, but a good deal above frogs. And there was little doubt she had been greatly mistaken about Lord Abingdon.

Even worse than being wrong, this new information would delay her plans for revenge.

This was not good, not good at all.

She should be angry. She should be annoyed.

Oddly, instead, she was *relieved*.

Lord Abingdon was not her sister's seducer.

She would not go so far as to admit this knowledge made her happy. Her sister was still dead, and the man responsible for that was likely frolicking through the countryside, seducing other gently bred maidens.

Even so, Alice was relieved. She felt as though a heavy weight that had been pressing hard against her breast had suddenly lightened—not been removed altogether, but at least she could breathe a little more deeply.

But why should she feel so?

She was not in love with Lord Abingdon, she was quite sure of that. Perhaps it was merely relief that a genuine puzzle had been solved. Perhaps, too, she had been uneasy at the thought of harming Lord Abingdon or his reputation. He was such a quiet, bashful man that it would have been akin to slaying a field of bunnies. Alice did not like to slay bunnies.

Now she could avenge her sister's death with a clear conscience.

Except for one tiny, very significant detail. Where, exactly, was Nicholas Eastwood?

She did not think he was in London. If he were, surely their paths would have crossed, would they not? At Almack's or Hyde Park or some such place. He had not attended Lady Freesia's coming out, which would be odd, indeed, if he were in town. That would have set the gossips' tongues wagging.

Although...come to think of it, had anyone ever spoken of Lord Abingdon's brother in her presence? She furrowed her brow. She could not recall a single instance, until Lord Abingdon did so himself. It could not be that Eastwood was simply a boring topic of conversation. A son of an earl, even a second son, was always a fascinating specimen to unmarried ladies.

How very strange.

The man existed, and yet somehow, he also did not.

How could she find someone who, for all intents and purposes, did not exist?

The only person to acknowledge the man's existence was Lord Abingdon, and she could not ask him. He had clearly been disinclined to tell her he had a brother at all. But even outside of that, one could not say, "My lord, please tell me the whereabouts of your brother so I may bash his brains out with a frying pan." Even estranged brothers would not wish each other death or destruction.

Would they?

Not that she was planning to murder the man. Lord, no. That would be beyond the pale, even for such a well-deserved revenge. She would ruin him, somehow, along with his reputation and his entire future. She hadn't quite figured out *how* she would accomplish all that, but she had no doubt something would come to her.

She tapped her chin with a finger and pondered the puzzle of Lord Abingdon and his mysteriously estranged brother. For the expression on his face as he'd told the story of the Stone had said it all.

Something was amiss between the two brothers.

She must discover what that something was. Perhaps it would serve to aid her revenge, or perhaps it would be an added complication. Either way, she could not allow the question to go unanswered.

She pursed her lips. The only way to solve the puzzle would be to stick close to Lord Abingdon. True, he seemed deeply reluctant to share his secrets. But no matter.

Slowly, she smiled.

It would be such fun to make him talk.

Chapter Thirteen

The social season of London was in full swing. Visitors left calling cards, gentlemen brought Alice flowers, and no one spoke of anything but the prior ball, except perhaps to discuss the upcoming ball at Almack's, to be held at the end of the month.

Tonight, she was to attend the theater with Aunt Bea and Lady Claire and her mother, the Marchioness of Chatwell. It would be, Alice had no doubt, another endless night of discussing beaux and balls. She was only looking forward to it on the assumption that during the play itself, at least, there could be no conversation.

London was so very *wearying*.

She was homesick, that was the truth of the matter. Her very bones ached with yearning for her quiet life by the sea. London was all right in small doses, but the constant hustle and bustle made her restless. She could scarcely breathe from feeling so closed in. She did not want to spend her days sitting with this lady or that, discussing this ball or that, until her body weakened from lack of exercise and her mind weakened from lack of thought. She longed to walk the cliffs of Northumberland, to gallop across its grassy hills, to hear the rolling thunder of the North Sea.

She sighed. Revenge came at a very dear price.

When she and Aunt Bea arrived at the Drury Lane Theater, they took their seats in a private balcony with Lady Claire and her mother.

Lady Claire sprang to her feet. "Oh, Alice, I am *so* glad you are *here*! Tell me, *what* did you *think* of Lady Freesia's come-out ball?"

Alice lifted a gloved hand to her mouth to stifle a groan. In theory, she liked Lady Claire. She was a kind girl with a good heart. But, heavens! She was so dreadfully dull. "I thought it was very lovely. Lady Freesia could not have asked for a more splendid coming out."

"*I* thought so, *too*." Lady Claire tucked her arm through Alice's. "Let *us* sit together back here, and leave *my mother* and *your aunt* to take the two front seats."

When they were thusly arranged, Alice glanced about her. It was her first time at a real theater, and despite her homesickness, she was eager and fascinated by her surroundings.

She glanced at the playbill. "Amoroso, King of Little Britain," she murmured. "A serio-comick bombastick operatick interlude in one act." She tapped the bill with one fingernail. "That sounds promising, don't you think, Lady Claire?"

"Hmm? Is *that* what we are to see?" Lady Claire leaned closer to Alice to examine the playbill. "Ah. I suppose there is not much difference between one play and another. I saw you *dancing* with *Colonel Kent* at the ball last night. Did he call on you today? They say he is quite *smitten* with you."

"Yes, he did call." Alice felt the speculative gaze of Lady Claire and felt obliged to add, "He brought me flowers."

"Oh!" Lady Claire was all excitement. "What kind did he bring?"

Alice thought rapidly. Well, goodness, what *had* he brought? She couldn't remember for the life of her. Colonel Kent had proved to be a wonderful dance partner, and it was kind of him to bring flowers, but she had no intention of being courted. She had forgotten the flowers almost as soon as they arrived.

"Roses, I think." Very likely they *were* roses. Most gentlemen sent roses, didn't they? The colonel didn't strike her as one to deviate from tradition.

Lady Claire nodded her approval. "An *excellent* choice." She sighed contentedly as she glanced around the theater. "I *also* danced with Colonel Kent. He did *not* send *me* flowers."

Alice sent a worried look to her friend, but it did not appear that Lady Claire was at all perturbed. Still, Alice did not wish to discuss him further. She had much more important matters on her mind.

"Have you ever met Viscount Abingdon's brother, Lady Claire?" She kept her eyes on the playbill, lest her friend suspect the question was not casual.

"Goodness, *does* Viscount Abingdon have a brother?" Lady Claire frowned and tapped her fan on her leg. "I cannot recall being introduced to such a gentleman. Perhaps he is dead?" On this cheerful note, she turned the topic back to the ball. "I danced the *first* set with Mr. Billingsworth. He is not *titled*, but he has an *estate* in Hampshire and is an *excellent* dancer." Lady Claire looked around the theater again. She waved to Eliza, then turned back to Alice and smiled.

Despite her whirling thoughts—heavens, did no one truly know of the brother?—Alice smiled back. Lady Claire took that as encouragement.

"The *second* set I promised to Baron Dillingham. He is such a *pleasant* man, is he not?"

Alice busied herself with the hem of her glove rather than answer. Dillingham was tedious.

"A *baron* is not so good as a *viscount*, of course, but he *is* quite wealthy. And pleasant, as we just agreed. He had such a problem choosing his cravat this evening! I had him list all the choices in great detail so I could give him my honest opinion. I daresay he chose correctly."

"I'm sure," Alice said drily.

"The *third* set was a waltz. As you know, I danced that one with Colonel Kent."

No, Alice did not know. Moreover, she did not care.

Claire tapped her spyglass in her palm. "Colonel Kent is a *good* height, I think. He is not too *tall*, nor too *short*. Medium height is best, don't you agree? And his *uniform* is so *dashing*! Now that the *wars* have ended, he is a *safe* choice once *again*."

Dear God.

Suddenly, Alice understood the full horror of what was upon her. Her friend intended to name every dance and discuss each partner in detail. She looked desperately for an escape.

"The *fourth* set was with Lord Hemsway. He is a *second* son, to be sure, but so *handsome*. All that *blond* hair! And such *green* eyes! I daresay I was *half in love* with him by the second dance." She closed her eyes rapturously.

Alice gave a silent scream of agony.

"The *fifth* set—"

Alice jumped to her feet. She could take no more. "Please excuse me, Lady Claire, but I believe I dropped my spyglass in the entryway. I must go retrieve it."

Lady Claire stood. "I'll go with you."

"No!" Alice nearly shouted. Lady Claire's eyes widened, and Alice immediately regretted her harsh tone. "No, thank you," she said in a calmer voice. "Please do not trouble yourself. I will only be gone a moment."

She made her escape with a barely concealed sigh of relief.

How on earth would she survive the night? Where was the strong, very *silent* Lord Abingdon when one needed him?

Chapter Fourteen

From two boxes over, Nathaniel watched Miss Bursnell dash from her seat. Too bad. It had amused him to see her growing desperation as her friend prattled on. He had almost laughed out loud, but had not wanted to draw their attention. He preferred to listen unobserved.

So, Colonel Kent had brought flowers to Miss Bursnell. What of it? It was of no concern to Nathaniel who brought her flowers. He would stop thinking of it immediately.

Roses, indeed. He let out a noise of disparagement. *He* would have brought her violets. She reminded him of a violet, all dark along the edges with a creamy white center.

His aunt's advice notwithstanding, he would do well to put a good distance between himself and Miss Bursnell. Their meeting last week at the abbey had proved that much, for certain. Clearly, he couldn't trust himself around her. It was bad enough to say too little, but it was far worse to say too much. And, good God, had he said far too much.

She was best avoided altogether.

"Excuse me, I must—" He broke off. His companions

paid him no mind. Ah, well. He slipped unnoticed from the box.

She was several steps away from the balcony doors, examining a large portrait hanging on the wall. Despite the vividness of her coloring—the darkness of her hair and eyes, the redness of her lips and cheeks against her very white skin—she looked wilted, somehow. It was her expression, he decided. She looked wistful.

He took an involuntary step closer, and then another.

She heard the soft step of his foot on the carpet as he approached and turned to face him, looking vaguely startled. "Lord Abingdon! It is good to see you." She glanced around. "Are you waiting for a friend?"

"No. I came to find you," he said, and immediately wished he hadn't. Why couldn't he lie like a proper gentleman?

Her mouth formed a small *O*, and for a moment she looked even more bewildered. But the moment passed quickly, and she shook her head. "I am not very good company at the moment, I'm afraid. You should rejoin your friends, who are undoubtedly in better spirits. I will not be offended."

He continued his approach slowly, as though she would dart like a startled doe if he frightened her. No, not a doe. Like a cornered wildcat. She was more likely to scratch his eyes out than run away.

"Why? Is something troubling you, Miss Bursnell?"

"Ah. Yes. I am suffering from a rather embarrassing malady." She smiled ruefully. "I am homesick."

He was right beside her now. "Homesick?" he asked, distracted. She smelled like lemon verbena, sweet and sharp.

"It is not at all the thing, is it? I fear I am woefully unsophisticated." She shook her head in mock despair. "But there you have it. I miss the country. I miss my mama and papa. I miss my horse and the ocean and the cliffs of Northumberland. I miss everything that is not London." She turned her black eyes to his. "I must seem horribly provincial to you."

He desperately sought words to show he understood, that he commiserated with her longing. "No."

Lord, but he was an idiot. Could he not manage eloquence just once in his life?

But she just smiled, as though she hadn't noticed he was a dunce. "No?"

He forced his lips to action. "I much prefer the country, too."

"Do you, my lord?"

He nodded. She watched him for a moment, perhaps waiting for him to say more, he realized. A fresh wave of agony seized him. She must think him little better than a monkey. Or more likely, a little worse. A monkey could peel a banana, after all—a feat he had reason to doubt he could manage at this precise moment.

Why the devil was he thinking of monkeys instead of making proper conversation?

Because he could not think with her standing so close, with her perfume invading his senses and the white cream of her neck demanding a nibble. He simply could *not*.

She turned back to the painting of Mrs. Edwin, to his great relief. "She is certainly lovely. A perfect bosom, shown to its best advantage by a chaste cross on a string of pearls. I should probably not say such things, I suppose, but her bosom is there and finely displayed whether I mention it or not. Tell me, what do you think of her smile?"

Good God.

For a moment, he could only stare blankly, completely thrown by her use of the word bosom—twice!—and could not force his mind round any other thought. Heat saturated the back of his neck. He could feel her eyes, black and velvety, on his face, waiting for an answer. She had asked him a question, had she not? And not about bosoms. Very well, then. What *did* he think of Mrs. Edwin's smile? He turned his eyes to the painting.

"Otherworldly," he said after a moment's perusal. "She entertains us, but she is not one of us. She is apart." He considered the subject more closely. "Perhaps she is laughing at us, because we are so easily amused by her beauty. The Mona Lisa of the theater."

Miss Bursnell's lips curved in a slow smile. "An excellent analysis, Lord Abingdon."

The heat of his flush deepened. No one ever thought his analysis on artistic endeavors to be excellent. Oh, he knew that he was well-regarded, that the *ton* held him in high esteem—for being so devilishly clever as to be born the first son of an earl, if for no other reason. All in all, he was well recommended...but never sought out. Nor were his opinions.

Yet, here was Miss Bursnell, asking for his views and declaring them to be excellent. It felt...bloody *good*.

"Have you ever seen Mrs. Edwin perform?" she asked.

"Yes. Have you?"

"No. She performed here at Drury, did she not? And then elsewhere in London, after the theater burned. I spent several summers in Cornwall, but this is my first time in London." She continued to study the portrait. "I suppose I have missed my chance, as she is now retired."

He arched his eyebrows. "You had never been to London before this season? But you are the daughter of a peer. How is that possible?"

"There was never a reason, my lord," she said quietly. "Northumberland is far from London, and I did not desire nor need a season. I was betrothed, and believed I would marry and spend the rest of my life happily in Northumberland. Unfortunately, my fiancé did not come back from Waterloo."

"I am so sorry." If only there were a cudgel lying about so

he could give himself a good whack to the head. "I seem to be in the habit of making you speak of unhappy things. Please forgive me."

She caught her lower lip between her teeth. "You do not need to apologize for things outside your control. You could not know the reason before you asked."

Her eyes were darker than ever as she looked up at him. He could not tell where the iris ended and the pupil began. How could a man ever prefer blue eyes to these velvet pools? Blue eyes were well and good, but one could not lose oneself in their depths. He had seen scores of blue eyes in scores of beautiful faces, and not once had he ever been in danger of drowning, as he was now.

The heavy fringe of her lashes swept downward, obscuring her expression. Her white teeth sank into her bottom lip, causing the rosy color to heighten. The movement captivated him. He wanted to cup her face in his hands, rub his thumb over that lip, and replace her nibble with his. Not hard enough to hurt her, just enough to see what it felt like. He wanted a taste, that was all.

He shook his head to clear the madness, but the madness would not clear. It was her scent, the bittersweet of lemons. Why could she not wear roses or gardenia, like every other woman of the *ton*? Why must she insist on wearing a perfume that begged him to lick her from head to toe?

Oh, he was most certainly mad. A gentleman did not *lick* a lady.

"I must return to my friend, Lord Abingdon," she said, still not meeting his gaze. "I am sure she is wondering about my absence."

"Yes. Yes. No doubt you are eager to finish Lady Claire's catalogue of dances," he said absently, paying no heed to the words coming from his mouth. He was too busy attempting to control his breathing so he did not pant like a rutting dog.

The dark fringe swept up abruptly, and her startled eyes met his own. She threw back her head and laughed, revealing even more of that slim marble neck. Another wave of her scent hit his nostrils. Blood pounded in his veins, roared in his ears. He could not take another moment of this.

He pounced.

Chapter Fifteen

Alice was still laughing when she felt Lord Abingdon's hand clamp firmly behind her neck, bringing her body up against his with surprising force. His mouth was on hers before she could protest—although she wasn't entirely sure she *would* protest, if given the opportunity.

She dizzied from the speed at which he pulled her from laughing into kissing. His mouth was warm and insistent, demanding something she did not understand and could not give.

Or could she?

Then she felt the gentle nip of his teeth on her bottom lip. She gasped.

He took full advantage. His tongue darted into her mouth, gently running over her teeth and playfully nudging against her own. She shrank back from the sudden intimacy, but he followed her, his mouth never leaving hers, until her back was pressed against the wall and she could feel the full length of him hard against her body.

The smell of him surrounded her, spicy and oh so male.

Her hands fluttered against the hard planes of his chest, unsure whether or not to land there. Decorum and self-preservation insisted that she should push him off—they could easily be seen by anyone leaving the theater—but instead, her arms twined around his neck, seemingly of their own accord.

His mouth roved her face, kissing her temple and eyelids before nibbling her jawline. He stopped at her pulse point, and his tongue swept it lightly, testing the rapid heartbeat that throbbed there. She whimpered, and his mouth once more found hers. Again, his lips coaxed hers apart, again his tongue invaded. But this time she understood. She brushed her tongue against his, explored the silky, piquant underside.

He moaned and crushed her harder against him.

"You taste sweet," he murmured. "So damn sweet."

A great swell of chatter rose through the theater. She struggled to make sense of it through the haze of passion.

Intermission! Soon the hall would fill with hundreds of people.

"Lord Abingdon!" she warned.

He seemed not to hear and continued to nuzzle her neck.

"Lord Abingdon!" She pushed hard against his chest.

"Hmm?" He blinked slowly, his eyes drugged and dreamy.

"Please, my lord. It is intermission. People will see us."

With sudden understanding of the danger, he released her and took a rapid step backward. She did not wait for him to speak. She picked up her skirts and fled.

Dear heavens.

What on earth had just happened? What had she done?

Chapter Sixteen

Alice shivered as she escaped the overheated theater and cannoned out into the cold, dark night. She had not stopped to collect her cloak, nor to inform Aunt Bea of her departure. She had not thought of anything other than fleeing her own mortification.

What undiscovered, terrifying weakness had Lord Abingdon laid bare within her heart? If someone would be so kind as to hand her a knife, she would gladly cut out the traitorous organ.

She heard footsteps running toward her over the cobblestones and immediately hastened her step.

Not quickly enough.

A warm hand clamped down on her upper arm, bringing her to a halt.

"Alice, stop!" Lord Abingdon panted.

She tried to shake him off, but his grip was like iron. She glowered up at him. "Do not presume to call me that!"

He eyed her warily. "My apologies. That was inappropriate of me."

She barked a laugh. "Perhaps you thought, after mauling me in a public place, you could dispense with other formalities, as well."

He had the good grace to blush deeply. His hand dropped from her arm. "Miss Bursnell, please come back to the theater. It's cold, and you are unprotected. You must allow me to escort you back."

"I most certainly will not. I have had quite enough of your company for one evening. Good night, my lord." She turned and marched swiftly in what she dearly hoped was the direction of home.

She sensed his hesitation as he debated his next course of action. When he fell into step beside her, she groaned loudly, not bothering to hide her dismay.

"You leave me no choice, Miss Bursnell. I cannot permit you to wander the streets of London alone, especially not at night."

"You are neither my father nor my husband. You cannot permit nor forbid me to do anything."

"Your point is well taken," he said cheerfully. "Yet, why argue semantics? You have no hope of outrunning me in those slippers."

Anger simmered in her stomach. She whirled toward him. "You arrogant, insufferable creature!" She shoved at his chest, but she might as well pound on a brick wall for all the good it did. Why would he not go and leave her to her shame? For she was ashamed—deeply so. He was, after all, just a man and couldn't help himself. It was *she* who should have restrained herself, as a true lady ought.

"Are you quite finished?" His lips quirked, fueling her acute displeasure.

"No, my lord." She brought her foot down hard upon his boot with righteous indignation, grinding her heel on his toes. "*Now* I am finished."

He grunted and stumbled backward. "*The devil.* You did not protest this much while I kissed you."

She snatched desperately at the shreds of her dignity and managed to send him a haughty look. "Really, my lord, you hardly gave me a chance!"

The remark hit home, she could see. His gaze faltered, and he rubbed anxiously at his cheek. It was not at all the response she expected. He may not have seduced her sister, but that did not mean he was inexperienced. He was the Duke of Wessex's closest friend, for God's sake! And—judging from the past few minutes alone—the man clearly knew how to kiss. She had most certainly not been his first.

He, on the other hand, *had* been her first. Unless one counted a handful of innocent pecks from her late fiancé.

Who knew kissing could be so...so...very pleasant? It gave her a whole new perspective on the reasons a young lady might find herself...in a spot of trouble.

He gave her a slight bow. "It will not happen again, Miss Bursnell. You have my word on it."

She searched his face suspiciously. Was he mocking her? But his blue eyes were serious, with not even a spark of laughter lurking in their depths. Which in no way explained the brief jolt of regret that went through her at his gallant promise. "Thank you, my lord."

"Will you return to the theater now? Please?"

She bit her lip. She did not truly want to walk home. Her delicate slippers would be torn to ribbons. And how would she explain her disappearance to Aunt Bea? There must be a way to give in without further bruising her pride.

As he watched her worry her lip, the sparkle returned to his eyes. She found that slightly ominous.

"If you wish to continue home, I will be happy to accompany you," he said. "You would be burdened with my company slightly longer than if we were to return to the theater now, of course, but that is no matter. It is a scant eight kilometers to Mayfair. I shall have you warm and safe at home in no more than…oh, two hours."

She blanched. Eight kilometers! The distance had seemed so much shorter traveling by coach. "Oh, very well! I will return to the theater. I cannot stand ten minutes more of your company, let alone two hours."

He made a sound suspiciously similar to a laugh being smothered by a cough. She glared.

"Will you take my arm?"

She hesitated. The very last thing she wanted was to touch him again.

Honestly, she didn't dare.

He closed his eyes briefly. The lines of his throat quivered as he swallowed hard. "I understand your reluctance, Miss Bursnell, but I swear you are safe with me."

She had serious doubts about that. But with little choice, she took his arm and allowed him to lead her back to the theater.

I understand your reluctance…

No, he did not.

She had lived her life with the belief that only a *certain type* of girl could be ruined. Not girls like her. To be seduced, a girl must be weak both of mind and of character, and Alice was neither of those things. Neither was Adelaide, however, so there must have been extenuating circumstances. Perhaps the man had tricked her into believing he would marry her immediately.

But sometimes—not often, but sometimes—she'd wondered…*had* Adelaide been weak? Alice had always banished the unsisterly, uncharitable thought immediately to the darkest corners of her mind. But she'd known it was there, this thought, and it had always troubled her.

Until now.

Now, she understood.

How could a lady *not* be seduced by such deep, sweet kisses that threatened to steal one's very soul from her body? Until Lord Abingdon's mouth had claimed her own, she had thought she knew what kissing was. But the chaste kisses she had shared with her fiancé had as little in common with Lord Abingdon's searing heat as a kitten had with a lion.

No, she no longer wondered how Adelaide had been seduced. She had likely been thoroughly kissed herself, and then things went on from there.

Which begged an even more troubling question.

Just how was Alice to find the seducer...without being seduced herself?

Chapter Seventeen

Nathaniel put forth a monumental effort to avoid Miss Bursnell for the next fortnight—a Herculean task if ever there was one. In a city of over a million people, how the deuce was it possible to continuously find himself in the same place as one small lady? Surely, she ought to be…somewhere else.

But no, wherever he was, there Miss Bursnell was sure to be. When he went with Wessex to Tattersall's, she was there with Miss Benton. When he escorted his sister and aunt to Bond Street for a new bonnet, there she was, shopping with Lady Claire.

Most disconcerting of all, here she was now, in Hyde Park, strolling arm in arm with Miss Benton. It was too much!

"Miss Bursnell is following me," Nathaniel muttered to Wessex as they rode side by side. "She is everywhere. I cannot escape her."

Wessex looked dubiously at him. "Yes, how obvious. Why else would she be here, in Hyde Park, during the fashionable hour? She must be plotting your murder even as we speak. And how clever of her to arrive before us!"

"If this were the only time I had seen her, I would agree it's just a coincidence. But it is not. It has been a fortnight of such coincidences, and judged as a whole, you must agree that these meetings are no accident."

Wessex rolled his eyes heavenward. "Very well. Let us hear it."

"We met last Tuesday at Bond Street, for example."

"You were in a ladies' hat shop. How on earth could she have expected to find you there?" Wessex demanded.

An excellent question, but Nathaniel was not so easily persuaded. "What of Tattersall's, then?"

Wessex sighed deeply. "My dear man, that was not a case of Miss Bursnell following you. That was a case of me following Miss Benton. You and Miss Bursnell were simply innocent bystanders."

This gave Nathaniel pause. "Oh." He gave Wessex a sidelong glance. "Wessex, if you don't mind my asking—"

"I *do* mind," Wessex snapped.

"Hmm. I see." Nathaniel tipped his hat in greeting to Colonel Kent and Baron Dillingham but urged his horse forward without stopping. "He sent her roses," he said under his breath.

"Perhaps," Wessex said sardonically, "Miss Bursnell is following *him*."

Nathaniel growled, to which Wessex just laughed.

"If you are so sure she is set on murdering you, why do you care if she is here for another man? You should be relieved."

Undoubtedly. And yet, Nathaniel was not relieved. He felt a certain possessiveness when it came to Miss Bursnell. If she was following any man, then it should be *him*, damn it! He actually liked her, and that was the worry of it all.

He frowned uneasily at his horse's ears. She said inappropriate things, laughed at inappropriate times, and was not above stomping on a gentleman's toes if he offended her. But he liked her scent of crisp lemons, the sweet taste of her lips, the sturdy feel of her in his arms. He closed his eyes, remembering. Beneath her dress he could feel the firmness of her bone and muscle. He could—

"For God's sake, man, open your eyes before you trample Miss Benton!" Wessex said.

Nathaniel's eyes shot open just in time to see Miss Benton do a quick sidestep to the left, nearly knocking Miss Bursnell to the ground as she did so. He tipped his hat to the ladies as nonchalantly as possible, as if he hadn't been caught riding a horse in the most foolish way imaginable. "Miss Bursnell, Miss Benton. How do you do?"

Miss Benton's eyes danced with mirth. "Very well, my lord. And yourself?"

"I am well." He tapped his crop nervously on his thigh. Miss Bursnell had not yet spoken. Was she still angry from his kiss? "It is fine weather for walking, is it not, Miss Bursnell?" he ventured.

Her obsidian eyes stared stonily back at him, but he knew she could not ignore a direct question. "Yes, my lord."

Miss Benton glanced wryly at her friend. "We were searching out the spring flowers, my lord, but Miss Bursnell complains that London gardens are too tame."

"Ah." Wessex gave an understanding nod. "Northumberland is blooming with fields of wild daffodils right now, is it not?"

"Yes, Your Grace." Miss Bursnell's cheeks turned pink with pleasure. "There is no sight more beautiful." She smiled at the duke with her whole face, rather than merely turning up her lips while sending him to the devil with her eyes.

Apparently, *that* particular grin was reserved for Nathaniel.

The side-eyed glance he gave to Wessex was one of supreme annoyance. What had *he* done to deserve her goodwill?

"I am hosting a house party at Haverly in two weeks'

time," Nathaniel said abruptly, ignoring a sudden assessing stare from the duke. "Perhaps you and your aunt would care to join us, Miss Bursnell? And Miss Benton is welcome, too, of course. Hampshire is not Northumberland, but perhaps the country air will ease your homesickness somewhat."

Miss Bursnell lifted her chin and gazed at him with the intense concentration of a lady determined to solve a complex riddle. Finally, she lowered her lashes, although he could not say if she had solved the question or merely admitted defeat. "Will your family be there, as well?"

Why had she asked that? Of whom, in particular, was she inquiring? "Lady Freesia prefers to stay in London," he said.

"I shall speak to my aunt." When she looked up again, her expression had changed from puzzlement to one of joy. "I should like very much to go to Hampshire, Lord Abingdon. Thank you."

"What of you, Miss Benton? Will we see you at Haverly?" Wessex's voice was cool and pleasant, even a trifle bored, but Nathaniel noted his fingers were fidgeting on his thigh.

"I should like nothing better than to join my friends in the countryside," Miss Benton said. "I fear you will be quite alone here in London, Your Grace."

Wessex had the look of a man who knew he was walking into a trap. "Parliament is closed for Easter. I will be at Haverly...if I am fortunate enough to receive an invitation." He coughed into his hand and looked slyly at Nathaniel, who glared back.

"Ah!" The corners of her mouth tucked up in almost a smile. "Then it will be friends and *you* at Haverly."

If the setdown stung, Wessex did not show it. "How delightful that we shall be there together," he said in a tone so smugly self-satisfied that her eyes widened. "Is there anything more romantic than the English countryside in the spring?"

"I am sure I do not know," Miss Benton demurred. "I

will leave you to discover that by yourself."

Miss Bursnell's eyes darted from her friend to the duke and back again. Her chin quivered with suppressed laughter. "Come, Eliza, I think I see meadowsweet. Shall we investigate?"

The ladies curtsied, and he and Wessex rode on in silence.

Uneasiness settled in the pit of Nathaniel's stomach. Had he really just done that? Yes, he had, and he could not take it back now.

He nearly groaned out loud. He had better tell his mother. His father likely would not notice half a dozen extra persons parading through the estate, but his mother would fret.

"Well. That was interesting," Wessex said, finally breaking the quiet.

Nathaniel said nothing.

"Exactly how long have you been planning this house party?" When he did not answer, Wessex continued. "My guess is that the idea flitted into your brain at the exact moment Miss Bursnell wished for daffodils."

Still, Nathaniel said nothing.

"I seem to remember a field of daffodils in the park at Haverly, do I not? To the west of the lake, I believe."

Nathaniel gritted his teeth. "Wessex."

"Yes?"

"Do shut up."

Wessex bit back a retort, closing his mouth so hard his teeth clanked, but he did nothing to constrain his smirk.

Nathaniel twitched the reins as unease spread through his belly. No, not unease.

Anticipation.

In a fortnight's time, she would be in his home. Not in his bed, but in a bed under the very same roof. The thought alone was enough to make his pulse quicken.

Two weeks.

Chapter Eighteen

Nathaniel was correct. Lady Wintham was, indeed, put out.

He had left immediately and made the day's journey to Haverly in order to inform her himself rather than depend upon the mail.

"You cannot be serious, Nathaniel!" his mother protested. "A house party in a fortnight? It cannot be done! The rooms must be prepared for guests. The cook must hire help—she is not prepared to make meals for a dozen extra mouths. Entertainment must be decided. No, my dear, it cannot be done!"

Nathaniel took it as a good sign that she had begun scribbling lists even as she protested.

"Who will be delighting us with their company, if I may ask?" his mother demanded as her pen flew over the page. "Colonel Kent lent support to one of your father's pet projects, so he must make the cut."

Nathaniel frowned. He had certainly not intended Kent to join them. "Lady Claire and the marchioness, Miss Benton, their friend Miss Alice Bursnell with her aunt, and

Baron Dillingham," he answered. The baron was the dullest man ever to burden London with his presence, but he seemed to be good friends with Lady Claire's set, so he could not be avoided. "And Wessex," he added as an afterthought.

His mother let out her breath in a sharp hiss. "Duke Wessex is coming? You want me to organize a house party at which a *duke* will be in attendance, and I am to do this in less than a fortnight?"

"Come now, mother, it is only Wessex."

"*Only* Wessex?" Lady Wintham put her pen down carefully and clasped her hands as though in prayer. "Heaven grant me patience. My dear son, there is no such thing as *only* a duke. A duke is always of the highest importance."

Nathaniel opened his mouth to remind his mother that she had met Wessex several times since Oxford, and that her own husband was an earl, a mere two steps lower than a duke…and a rather important earl, at that. But she had gone back to her list and was muttering busily. He did not wish to impede her progress.

He stooped to kiss her cheek. "Thank you, Mother."

She patted his hand distractedly. "Go see your father. He does not know you are home."

Nathaniel nodded his assent and left her to her list-making. His father was bound to be in the library, his usual haunt, but Nathaniel did not go there straightaway. Instead, he went outside to the garden, to the old oak tree that stood guard at the gate. He sat down unceremoniously in the dirt amongst the roots and rested his back against the rough bark of the trunk.

It was the same oak tree he had fallen from as a boy.

Perhaps "fallen" was the wrong word, since Nicholas had pushed him, thus securing his banishment from the family. Nathaniel had survived with only a broken ankle. It was a clean break and mended quickly. However, combined with their bloody family history, his parents' faith in the integrity of brotherly love was irreparably shattered.

It made no difference that it was an accident—well, not a complete accident, exactly. He *had* intended to push Nathaniel...but he *hadn't* intended for him to break his ankle on the landing. He wouldn't have pushed him at all if Nathaniel hadn't first called him a fatheaded dandy. And even if he *had* pushed him, Nathaniel wouldn't have fallen if he had been using his arms to hold on to the tree rather than to demonstrate what, exactly, a fatheaded dandy looked like.

The trouble was that Nicholas and Nathaniel hailed from a long history of fratricide. Their father, an only son, had not participated in the tradition, thank God. But prior generations... Well. Nothing had ever been proven, but it was suspicious, was it not, that in six generations, five first sons had died under peculiar circumstances, leaving five second sons to inherit the title?

Nathaniel, having had several narrow escapes over the years, was, indeed, suspicious. There had been cut leathers and broken ladders and curricles that had mysteriously fallen apart. Most disturbing of all had been a ballerina intent on stabbing him to death. But he had survived, and no one had ever proven Nicholas responsible. For any of it.

Nathaniel stared up at the soft evening light filtering through the fresh green leaves. Someday, he hoped, there would be children playing in the branches once again— although preferably without suffering broken ankles. There could be cousins and laughter and jests.

Someday.

If only Nicholas would forgive him. Or at least stop trying to kill him.

If it was, in fact, him. Nathaniel preferred to think it was *not* his brother attempting to rid the world of him.

Then again, who else could it be? Who else had motive

enough to see him dead?

Still, he did not want to believe it of Nicholas.

He wrapped his arm around one bent knee and closed his eyes. He felt a headache coming on. It nearly always happened when he thought about the brotherly conundrum of his life. He focused on the sundry sun-dappled shapes that flitted across his closed eyelids, and took deep, calming breaths. Eventually the pain receded.

A large black shadow suddenly blocked the sun. He cracked his eyes open and saw his father looming over him.

"Ah, so you are home. Your mother assured me it was true, but as you were nowhere to be seen, I thought she must be mistaken. But, no! Here you are. And that is a very good thing, because even as we speak, your mother is conspiring with the housekeeper and the cook, and I would hate to spoil her fun. So, we are to have a house party in a fortnight's time, I hear?"

"Yes, sir." Nathaniel clambered to his feet and braced himself for what was coming.

His father raised a quizzing glass and focused on him. "Does this have anything to do with a lady, perchance?"

"No, not at all." A lie was better than attempting to explain Miss Bursnell. Miss Bursnell was simply unexplainable. Quite marvelously so…for reasons that remained a mystery.

"Pity." His father tsked softly. "By the time I was your age, I had done my duty twice over and ensured the continuance of our line. You do not mean to shirk your duty, do you, lad?"

Nathaniel could not resist such an opportunity. "You did your duty so well, Father, that it doesn't matter in the slightest whether I do mine. If I do not provide an heir, Nicholas will. The earldom is in no danger."

Wintham snorted brusquely. "Nicholas is no closer to settling down than you are. And the earldom is always in danger of those terrible cousins inheriting."

"Gordon and John are not as bad as all that," Nathaniel said mildly. "I daresay, they might even make improvements. Gordon is a very imaginative man."

His father clasped his hands behind his back, legs akimbo, and glowered. "Do not even jest. They're Scots."

Nathaniel chuckled. "Very well, Father. Send word to Nick that he must hurry along with creating the next generation. You cannot look to me. Women do not like me." He kept his tone jocular, masking the strength of his feelings.

Not for all the earldoms in England would he tell his father the truth—that it was possible his brother *was* attempting fratricide, and that Nathaniel could not trust that any woman who showed interest in him was not in league with the plan. He and Nicholas had been separated to prevent such a fate, and yet, that fate seemed to be an ever-present stone upon Nathaniel's back.

How could he trust his safety to a woman when he couldn't trust his own flesh and blood?

His father rolled his eyes. "Women don't have to like you. You are a viscount and the heir to an earldom. Any personal preference is quite beside the point. And as for Nick... Well, he would marry a French gel just to spite us, I'm sure. Imagine a half-French Earl of Wintham!" He shuddered. "Worse than a Scot."

Nathaniel laughed and stood. "I must dress for dinner."

His father laid a hand on his arm, halting him. "A moment, son. Just a moment."

Nathaniel looked at him sharply. When had his face taken on that gray cast? "Are you quite well, sir?"

"Quite." His father smiled faintly. "But we must speak of something rather important, I'm afraid."

Nathaniel waited, frowning, as his father gathered his thoughts.

"It seems there is an issue with my heart. Sometimes it

beats off tune. The doctors have advised rest, although not too much of it, and other than that…" He shrugged.

Nathaniel stared at him blankly. "Your heart? Surely not." He had sincerely hoped the Earl of Wintham would outlive them all.

"It is likely nothing serious. A mere oddity, that is all."

How could an oddity that affected one's heart not be serious? One could not live without one's heart, after all.

"I have been, I think, a loving and lenient parent. I have not asked much of you—not too much, I hope." His father paused. "But I find now that I wish I had done some things differently, and I must make a few demands, after all."

Nathaniel looked at him warily. "What demands?"

"You must marry expediently and follow that with an heir."

He paused, his expression somber.

Nathaniel waited for the other boot to fall.

"And you must bring Nicholas home."

Chapter Nineteen

Alice was having a crisis. She should have been packing for a glorious two weeks in Hampshire, but instead she was pacing the plush gray carpet of her dressing room while Eliza watched in bemusement from the window seat.

On the one hand, Alice would like nothing better than to escape the clogged London streets and inhale the sweet spring country air of Hampshire. On the other hand, that sweet Hampshire air would be inhaled at the estate of a man who had done something entirely inappropriate to her mouth, and must therefore be abhorrent to her.

But she must go to Hampshire if she wished to solve the riddle of Lord Abingdon's brother, Nicholas. Surely their childhood home would afford some clues. Even if Lord Abingdon was abhorrent to her, she must go.

Unfortunately, she was not completely convinced that she abhorred Lord Abingdon quite as deeply as she ought. She was rather afraid she liked him, which was quite unacceptable and ought not to be encouraged…if she had any hope of keeping her virtue intact. It would be far safer to stay away.

But what of Adelaide's revenge?

Unless she intended to murder her sister's seducer—which would definitely be going too far—she needed to glean as much information about the man as she could. At Haverly, she could go places she should not, read private papers not meant for her eyes, and search high and low for clues about the man who had once lived there and where he might be now.

It was, admittedly, a bit of a pickle.

"Alice, dear, stop that infernal pacing and finish your packing! We should have left this morning. Now we will arrive at least a day later than the other guests," Eliza said impatiently.

Alice slumped onto her bed. "Perhaps I should not leave London just now. There is ever so much to do here, and I have never explored London before. You had better go without me."

"Nonsense! You are *dying* to escape the city. Anyway, the entire *ton* will be away until after Easter. London will be deadly dull." Eliza studied her with narrowed, searching eyes. "Whatever is the matter, Alice?"

Alice stared miserably at the floor. *How to revenge without being seduced, that was the question…*

But she couldn't very well confess her confusion to Eliza.

Well, not on *that* point, at least.

"Lord Abingdon kissed me," she said bluntly, then immediately clapped a hand to her mouth, wishing she could take back the words.

"No! Did he?" Eliza rocked backward and clapped her hands gleefully. "Oh, was it dreadful? He is such a sullen man. I imagine his kisses must be terribly polite." She leaned forward eagerly. "Tell me all."

Alice made a sound like a strangled goose honking. A hot blush blazed across her cheeks.

"Oh! Oh, I see." An impish smile tugged up the corners of Eliza's mouth. "*Not* so polite, then?"

Alice found her voice. "It was…" *Hot. Wet. Fierce.* "Not polite."

"Dear me, I shall swoon!" Eliza lifted a hand weakly to her forehead and fluttered her silky lashes dramatically.

Alice laughed. "Oh, do be serious! You see why I cannot go to Hampshire. It would be…reckless."

Eliza blinked at her uncomprehendingly. "Why reckless? You are a lady of good family with a healthy dowry. He is a viscount, and will one day be an earl. You are not beneath him, and I do not think you have ambitions to go higher. You are both of an age where one must think seriously about settling down. Why ever are you in London for the season, if not to secure a husband?"

Alice saw her opportunity and slyly seized it. "Why ever are *you* in London, if not to secure a husband?" she countered. "You are the prettiest girl in England, and you have a large dowry of your own. And I do believe Duke Wessex is utterly smitten with you."

Eliza wrinkled her nose. "Wessex is utterly smitten with his own ego. He cannot understand how any woman under the same sun and stars as he can be ambivalent to his charms. As for the rest, very well. It is true that I could be married, if I so chose." She stood and turned to the window. "But I do *not* so choose. I most emphatically do not. I have a cottage of my own in Surrey and enough money to live comfortably for the rest of my life. My parents are dead, and my brother is kind and lets me do as I please. Trust me, I would find no such freedom in marriage." Her knuckles turned white as they gripped the back of the chair.

Alice got to her feet. "What if it were a love match?"

Eliza laughed softly. "But, my dear, a love match would be the worst shackle of all. How terrible to put a man's needs and desires above your own! How terrible to wait for him at night while he is with his mistress! Even in a love match, a man is not easily satisfied with just one woman."

Alice frowned in annoyance. "If marriage is so terrible, you needn't be so eager to throw me into it! No, I shall stay in London."

Eliza's eyes glinted. "Surely, you can manage a fortnight without compromising yourself? Lord Abingdon is not as alluring as all that. But I suppose you know best. If you truly believe you cannot be trusted within the same county as the tempting Lord Abingdon, then perhaps you better stay, after all."

Alice let out a huff. Well, when put thusly…

Was she really such a weakling and a nitwit that she would allow history to repeat itself? Abingdon's brother may have seduced her sister.

But Alice would *not* follow in her footsteps.

Soul-shattering kisses notwithstanding.

Chapter Twenty

Few people would disagree that Haverly was one of the more unique estates in Hampshire. The manor itself was an odd-looking thing, with three large wings, each of a very different style. The structure began as a beige, honeycomb color, moving on to pale-pink sandstone, and finally ending in a deep-red brick. Three turrets clustered against the right wing. It was not a balanced or remotely symmetrical design.

Alice proclaimed it utterly charming.

"After a twelve-hour carriage ride, anything that is not a carriage is positively delightful," Aunt Bea said frankly.

Eliza grinned. "It is lovely, is it not? The lady who becomes mistress of such a place will be fortunate, indeed."

Alice glared at her, but Eliza's grin only widened.

It was early morning when they arrived, having stopped the previous night in a town a mere hour away. Alice and Eliza would have preferred to finish the journey, as they were so close to Haverly, but Aunt Bea had insisted on stopping. Her body had endured enough, she'd declared, and demanded a rest.

This morning the manor was silent and still. The servants saw to their bags, and the butler showed them to their rooms after informing them that the earl and countess, as well as the guests, had not come down yet.

Aunt Bea promptly sat down to write her letters, a task she dearly loved.

"Would you mind terribly if we parted?" Eliza whispered. "I crave a moment of solitude, and I have several letters I must write, as well."

Alice shook her head. "Say no more. I feel the same. Traveling is so very *together*, is it not? And I doubt a house party will offer much in the way of solitude for the next fortnight. I believe I shall take a walk." Espionage and revenge could wait until after she had stretched her legs.

Eliza squeezed her hand. "Thank you. If memory serves, there is a charming patch of daffodils that crops up every year. To the west of the lake, I believe."

Alice set off immediately in the direction of the lake. When she was clear of the manor, she removed her bonnet and breathed deeply. The air smelled of spring—of damp earth and new grass and ripe wildflowers. The Hampshire sky was a deeper, *bluer* blue than in London. Surely, it could not be the same sky, at all.

She tramped along, arms swinging, turning this way and that to admire wild primrose and delicate blue damselflies flitting by. At last, she came to the daffodils, their golden trumpets lifting merrily to the sun. She unbuttoned her pelisse, spread it on the ground for a blanket, and sat. She closed her eyes and tilted her face skyward like the daffodils that surrounded her. She would get horribly brown, she supposed, but it was worth it for this single marvelous moment.

She would have been happy to remain so for the rest of the day, had her eyes not been jerked open and assaulted by the vision of a man, bare chested, running through the field.

No. Assaulted was the wrong word. Her eyes were *blessed* with the sight.

He was a remarkable specimen, with his taught, well-muscled physique glistening from exertion. The distance was too great to see his face, but then he turned along a curve in the path, and she saw the queue of red-gold hair glinting in the morning sun.

Good God.

Lord Abingdon.

She should return to the house immediately. At the very least, she should avert her eyes, for heaven's sake.

She did neither.

Had she once thought him too thin? Had she thought him gangly and clumsy? He was none of those things. He was not too thin—he was lean and sleek, like a well-sprung lion. He was not clumsy—his arms and legs pumped with perfect grace.

He was magnificent.

The trick was that the current men's fashion simply did not suit his figure. Or perhaps he needed to pay a visit to a better tailor. How was she to have guessed that under those excessive folds of fabric lurked such a marvelous body? It was to his advantage to wear as little as possible, that much was clear. Could anything be more glorious than his naked back? The muscles that rippled around his shoulders and along his spine were so virile, so male, that her breath caught.

She watched as he rounded the far side of the lake. If she squinted and tried very, very hard, she could still make out his lithe form. Oh, dear. He was coming around the east side now, his long strides bringing him closer to her at a rapid pace.

What on earth was he about? He was not running *to* something, and he did not appear to be running *away* from something. He was merely running…for the sake of running?

Why ever would one do such a thing?

As he neared her spot amongst the daffodils, his eyes suddenly darted in her direction. Horror filled his face and down he went, tumbling feet over head in the tall grass.

"Lord Abingdon!" She sprang up and rushed to his side. She peered anxiously down at the man who lay sprawled at her feet. "Lord Abingdon?"

He blinked up at her. "Miss Bursnell." He blinked again. "Miss Bursnell, would you be so kind as to pretend this never happened?"

Her gaze, which had been sneaking down the line of golden bronze hair over his stomach to his waistband, snapped back to his face. She choked on a giggle. "I beg your pardon?"

"If you please, Miss Bursnell, you may return to the spot where I saw you. I will set myself to rights and come join you. We will speak of the lovely weather, and the daffodils, and everyone's health, and not"—a laugh escaped her lips, and he looked at her sternly—"and *not* of this incident in which we find ourselves."

"Very well." She covered her grin with a gloved hand and turned, marching purposefully to her pelisse on the grass.

As she reclaimed her seat, she managed a quick, furtive glance back, just in time to see him scrub a towel over his stomach and arms. He pulled a shirt over his head and walked toward her, if not fully clothed then at least fully covered.

She frowned at the daffodils.

"Good morning, my lord," she said as he approached. And then, mindful of his request, she added, "What a surprise."

"A pleasant one, I hope."

She felt heat rise from the roots of her hair to the toes of her feet. *Oh, yes, very pleasant.*

Her flaming face caught him off guard. "I did not mean—

That is, I only meant— Oh, damn," he muttered.

She howled with laughter. "Oh, Lord Abingdon, I do not think I can pretend!" she gasped out. "I must tell Miss Benton. She will—"

"You most certainly will *not* tell Miss Benton," he broke in. "An unchaperoned lady with a half-naked man? You would be forced to marry me."

Her laughter died on her lips, and her eyes widened. *Heaven forbid.* "You are right. I will say nothing to Miss Benton."

He shot her an aggrieved look. "You needn't look so frightened. I have no desire to trap you."

"Of course not, my lord," she murmured. She fingered the ribbons of her bonnet and, with a sigh, placed it back on her head. They had dispensed with propriety enough for one day. "It is a fine morning, is it not?"

He was still frowning. "What? Oh, yes. A very fine morning."

"I trust that your mother is in good health? We arrived so early she had not yet come down."

"My mother is quite well. Thank you." He turned his gaze to the daffodils. "How was your journey?"

"Uneventful. Thank you for inquiring, my lord."

"And your aunt and Miss Benton are well?" He glanced around quickly. "They did not join you on your walk?"

Alice shook her head, a smile lurking on her lips. What, she wondered, would Aunt Bea have said at the sight of Lord Abingdon stripped to the waist and running circles around the lake? "Aunt Bea is resting, as she never sleeps well when she travels. Miss Benton went to the library."

"I am happy to hear that."

He exhaled.

She sighed.

They looked at each other, then looked away again.

The weather and everyone's health were proper topics, but dreadfully dull. She ought to inquire after his brother. Would he withdraw as he had at the abbey? Or would he tell her something useful? But, somehow, she could not force the words through her lips. The day was too beautiful, and Lord Abingdon was…well, he was wonderful, too.

"You know, I once saw a man running around a lake," she said conversationally. She glanced at him sideways to see how he would react. He nodded slowly. Taking that as encouragement, she continued, "He did not seem to have a destination, nor was he being chased. At least, I do not believe so."

Lord Abingdon laughed softly. "Oh, you think not?"

She whipped her head around. "He *was* being chased?"

"Perhaps not in the sense you mean. Perhaps he was practicing."

She narrowed her eyes at that. "Practicing…being chased? Would that be a likely thing to happen to him, that he must practice and prepare for it?"

"Perhaps." The viscount shifted uncomfortably. "Or perhaps he runs because he loves the feel of the exercise?"

"Ah." It did look like glorious fun, to move one's body as fast as one possibly could. "What does it feel like, I wonder?"

"Like death. And then superb, once you get past that part."

She laughed, and he laughed with her. For a moment, it seemed to her that all was right with the world.

"A man might run every morning to strengthen his heart and lungs, and quiet his mind," he said. "When he is not in London, that is. It would not do to dodge hacks and ladies without one's shirt on."

She laughed. "Heaven forbid." She gazed out at the lake. Her legs ached with longing to try it for herself, to move until exhausted. "Blasted skirts," she muttered.

His eyes danced with laughter. "I daresay, I would feel the same."

"How lucky for you that you will never have to test that theory."

He smirked. "Indeed."

She looked at him and grinned, and felt the smile blooming all over her face. The look he gave her in return—a look of startled wonder—caused her breath to stutter in her throat. She was suddenly filled with an odd sensation—a feeling of fierce protectiveness. Why should he be so surprised by a smile?

She longed to pull his head into her lap and stroke the burnished gold hair. She wanted to coax him, tease him, until he spilled all his stories of when he was wicked and when he was good. She knew instinctively he was a good man. His behavior toward her had never hinted at anything else.

Well, other than when he'd kissed her. And that had been *very* good.

But if he was good, then what was she?

For the first time, it occurred to her to wonder if she was a good person. She had thought the issue of taking her revenge quite simple. A man had destroyed her sister and thus deserved to be punished. But Alice had not realized that the punishment would of necessity involve more than just the man himself. *Of course,* it would. He had a family, just as Adelaide had. Was Alice, herself, not here and involved because of his deed?

The thought made her deeply troubled.

Because was that, indeed, not why she had come here, intent on using a good man to help her exact revenge upon his brother?

It was, and she was.

She dipped her eyelashes down, obscuring the storm brewing in her eyes.

Would a truly good person ever do such a ruthless thing? Probably not.

And yet…and yet…

Her sister was dead.

How could she not?

Chapter Twenty-One

"Shall I accompany you back to the house, Miss Bursnell?" Nathaniel asked. "My mother will have come down by now. I am sure she is eager to meet the latest arrivals." He stood and after a moment's hesitation—he was sweaty and unkempt, after all—offered his hand.

"Yes, thank you, my lord." Miss Bursnell allowed him to assist her to her feet.

He did not know what to do next. Her small hand was engulfed in his large one. He knew he should release her. They could not walk along, swinging their joined hands between them like schoolchildren.

Could they?

He would very much like to.

How odd.

Instead, he tucked her arm through his and freed her hand. He looked at her downcast lashes and felt a stirring of unease. He never knew what to expect from her. One moment they were laughing together, and the next she was quiet and withdrawn.

But, oh, it was such a lovely feeling, laughing with someone. He could not remember the last time it had happened, other than with Wessex. Surely, that was merely a trick of his mind. It could not be that his life was so barren of joy that he did not laugh. Yet, try as he might, he could not recall the last time he had laughed with someone—not with the same camaraderie of spirit that he felt now with Miss Bursnell. Even with Wessex, it did not feel at all the same.

He pushed the thought from his mind and turned his attention to the lady walking by his side. Remembering her desperation to escape the crowded confines of London, he said, "I hope you find Hampshire refreshing to your spirits, though it is not Northumberland. It is soggy and damp this time of year, but Haverly is full of good walks if you don't mind the mud."

She tilted her head back and smiled. "I don't mind, as you can tell." She gave a comical grimace and lifted her skirt two inches to give him a glimpse of muddy petticoat and delicate ankle.

Warmth spread through his belly. It was a truly delicious ankle.

How did she always manage to make him feel like a ravenous beast? Yet, food could not fill his insatiable hunger. No, he needed…something else. He stared fixedly at the arm tucked neatly through his.

As though sensing sudden peril, she tensed and turned startled eyes to meet his. "My lord?" she whispered. "Are you quite well?"

Was he? He wasn't altogether sure. His brain felt thick and slow, and the heat from his core was spreading through his entire body with alarming speed. "Yes, quite."

They were quickly nearing the house, but it was not close enough. He was in imminent danger of doing something regrettable and getting his ears boxed.

"The daffodils were well worth a muddy petticoat," Miss Bursnell said in a rush. "Is anything so joyous as those golden heads bobbing and dancing on a spring morning? Do you know they are also called narcissus? The name does not suit them, I think. They are flashy and showy, but not vain. Don't you agree? Exuberance should not be mistaken for vanity."

He looked down at her face quizzically. Her cheeks were red with a blush.

Catching his questioning glance, she looked at the ground and her color deepened. "Pardon me, my lord. I tend to babble when I'm nervous."

Her words brought him to a sudden halt. She could not be serious. Men like Wessex made women nervous. *Nathaniel* didn't make women nervous. Uncomfortable, perhaps. Bored, most certainly. But never nervous.

Again, warmth spread through his body. No, it wasn't lust. Lust he was familiar with. *This* was something…different. It flowed through his veins, sweet and thick like honey. It was like standing close to a fire on a cold winter night.

He cupped her chin and tilted her face back, forcing her to look at him. "Why do I make you nervous, Miss Bursnell?" he asked, his voice low.

Her lips parted in a soft puff of air, but no sound came out.

He lowered his head closer to that beguiling mouth and waited.

Her breath hitched.

He dipped his head even lower, but still no reproof came. It would take nothing at all to close that last sliver of space separating her lips from his.

Perhaps his ears were safe? Perhaps—

The sound of voices startled him. Miss Bursnell jerked away and took several rapid steps backward. He reached out instinctively, mindlessly, to keep her close to him, but she eluded his grasp.

"My lord, please." She looked at him with wide, wary eyes.

Remorse stabbed him in the gut. Again, he had misstepped. Again, he had misunderstood her.

The voices came closer. He looked up to see his mother, Lady Shaw, and Miss Benton rounding the corner of the house. *Ah, lovely.* Just the ladies one wished to see when one was sweaty and inappropriately dressed.

His bad luck never ceased to amaze and embarrass him.

"Nathaniel! There you are!" his mother said. "I was showing our new guests the gardens." She offered her cheek for him to kiss.

"Mother, hello. May I introduce Miss Alice Bursnell?"

"Ah, Baroness Shaw's niece. I'm delighted to meet you." His mother clasped her hands and beamed when Miss Bursnell bobbed a curtsy.

"Thank you, Lady Wintham." Miss Bursnell turned to her aunt. "Did you rest, Aunt Bea?"

"I did, and I feel quite refreshed. Pray, don't worry about me, my dear." The baroness looked from her niece to Nathaniel and smiled again.

It occurred to him, just then, that he probably stank.

Miss Benton was standing very still, head tilted to the side, her eyes also darting from Miss Bursnell to himself and back again. He could practically see the wheels turning in her all-too-clever brain.

His own mother was doing the same, her expression a mix of hope and curiosity. He knew her desire to see him wed and settled was even greater than his father's—at least it had been before this pesky heart business. The Earl of Wintham merely wanted an heir. The countess wanted *grandchildren*. Nathaniel was sure she was imagining a good half dozen lads and lasses with Miss Bursnell's dark hair at that very moment.

Would they have blue eyes or brown? Some of each, he reckoned, if they managed six of them.

Good Lord! Now *he* was doing it.

His mother's expression turned dreamy.

He cleared his throat and gave her a warning look. "Perhaps some tea? I am sure Miss Bursnell would appreciate some refreshments after our walk." And while the ladies took their tea, he could make his escape.

"A splendid idea! I will tell Charlotte to make a tray. Nathaniel, will you please take our guests to the morning room?"

His heart sank, and he bit back a groan. No, he did not want to see the ladies to the morning room. He wanted a bath and clean trousers. But he could not be rude to his guests. "Certainly. Baroness Shaw, if I may?" he said, proffering his arm.

She took it, leaving Miss Bursnell and Miss Benton to fall in step behind them.

"How were the daffodils?" he heard Miss Benton whisper with a giggle.

His face heated.

And he felt suddenly contrite about every time he'd ever laughed at Wessex when he'd put a foot wrong over a woman.

Chapter Twenty-Two

"Eliza, shh," Alice hissed in reproach.

"Oh, very well," Eliza whispered back.

Alice was not foolish enough to think her friend's silence on the matter would be permanent. Eliza may make insinuations and sly asides, but she was discreet. She would let the matter drop—for now—but was sure to return to it when they had a moment alone.

Lord Abingdon led them to the parlor, where they were joined by Lady Wintham. A moment later the maid brought the tea tray.

"How did you find the park, Miss Bursnell?" Lady Wintham asked as she poured.

"It was lovely, thank you, my lady," Alice said. "How beautiful this part of Hampshire is!"

"Miss Benton said you were searching for daffodils," Aunt Bea said. "Did you find them?" To Lady Wintham, she added, "Alice has been homesick for Northumberland, where the fields would be full of spring flowers right now."

"Yes, I did find the daffodils. You should walk there

yourself—it will remind you of Colworth House." Alice turned to the countess and smiled. "It was very kind of Lord Abingdon to make space for us. I do hope our addition to the party didn't cause any trouble."

"No trouble at all, I assure you." The countess glanced thoughtfully at her son.

Alice was aware that Eliza was taking an unholy delight in watching Lord Abingdon squirm in his seat, but before she could puzzle out the meaning, Duke Wessex appeared and everyone's attention was diverted thither.

"Wessex!" the countess exclaimed. "How lovely to see you again. Do have some tea."

The duke smiled. "It's good to be back at Haverly. When I look at you, my lady, years lose all meaning and I feel like an Oxford lad again."

Alice caught Lord Abingdon rolling his eyes and smothered a grin.

Duke Wessex claimed a seat near Miss Benton, who shifted ever so slightly closer to Alice. This time, it was Alice who couldn't suppress a heavenward glance. Lord Abingdon caught her look with an amused sparkle in his eyes. She couldn't resist smiling back at him. Their friends' preferred method of courtship was ridiculous, to say the least.

"How was your journey, ma'am?" Duke Wessex asked her aunt. "I trust Miss Benton and Miss Bursnell were good travel companions?"

Aunt Bea clasped her hands, beaming. "They were delightful."

The duke sipped his tea. "I daresay they were better companions than Lord Abingdon, who always insists on driving straight through, with never a thought to one's stomach or..." His voice trailed off as he truly took in his friend's appearance for the first time. "Good heavens, man, why on earth do you look like you were toiling in the fields?"

The countess turned sharply toward her son, her face registering surprise and dismay. Likely, her brain had been too full of matchmaking to take note of things such as Lord Abingdon's appearance, and Aunt Bea and Eliza were too polite to demand an explanation for his rough attire.

Duke Wessex, however, had no such qualms.

"Were you running again?" Lady Wintham asked. "Oh, I do wish you would leave that be and take up a more gentlemanly form of exercise. Boxing, perhaps."

"I have taken several lessons with John Jackson already. But as I greatly prefer running away to hitting another man, I believe I shall continue with my current regime."

His tone was light, but there was a hard look to his face that made Alice take note. She frowned and sipped her tea thoughtfully.

Misunderstanding her expression, the duke rushed to defend his friend. "You mustn't think him a coward, Miss Bursnell. Lord Abingdon has never shown any hesitation to defend himself and his friends. Any man who knows him will tell you that."

"No, I do not think Lord Abingdon a coward. I was merely considering his choice of words." *I greatly prefer running away to hitting another man.* "He does not seem to fear harm to himself so much as he fears doing harm to another."

The room went still. Lord Abingdon sat as if turned to stone, his eyes riveted to her.

Finally, the countess spoke. "Nathaniel, do go make yourself presentable. And try not to let the other guests see you."

The tremor in her voice was so slight that one would miss it if one did not attend. Alice did not miss it.

Lord Abingdon got to his feet like a shot, bowed quickly, and was gone.

Alice shared a look with Eliza.

"What," Eliza muttered under her breath so only Alice could hear, "was *that*?"

Alice did not know. But she would find out, even if she had to drag the truth from his lips with kisses.

Chapter Twenty-Three

Blast it all, she had done it again!

Nathaniel stormed to his room and stripped the offending clothing from his body. He lowered himself into the bath that had been prepared and immediately got out again. He rang for his valet. "George!" he bellowed.

His valet appeared.

"Yes, my lord?"

"The water is cold, George."

"Yes, my lord."

"Why is it cold?"

George let out a long-suffering sigh. "Because you ordered the bath for when you returned from your exercise at nine o'clock, my lord. It is now eleven o'clock."

Nathaniel gritted his teeth. "I need a bath. A *hot* bath. Immediately."

George eyed him balefully. "Yes, my lord. You do. If I might be so bold, my lord, to suggest that if you intend to bathe at eleven, you do not order a bath for nine?"

Nathaniel glared. George departed hastily.

A quarter of an hour later, Nathaniel again lowered himself into the bath, and this time was rewarded with good, hot water. He sighed and leaned back, relaxing in the steam. He tried to clear his mind, but his mind wouldn't clear. Try as he might, he could not budge Miss Bursnell from his thoughts.

Of *course* he would rather run away than stay and fight. In a fight, he would be forced to either kill his brother or be killed himself, neither of which was a palatable option. Especially not now, when he had given his father his word that he would mend the divide and bring Nick home.

Somehow, without knowing the particulars, Miss Bursnell had understood that. She instinctively understood *him*. It seemed he was naught but an open book to her, and she might thumb through the pages of his heart and mind at her leisure.

A terrifying thought if ever there was one.

After all, she might be here to kill him. As much as he wanted to reject the idea, he was still not 100 percent convinced she wasn't working with Nicholas—or some unknown party—to bring about a change of heir for the Abingdon earldom.

Still…if that were truly the case, she was, indeed, a consummate actress.

How long had it been since she had looked at him with loathing, as though he was a worm she would dearly love to trample if not for the fear it would soil her slippers? He had certainly not felt it today.

No, today had been…different.

The evening at the theater, he decided after due consideration. After that kiss was the last time he had felt the full force of her hatred. Since his promise that night to refrain from taking such liberties, she had slowly, slowly warmed to him. Which wasn't to say she was never angry. Because he'd nearly slipped a couple of times.

He should probably stop trying to kiss her. Then she couldn't be angry with him.

He frowned into the bathwater. That plan did not seem at all appealing. Surely, there was another way to avoid her ire.

A way that involved *more* kissing, perhaps.

After he finished washing, George dressed him and he joined the other men in the billiards room.

"Ah, there is the man himself!" Sir Bellamy declared. "Lord Abingdon will agree with me."

Nathaniel doubted that. Sir Bellamy was a neighbor and therefore an old family friend, as pompous as he was fond of spirits—which was to say, very—and he had yet to espouse a single belief that Nathaniel agreed with.

"I was just explaining to Colonel Kent why we cannot simply remove larceny as a capital crime. Kent, here, wants a full repeal of the Bloody Code. Can you imagine! A full repeal!" Sir Bellamy puffed out his stomach and harrumphed.

That made Nathaniel pause. A full repeal? *Should* a murderer be allowed to keep his own life after taking the life of another?

He studied Colonel Kent. He did not wish to agree with the likes of Sir Bellamy, but he would not mind sparring with Kent. "You don't agree with hanging a traitor, Colonel?"

The colonel shrugged as if it were all the same to him, but there was a sudden tension in his jaw. "I don't believe in a mandatory death sentence. Juries should be free to weigh extenuating circumstances. As for treason and murder...well, I am perfectly happy to start with larceny. I have yet to see an item that I thought worth a man's life."

Dash it all, why did the man have to be so sensible? Nathaniel had voted—unsuccessfully—four times in as many years to remove larceny from the Bloody Code.

"I agree," he said, if inwardly grudgingly.

Sir Bellamy's jowls quivered in his fleshy face. "You

cannot be serious, my lord!" He looked about the room for support. "Consider the words of the greatly esteemed George Savile. 'Men are not hanged for stealing horses, but that horses may not be stolen.' If the rabble know they will no longer face the noose for theft, they will take everything that isn't nailed down."

Nathaniel gave a wry smile. "For over a century they have faced that threat. It has not seemed to dissuade them. All it has done is inspire juries to lower the value of the goods taken, so as not to reach the level of grand larceny. Men do not want blood on their hands for the price of a paste necklace."

Sir Bellamy fairly bristled, but the man dared not continue the argument. A viscount—particularly a viscount who counted a duke among his closest friends—was not a man Sir Bellamy wished for an enemy.

Nathaniel was aware of Colonel Kent watching him closely. He knew the man was friendly with his father, having supported his project of bringing the Parthenon sculptures to the British Museum. He also knew Kent's reputation as a Waterloo hero, and while not a member of the peerage, he had a sizable enough fortune to tempt any scheming mama. And now it appeared he was also the champion of the poor and downtrodden.

Nathaniel clamped his jaw in irritation. Very likely, the colonel never found himself prostrate at the feet of any young lady with nothing to blame but his own clumsiness, much less found himself in such a position three times.

Had the colonel seen Miss Bursnell since the ball? If so, had he brought her flowers again? More roses, perhaps? The very thought made Nathaniel's stomach clench.

There was nothing so galling as discovering one's biggest rival was the better man.

Chapter Twenty-Four

The tedious Baron Dillingham was, at that moment, chasing Eliza round the drawing room, much to the amusement of Alice. She watched from a safe distance so as not to be pulled into the conversation by a desperate Eliza. For every step her friend retreated, Dillingham advanced two. Round and round the room they went.

Alice couldn't help but wonder what had prompted Lord Abingdon to invite the roué to his house party. It was an odd conglomeration of guests, to be sure.

"Mr. Ellsworth claimed that four inches is the proper width of a lapel," Dillingham said as they passed Alice. "Four inches! But I explained that, no, four and five-eighths was the ideal."

Eliza took a long step back. Dillingham took two mincing steps forward. And thus the dance continued.

Next to Alice, Lady Claire sighed. "Dillingham seems *quite* infatuated. Did you know? He walked with me from St. James's to Drury Lane, and spoke of *nothing* but Eliza's *pink gown*. Can you *imagine*?"

Alice laughed. Yes, she could imagine. Dandy Dillingham likely had quite a bit to say on the matter. "His opinion is worth at least as much as Beau Brummell's. Did you say you walked? Whatever possessed you to walk such a distance?"

Lady Claire dismissed the remark with a wave of her hand. "It is scarcely a kilometer, and the day was fine."

Alice's jaw dropped. Well!

"Lord Abingdon claimed it was much farther," she said as she snapped her mouth closed and narrowed her eyes. *Eight kilometers, to be exact.*

Lady Claire pried her gaze away from Baron Dillingham, and Eliza and turned to look at Alice, eyebrows raised. "How very *odd*! Why ever would he say such a thing?"

Why, indeed?

Alice was spared from answering by Eliza, who had, at last, managed to free herself. "Drat that man!" she muttered crossly. "Why is he not playing billiards with the other gentlemen?"

"Come now," Lady Claire protested. "*Surely* his company is not so *odious*."

Eliza's glare was murderous. "Then *you* converse with him on the width of men's lapels and the proper cravat knot."

Lady Claire pursed her lips. "Oh, very well." She wandered away from them and joined Dillingham by the bay window. Soon the two were deep in conversation.

"Well. That is much better." Eliza linked arms with Alice. "Come. Let us escape to the garden before she changes her mind."

They had scarcely left the room before they looked at each other and burst into giggles.

"Oh, heavens, that man!" Eliza gasped out. "If he has a single word to say on any topic that is not cravats or waistcoats, I have yet to hear it. Is he really so foolish as to think I find such conversation enthralling? Can he not see I am bored to tears?"

Alice patted her arm. "It is your lovely face, my dear. He cannot see the wicked thoughts behind the angelic countenance."

Eliza gave an exasperated huff. "Bother my face! I was practically running backward to escape him!"

They looked at each other and laughed again.

The garden path wound through pretty beds of spring flowers. Crocuses, snowdrops, and pansies poked shyly through the grass. They stopped at a terrace surrounded by rose bushes. The roses were not yet in bloom, but there was a stone bench for resting.

Eliza sat down. She smiled up at Alice. "I am so glad you are here with me. It would be dreadfully dull without you."

Alice laughed. "Oh, yes, how ever would you manage such dreadfully ugly scenery with only Duke Wessex to entertain you?"

"Never mind Wessex. He is tolerably amusing, but a man cannot be just friends with a woman. Friendship requires mutual respect and liking, and men simply aren't capable of having such feelings for a woman. It takes a depth they are sadly lacking."

Alice considered the point. She remembered the day at Westminster Abbey when she and Lord Abingdon had laughed together. She thought of the moment in the daffodils, when they had laughed again. It *felt* like friendship, or something akin to it.

Then again, she was still determined to avenge Adelaide, even knowing it would cause him pain. *And* he had kissed her. Revenge and kissing were not the stuff of friendship.

Very likely Eliza had the right of it.

"You have no idea how tedious London had become before you knocked down Lord Abingdon," Eliza continued. "This is my fourth season, and it is always the same. First come the girls in white dresses. They never say anything interesting for fear a marriageable man will overhear. Lady Claire is the best of the lot this year, but even she thinks I should be married by now."

The impassioned speech surprised Alice. How could Eliza, the toast of the beau monde, possibly be lonely? She clasped Eliza's hand in hers. "I am grateful for your company, as well." She paused, her gaze drifting about the garden, suddenly sad. "Do you know, I don't think I have had a friend like you since Adelaide."

Eliza eyed her cautiously. "Your sister? You never speak of her. Do I remind you of her?"

Alice shook her head with a smile. "No, quite the contrary. We were twins, you know, both of us as dark as you are fair. But more than that, she was so very sweet and demure. She never had a harsh word for anyone, and she was infinitely patient." She gave a rueful grimace. "My complete opposite, I was often told."

"Then mine, as well, I'm afraid. No one has ever accused me of infinite patience. You must miss her terribly."

"It is more than missing her. It is an emptiness that can never be filled. And yet, there are moments when I forget she is gone. I see something and I turn to point it out to her, and she is not there. I laugh and expect to hear her laughing with me. I smell her lilac perfume in the air. I hear a funny story, and I think, *I must tell Adelaide*. Then I remember, and it's like learning of her death all over again."

Eliza squeezed her hand. "I cannot replace your sister, but I do hope I can be of some comfort to you. If you need someone to talk or laugh with, or…or be sad with, I am here. I am *glad* to be here."

Alice blinked against the sudden tears in her eyes. "You have no idea what your words mean to me. My family is good and kind, but they cannot bear to hear Adelaide's name spoken.

It is still too painful for them, and when I try to speak of her, I am called maudlin. I do not wish to hurt my parents, but sometimes I feel like her name must simply burst from my lips."

"I understand. One cannot be expected to continue on as one did before, after such a catastrophe. I would never think you maudlin."

A meadowlark trilled, its cheerful call echoing in the distance. Alice felt like singing along. She felt lighter, somehow, as though a rock that had been pressing on her chest was suddenly lifted. It had been such a burden, carrying the memory of Adelaide silently and alone. She had not realized how much she'd needed to share her sister's memory with someone. She had been so very lonely, with nothing but a ghost and dreams of revenge to occupy her mind.

Now she had a friend.

Her mind drifted back to the daffodils, and her smile widened.

And yes, just possibly, two…

Chapter Twenty-Five

Alice was by temperament an early riser. She had always awoken with the first rays of dawn, much to the consternation of her sister and mother. Waking early had the advantage of freedom—she could indulge in whatever suited her fancy, for there was no one else awake to care and lecture. In Northumberland, she had used the time to ride her horse, and in London she had spent the time reading.

In Hampshire, she decided to spend the time snooping.

Lord Abingdon may have asked her to this house party so she might seek out his daffodils, but she had accepted the invitation for the sole purpose of seeking out the whereabouts of his treacherous brother.

Did she feel guilty about taking ruthless advantage of Abingdon's kindness for such nefarious purpose? Possibly. Fine, yes, she did. But someone had once said something about the end of an enterprise justifying the means, and avenging Adelaide's cruel fate was far more important than qualms over using an innocent to further that goal.

No matter how much her conscience pricked.

She felt vaguely like a criminal the first time she rifled through the papers in Lord Wintham's private study. Worse, she was an inept criminal, for she found nothing useful. When the household finally began to stir, she crept back to her room.

Breakfast, at least, was…entertaining. The food was of the usual sort—tea, toast and jam, sausages, bacon, eggs, and more tea—delicious, but not entertaining. The room itself, likewise, was lovely, in shades of creamy yellow and pale green, but not what one would call entertaining. No, the entertainment was provided by persons named Dillingham, Wessex, and Eliza.

Alice happily munched on her toast. She so enjoyed a good farce.

"White, you see, pairs well with black. But brown requires off-white if it is to be shown to its true advantage," Dillingham explained earnestly. "Just a shade or two south of cream."

Eliza's face was impassive. "Oh, yes, just so."

Anyone would have thought she was sincerely interested in Dillingham's analysis of the proper color pairings of gentleman's attire. But Alice noticed the miniscule twitch of her right eyelid and grinned.

Wessex, who sat to Eliza's other side, did not grin. He glowered.

That just made Alice grin all the more.

"Dare I ask what has you so amused, Miss Bursnell?"

The rough velvet of Lord Abingdon's voice gave her the tiniest ping of pleasure. "You may, but I would not be so indelicate as to answer. Watch for a moment, and perhaps you will also find a reason to be amused."

He hiked an eyebrow. "How intriguing." He heaped a plate with food and sat down at the table next to her to watch.

She poured him a cup of tea, added milk, no sugar, and

passed it to him. He took it but did not drink, instead staring down at the pale brown liquid with a curious expression. Like a child who was given a puppy on Christmas morning—overjoyed, but somewhat suspicious that it might bite him.

Something stabbed in her chest. "Did you not want tea, my lord?"

He looked confused by the question. "I—" He was, after all, English. His brow furrowed.

"Lord Abingdon? You are not watching," she chided gently.

"What? Oh, yes." He looked up from the perplexing tea and fixed his attention on the guests milling about the breakfast room.

He looked tired. What kept him from sleep?

She watched his gaze roam casually about the room, flitting from face to face before returning sharply to Wessex with yet another puzzled frown. He drank his tea. His frown smoothed. The corners of his eyes crinkled with a smile. Then he laughed outright, though he did his best to cover it.

He turned to her, his lips twisted comically.

"Yes, exactly," she murmured over the rim of her teacup. They were both being very naughty.

Eliza was turned squarely to face Dillingham, shutting Wessex out of the conversation completely—as much as Wessex could ever *be* shut out from anything. "Tell me, sir, do you think pink could ever pair with red?"

Wessex snorted derisively. "Oh, please—"

"Now, now. Let's not be too hasty. I wonder if..." Dillingham tapped his chin thoughtfully, clearly determined to give the matter its due consideration. "Yes, I think it might do. One would have to be extremely cautious in selecting the exact shade of red to carry it off."

Eliza leaned forward with round blue eyes. "*Do* you?"

Alice suppressed a giggle. Watching Eliza feign interest

in the minutiae of men's fashion and Wessex feign apathy—with far less success—toward Eliza's interest in Dillingham was the most fun she had had since…well…since she had stumbled on a half-naked man in the daffodils.

Even now that memory brought heat to her cheeks.

But not unpleasantly so.

"It is most satisfying to see Wessex so utterly discomfited by a baronet," Lord Abingdon muttered. "I would walk from one end of London to the other just for this."

Ha!

She took a demure sip of tea. "Or perhaps from Drury Theater to St. James's?"

His gaze snapped to her. "Pardon?"

"To be sure, it is no great distance, although I once heard it described otherwise. Why, you would have to walk there and back again *four times* to make eight kilometers."

He rubbed his cheek. He did that, she'd noticed, when he was anxious.

Again, she felt the slight stabbing in her heart.

She ignored it. "Back and forth, back and forth, back and forth, and back and forth *again*." She waved her arm to and fro in the air as she spoke. "Really, it would make one quite dizzy."

He looked down at his plate. She sipped her tea.

Finally, he asked, "Are you angry with me, Miss Bursnell?"

She pierced a bit of sausage with her fork. "No."

"No?"

"Good heavens, what kind of man would you be if you let me traipse even *one* kilometer through London in the middle of the night? In satin slippers, no less."

He blinked. "Quite right."

"Nevertheless, you should be prepared for retaliation. More tea?"

"Yes, thank— W-what?" he stammered.

She made a soft clucking sound with her tongue. "You were well aware I have no sense of direction. I told you my weakness in confidence, my lord, and you used it against me. Surely, you do not expect me to let that pass?" She poured the tea.

"What— Um. What are you going to do?" he asked warily.

She smiled sweetly. "Why, discover your weakness and use it against *you*."

He gaped at her. Then he closed his jaw, only for it to drop open again.

She tapped her fingers on the table in anticipation. Her smile widened. "This will be such fun. I do enjoy a new challenge. It is so thrilling, don't you think?"

"No."

She laughed merrily. "I meant thrilling for *me*. First, though, I must learn your weakness, since I do not know it already."

His expression shifted slightly, and he leaned forward, his voice low. "Do you not?"

She froze. Slowly, she raised her gaze to his. Why, why, *why* was he looking at her like that? As though she— As if he— Well. She did not know what. She only knew it made her skin feel itchy and prickly and hot.

Then he looked away.

And that was worse.

The room spun dizzily around her, and she reached desperately for the one thing that still made sense in her world. Her hand shook as she brought the teacup to her lips.

"Ah, good morning, Miss Bursnell. Lord Abingdon." Colonel Kent bowed. "May I join you?"

She smiled and thanked the heavens for the interruption. "It would be a pleasure."

Lord Abingdon said nothing.

"Miss Bursnell, I seem to recall you are an equine enthusiast. Would you care to walk over to the stables after you finish your breakfast?"

"I should like nothing better. I am done now, but please take your time."

"Oh, I ate ages ago. I keep country hours, you know." He stood and offered his arm. "Shall we?"

She took it. "We shall. Let me tell my maid to follow us."

She refused to look back.

She didn't want to ponder the look of recrimination on Lord Abingdon's face.

Or had it been...hurt?

Chapter Twenty-Six

The next morning, Alice had a strong hankering for daffodils. Was anything so lovely as the golden trumpets in the hazy shimmer of dawn? She thought not. So, of the ten hours of daylight during which she might wander, she chose the first. She donned her blue pelisse and a straw bonnet, and set off in the direction of the lake.

The morning was still and quiet, save the calls of birds and humming crickets. Certainly, there was no half-naked viscount running circles around the lake.

Not that she expected there would be.

She was *not* disappointed. Not at all.

She raised her hand to her forehead, shielding her eyes from the rising sun as she looked about the lake. No, there was no man. But there was an odd, lumpish pile of something. She walked closer to investigate and discovered a white linen shirt, a towel, and a flask of water—just the sort of things a man would need if he were to go for a morning run.

She looked about again, but saw no trace of Abingdon. Not on land, nor in the water.

The back of her neck prickled. Something did not feel right.

"Lord Abingdon?" she called tentatively. Then, louder, "Lord Abingdon!"

"Here," came the muffled return.

She moved toward the sound. "Where?"

"Down here."

She scanned the path anxiously until her eyes landed on a dark hole. She gasped and hurried forward. When she reached the hole, she knelt by the rim and peered down. "Lord Abingdon! Good heavens!"

He looked up at her with wide eyes and a pale face. "Miss Bursnell. I thought it was your voice. Hello. It's a lovely morning, is it not?"

She choked back a laugh. The man was ridiculous, making pleasantries while clearly stuck in some kind of trap. "Are you all right?"

"I believe so. My ankle is injured, and this blasted hole is too deep to pull myself out of, but I am all in one piece."

She got to her feet. "I will go fetch help."

"I would rather you didn't," came the swift reply.

She paused in disbelief. "I beg your pardon?"

"I would rather not wait here alone, is what I mean." He hesitated, then explained, "The hole was hidden, covered over with cloth and dirt, and the walls are unnaturally slick."

She knitted her brow. The excavation was just large enough for an unsuspecting man to fall into—and it had been dug smack in the middle of Abingdon's running path. It was so deep she could not even see the bottom in the darkness. The walls did seem to be coated with some type of slippery oil, making a climb out nearly impossible. The whole design was certainly deliberate, which meant that whoever had made it would likely return for their prey.

Lord Abingdon would not wish to be trapped there,

helpless, when he did.

"I see."

"Yes, I thought you might."

She planted her hands on her hips. "Well, how the devil am I to get you out?"

Her unladylike language did not seem to bother him in the slightest. "You told me once that you were fond of puzzles, did you not? You will think of something."

"Your faith in me is touching." Her tone was sarcastic, but no sooner had the words left her lips than she was casting about for ideas. His faith *was* touching—and inspiring. He believed she would think of something, so she jolly well would.

"How far up can you reach?" she asked.

He stretched his arms as far up as he could to demonstrate. His fingertips barely grazed the top edge of the hole.

"Not far enough for me to pull you out. Hmm."

He laughed. "Even if you could get a good grip on my arms, I don't think you could pull me out. I'm a full-size man."

"Oversize, I'd say."

He laughed again. She took this as a good sign. The danger could not be too great if he could still laugh.

She looked around again. She could use her pelisse as a rope, but there was no tree or log nearby to tie it to. She would still have to pull him up, or his weight would pull her down. If only he could get a toehold, he could scramble up a bit…but the walls of the hole were slick and smooth, and his ankle was injured. She kicked a rock in frustration, sending it sailing to the lake.

And that gave her an idea.

She ran to the lake, grabbed four fist-sized, long but flattish rocks, and returned to him. When she looked down, his face was pale and pinched, his eyes closed. He was clearly in pain. She cleared her throat. His eyes opened.

"Do you think you are up for some digging of your own?" she asked.

He smiled slightly. "Are you suggesting I tunnel my way back home?"

"No. I'm suggesting you jam a few rocks in the wall so you can climb out." She handed him the first rock. "Make a staircase, of sorts."

He took the rocks one by one and worked quickly, creating four steps. The wall was too sheer and slippery to allow him to climb straight out, so she removed her pelisse and handed him one end, holding the other secure.

"You will have to put weight on your ankle, I'm afraid. Should I climb down and help you?"

"You will do no such thing. Then we would both be stuck in this damn hole, for who knows how long."

"Eliza and Wessex would find us eventually."

"Unless someone else did first."

"Ah, yes." That wasn't worth risking. Whoever did this was clearly unhinged. "Right, then. I'm ready."

She heard him grunt as he stepped on his sore ankle, and moments later he lay sprawled next to her in the dirt, breathing hard. Then he scrambled awkwardly to his feet, pulling her up with him so hard that she landed against his chest with a soft thud.

His *bare* chest.

She let out a startled gasp and pressed a hand against him to steady herself. Even through her glove she could feel the springiness of the coppery hair and the taught muscles beneath. She could feel his heat.

Blood rushed to her face.

She told herself to step back, but instead found her fingers curling in that delightful, springy hair. "You should let me look at your ankle."

He shook his head. "No time for that. We must hurry. May I lean on you? I need assistance walking."

"Wait a moment." She grabbed his shirt and threw it at him. "Put this on."

He did as he was told with only a grunt of protest. "I may be shot in the back for the delay, but at least I will die fully clothed."

"I am not going to wrap my arms around a half-naked man, no matter how great the danger."

Or the temptation.

She knew how *that* could end.

He wrapped an arm around her shoulders, and she wrapped hers around his waist. She fit snugly against him in the crook of his arm. He stumbled slightly, and she tightened her grasp.

His linen shirt was not nearly thick enough. She could feel every contraction of his muscles, every movement of his bones, even through the layers of his shirt and her dress.

"Damn," she muttered, searching desperately for another layer. "I forgot my pelisse." It was still lying in the dirt by the hole, utterly useless. She looked at him sideways. "Pardon my language, my lord."

"Nonsense. If one cannot use foul language in a situation such as this, foul language might as well not exist. Your language is nothing compared to what I said when I fell in that hole, let me assure you."

She winced. "You must have been terrified."

"Do you know…I wasn't," he said thoughtfully. He sounded rather surprised by the knowledge. "I should have been." He paused. "I remember thinking, *No matter. Miss Bursnell will find me.*"

She turned to him, startled. Had he *expected* she would seek him out? "Pardon?"

"Not that I had any idea you would take an early walk.

You must have wanted to see the daffodils again," he mused. "But it seems to me that every time I find myself in an embarrassing fix, you are always on hand to witness it. So, naturally, you would be the one to find me in this morning's predicament."

She laughed in relief. "Strangely, I do seem to have a knack for it, my lord."

"So, I was not scared, because I knew you would come. It was a very comforting thought because I knew if you came, you would fix everything."

His words made her glow. She was ridiculously pleased by the compliment. All her life people had said, "Oh, *Alice*," in disapproving tones as she got into one scrape after another. No one except Adelaide had given much thought to how she had managed to get herself *out* of those very same scrapes, much less thought well of her for doing so.

Adelaide was the only scrape she hadn't been able to fix. *Yet.*

She tightened her grip around Abingdon.

He might be merely her means to achieve that end. But she would not let him fall.

Not until he'd served his purpose.

After that, once he'd discovered what she was about… Well, she was fairly certain no more compliments would be forthcoming.

Chapter Twenty-Seven

Nathaniel had never been so happy to see his home as he was after the morning's misadventure. His ankle hurt like the devil, and he wanted a hot bath and tea. Or possibly something stronger, despite the hour.

He was less happy to see his mother sitting at a table outside, taking tea with Baroness Shaw in the mellow sunshine. Both ladies jumped to their feet when they saw his hobbled approach, leaning heavily on Miss Bursnell.

His mother shouted for a footman then rushed forward. "Nathaniel! What in heaven's name…?" She caught him under his free arm to help bear his weight.

"It's only a bad sprain, Mother. That ankle has been weak since I broke it falling from the tree. I'm all right."

The two ladies helped him to a chair, and he gratefully sank into it.

His mother peered at him with narrowed eyes. "I suppose you sprained it running around the lake."

He hesitated. He didn't like lying to his mother. "Yes."

Her gaze shifted to Miss Bursnell. "And I further suppose

that Miss Bursnell happened by at a convenient time, whilst out for a morning stroll." When Miss Bursnell stared blankly back at her, she sighed deeply and said, "Clearly, it was just a coincidence, since you did not leave together before breakfast, even though you have returned together. You were in each other's company for no more than a moment, correct?"

Miss Bursnell made a small wheezing sound. Nathaniel was certain she turned a shade paler than her usual paleness. Clearly, she did not like lying, either. Or more likely, she was not eager to find herself ensnared by the parson's mousetrap. Not with him. The realization stung more than it ought. She would not want to sully her reputation with the circumstances, but, surely, marriage to him wouldn't be as bad as all that…

"Just so, Lady Wintham," Miss Bursnell said quickly. "I always enjoy a morning walk when I am in the country."

His mother clasped her hands together and exchanged a look with Baroness Shaw. Her face relaxed. "I see."

"You should have woken me, dear." Baroness Shaw smiled reproachfully at her niece. "I would have been happy to accompany you. At the very least, take your maid with you when you go walking in future."

Miss Bursnell nodded. "I will."

The footmen appeared, and his mother gestured toward him. "John, Henry, please see Lord Abingdon to his room. He has injured his ankle." She paused. "Again."

"Yes, my lady." They bowed and each grabbed an arm, hoisting him to his feet.

"I will have a tray brought to your room," his mother said. "You need your rest."

"I do not need to rest, Mother. It's my ankle. It's not a concussion or a broken rib."

"Nonsense," she said.

He did not bother to argue. It was easier that way.

"Thank you, Mother. Tea would be fine." He turned back

to Miss Bursnell. "And thank you, for helping me home. I'm not sure how I would have done so without your assistance."

She bobbed a curtsy. "Not at all, my lord."

He allowed John and Henry to help him into the house. Behind him, he heard Baroness Shaw say to Miss Bursnell, "Now, then. Have some tea and *tell me everything.*"

He couldn't help but grin.

He was quite certain Miss Bursnell would do no such thing.

Chapter Twenty-Eight

Alice stared out through the morning room window, forcing herself not to pace in front of the other ladies. The beautiful gardens outside were merely a blur.

Good lord. Someone was trying to *kill* Lord Abingdon.

No matter how many times she turned the facts this way and that, they always added up to the same thing. The chandelier, the riding incident, the hole in the path... At three strikes, the argument for coincidence was laughable.

Someone was *definitely* trying to kill Lord Abingdon.

Not that he seemed overly concerned about the situation, oddly enough.

Therefore, it was up to *her* to find the would-be murderer and put a stop to it. As if she did not already have enough to do with finding his brother and plotting revenge.

She let out a huff. She was really quite cross over this unwanted distraction. But if Abingdon were to die, she would have no excuse to stay at Haverly, and therefore would have no chance of finding his miscreant brother. Her blossoming concern had nothing to do with her not wanting to see him hurt in any way. Not at all.

But who on earth could be trying to kill him?

It should not be too difficult to figure out. Abingdon must have *some* idea of who would like to see him dead. And if he didn't…

Well, he must.

She racked her brain for a plausible suspect. The trouble was, he was such a solitary man. Most of the *ton* took very little notice of him, neither praised nor condemned him. No one would turn down an invitation to a house party issued by Viscount Abingdon, heir apparent to the Earl of Wintham, but it did not seem that any of the guests were particular friends of his…any more than they appeared his enemies. Duke Wessex was his only steady companion.

Abingdon must be so lonely.

That thought came unbidden, and she hastily pushed it away again. She could not allow her concern to become compassion. It would cloud her judgment.

No. She would *not* feel sorry for him.

She refused to feel sorry for him as she requested a luncheon tray be brought to his room. She refused to feel sorry for him as she returned to her room and summoned her maid. She refused to feel sorry for him as she marched purposefully to his room an hour later and rapped on the door.

But when he bade her enter, and she saw him sprawled on his bed with his injured ankle propped on a pillow and a miserable expression on his face, all her refusals evaporated and she felt overwhelmingly, achingly sorry for him.

It was just a sprain, she reminded herself. He was not dead. And he would not die anytime soon, if she had anything to say about it.

A sprain was nothing. A scratch or other wound might at least fester. A sprain couldn't even do *that*.

He lit up at the sight of her. "You came."

She nodded. "Has your mother already visited?" she asked, noting the chair by his bed.

"Yes. She promised me tea, but only brought broth. Broth!" He scowled. "As though there is anything wrong with my stomach. This blasted ankle has not made an invalid of me, but I assure you my mother will if I am kept here much longer. I will wither away to nothing but bones."

Alice laughed and took the seat. "Does that mean you are hungry, my lord?"

"Famished."

"Good. I asked for a tray to be sent up. It should arrive momentarily. In the meantime…" She hesitated and nodded to her maid.

Mary nodded back. "I shall take my mending to the hall, miss, and leave the door open."

"Thank you, Mary." When the girl had left, Alice turned back to him. "Now, then. It seems to me that someone is trying to kill you, my lord."

"That certainly seems to be the case," he agreed amicably.

She waited, tapping her foot against the plush white carpet.

He said nothing.

"Well?" she finally broke out.

"Well, what?"

She let out another exasperated huff. *Aggravating man.* "Well, who would *want* to kill you? You must have some idea."

"No," he said quickly.

Too quickly.

Her eyebrows went up.

"I thought it might be you," he reluctantly confessed. "At one time. As I mentioned, you always seem to be nearby when disaster strikes. Your timing is really quite uncanny."

He grimaced, then continued, "But I've given the matter some thought, and I don't think it can be you, after all. If you wanted me dead, you wouldn't bother to rescue me, would you?"

She shook the momentary shock—and large sliver of guilt—out of her head and forced her lips up into a smile. "It seems unlikely."

Good lord. Had she been *so* transparent?

"Furthermore, the assassin's methods of choice seem rather unlike you. A falling chandelier, a broken stirrup, a deep hole that would have been deuced difficult to dig... These methods are all very impersonal, and they leave too much to chance. I believe you would just knock me over the head with an iron and be done with it."

"Or shoot you," she agreed amicably.

He paused, looking slightly taken aback. "Yes. Or shoot me."

"Or push you off a cliff."

He cleared his throat. "Or that."

"Or, perhaps poison..."

He gaped at her. "Clearly, you have given the subject a great deal of thought."

She widened her smile. "A moment here and there, perhaps."

The tray arrived.

"Thank the heavens. I suppose we can cross starvation off your list of murderous methods, then." He reached for a jam tart and happily popped it in his mouth.

With a chuckle, she poured the tea, added milk, and passed it to him. "That would take far too long."

He rolled his eyes, then regarded her thoughtfully. "You remember how I take my tea. Though I only told you once."

She paused, her own cup halfway to her lips. "There are only so many ways to take tea, and yours isn't particularly complicated," she averred.

His eyes lowered, and his fingers fidgeted with the ruffled edge of a pillow. "Of course."

Oh, this man! What was it about him that made her feel so protective?

She reached out to touch his hand, stilling his fingers with her own. "It is very easy to remember how you take your tea. Just as it is easy for me to remember that you enjoy history, that you prefer running to boxing, that you have a brother and a sister, and that you don't especially care for pink. I find I have a very good mind for such things. Although…now that you mention it, I can't for the life of me remember how Duke Wessex takes his tea."

She frowned, a memory tugging at the edge of her mind— not of Wessex's tea, but something about brothers…

Neither brother behaved well, and they tormented each other.

That was what Abingdon had said that day at Westminster Abbey when he told her the story of Jacob and Esau, and the Stone of Scone.

An uncomfortable thought struck her.

Did such torment include attempted murder?

Her hand tightened on his, and she leaned forward. "What of your family? Not your sister, or your parents, of course, and I don't see your aunt digging such a hole, either. But maybe—"

He looked from their hands to her face, his expression dazed. "You don't recall how Wessex likes his tea?" he murmured, completely derailing her train of thought.

She blinked. "No. But I do not see how that is relevant to the conversation." She removed her hand and leaned back. What was wrong with the man? How could he be so unconcerned about his own wellbeing?

"You said—"

She ground her teeth in frustration and cut him off. "I understand it has been a trying day for you, but please pay attention!" Who the devil cared about Wessex's tea when there was a *murderer* to catch? She was trying to save his life! "Tell me about your brother," she ordered.

He narrowed his eyes at her suspiciously. "Why?"

She did not think Lord Abingdon was a stupid man, for all his awkward blunderings. He was being deliberately obtuse. She summoned her patience. "I am trying to discover your would-be murderer, my lord. Do you think it possible that your brother might want to kill you?"

He leaned back on his throne of pillows and stared unhappily at the ceiling. A whole minute passed in silence. "I can see why others might think so," he said at last. "But I prefer to think it's not him."

She frowned. "Then… Is he a suspect, or is he not?"

Abingdon pushed out a breath. "I suppose it depends on who you ask."

"I'm asking *you*," she said in exasperation. "We are not discussing a preference for honey over jam. This is not merely a difference of opinion. Do you, or do you not, think your brother is trying to kill you?"

His gaze did not move from the ceiling. "He is my brother. It is unthinkable that Nicholas would try to murder me. And yet," he added, more to himself than to her, "I *have* thought it. More than once. I have betrayed him, doubting his honor like that."

The catch in his voice made her pause. He rubbed his cheek, and she folded her hands tightly together against the desire to soothe him with another touch. "Perhaps it is a betrayal," she conceded. "Although, I count it a rung or two lower than fratricide."

"Which he might not be guilty of attempting."

"One can always hope. So long as one is not stupid about

it."

"Yes, that is the trick of it, isn't it?" he mused sadly. "How to hope, without being a bleeding idiot."

She managed a smile. "Keep your hope, Lord Abingdon. It suits you. But why do you say *others* think he might wish you dead?"

Abingdon considered her question, then abruptly swung his legs off the bed and stood up. "It will be easier to explain in the Great Hall."

Chapter Twenty-Nine

Alice stood, somewhat bewildered. "Are you sure you can walk, my lord?"

Lord Abingdon shifted his weight, wincing slightly. "I can limp, so long as Mother never finds out."

Alice smiled. The man was incorrigible. "Very well, then. Lead on."

The Great Hall connected the library with the private rooms of Haverly's north wing. The floor was veined marble, the ceiling gilded gold. A pastoral mural covered the east wall, flocks of sheep grazing while yellow-haired shepherdesses daydreamed in pretty pink dresses. Along the west wall, the portraits of seven Earls of Wintham stared down at them.

Alice stared back. It was remarkable, really, how the cheeks and chin and nose changed from man to man, but the blue eyes and red hair all remained the same, passed from father to son throughout the generations.

Lord Abingdon stopped at the first portrait, a beast of a man with a cloud of dark auburn hair and a scowl to match. "Lord Geoffrey Eastwood, the first Earl of Wintham. He was granted the title for his…er…*assistance* in restoring Charles II to the throne in 1660."

She gazed up at the portrait. She could well imagine just what sort of assistance he had provided to earn the king's gratitude. Centuries of faded paint could not dull the ruthlessness of his expression. "How…noble he looks," she said.

Lord Abingdon's lips twitched. "Nobility…brutality… It's certainly one of those." He stepped to the right. "Next to him is Albemarle, the second Earl of Wintham."

Albemarle appeared a shade less barbaric, she decided, but only a shade. It was clear he was his father's son. His expression was downright bloodthirsty.

"Albemarle was a second son, but inherited after his elder brother fell off a cliff," Lord Abingdon said then took another step. "Now we come to Francis, the third Earl of Wintham. Also a second son."

A chill stole down her spine. She didn't like where this was going.

Lord Abingdon moved on. "This is Walter, the fourth Earl of Wintham. Another second son." Here, he stopped and considered his ancestor thoughtfully.

She shivered. "How did the elder brother die?"

He pursed his lips. "A riding accident."

"Oh!" She inhaled sharply. But men were always killing themselves on horseback. Wealth and privilege did not guarantee brains. "Well. That's not—"

"The leathers were cut."

She froze. "Ah."

"Charles is the fifth Earl of Wintham."

She was afraid to ask, but forced the words past her lips. "A second son?"

"Yes. His older brother, Morgan, drowned in a puddle." Abingdon tapped a finger to his chin. "To be sure, Morgan was very drunk, but the puddle was very small."

She bit back an inappropriate, hysterical choke of laughter. "Oh, dear."

Abingdon continued down the row of portraits. "Philip, now, was most certainly murdered. His younger brother, Stephen, became the sixth Earl of Wintham."

"How was he murdered?"

"Poisoned porridge."

She winced. "Was it actually proven to be Stephen?" she asked. He shook his head, and she ventured, "It might have been his wife. It seems like something a woman would do."

Lord Abingdon blinked at her. "Do you know, that is exactly what Freesia said. You ladies certainly make a man consider the vows of holy matrimony in a new light."

Alice shot him a coy look through her lashes. His face flushed in response. Adorable man.

She turned back to the portraits. "I understand what you're saying. But…what of your brother? Do you think he was born wicked and can't help himself? That the desire to murder one's elder brother is passed down from the father to his sons, like red hair? Or do you think he merely heard the bloody family tales and got ideas?"

Lord Abingdon had also been the intended victim of cut leathers.

"My parents do believe he was born wicked, through no fault of his own, and they are determined to save him from himself by keeping us apart. My aunt, on the other hand, suspects the latter."

"But what do *you* think?" Alice persisted.

"I don't think he was born wicked. I think he was good once, and if he is otherwise now, it is my own damn fault."

"*Your* fault?"

He gestured to a chaise—placed, no doubt, with the express purpose of allowing visitors to admire a particularly buxom shepherdess in the mural—and Alice sat down.

He sat next to her and glared at the rolling hills. "I have not seen him since we were boys. Nearly two decades now. After the tree incident, he was sent to Eton, and I was tutored at home, to learn how to manage the estate when the time comes. At eighteen, I went to Oxford. Eastwood men have always gone to Oxford." He paused. "My brother was sent to Cambridge."

She touched his shoulder. "I understand he must have felt the insult keenly, but surely, that is not enough to contemplate fratricide."

Abingdon shook his head. "That wasn't the worst of it. He was not allowed home for Christmas or holidays, except for two months every summer, when I was sent to travel abroad. He wrote and received letters from our parents and Freesia, but he was no longer one of us. He was an outsider. When the war with France broke out, he was stuck in Europe and couldn't get out. Meanwhile, I was quite comfortable in London. I took his home and his family, Miss Bursnell. And for what? A boyhood accident."

The anger in his voice squeezed her chest, for she knew all too well the loathing was directed at himself. "You cannot blame yourself. You were not the one who banished him."

He laughed roughly. "If a man witnesses an injustice and turns the other way, does he not share in its guilt? He was banished for my sake, and I did nothing to save him."

He rubbed his cheek, and she caught his hand with hers, stroking her fingers against his jaw. He froze, the muscles in his face clenching.

Then he looked at her.

And she knew instantly.

He was going to kiss her.

Chapter Thirty

Kissing Alice wasn't so much a choice for Nathaniel as a given.

If she was going sit there so cozily beside him, her soft hand on his cheek and her black eyes so full of concern, well then. She *would* be kissed.

The remarkable thing, he discovered as his lips brushed over hers, was that she kissed him back.

He had meant to be gentle, to give her time to say no, but her hands tangled in his hair, bringing him more firmly against her. Her mouth did more than simply yield to his— she pressed back willingly. Eagerly?

By God, he hoped so.

He licked lightly over the seam of her lips, and they parted for him, her sweet tongue darting out to touch his. The movement surprised him. He pulled back and looked at her incredulously. She looked back at him with glazed, sleepy eyes, and lips still dewy from his kiss.

Their first kiss had been a surprise attack.

Their second kiss hadn't actually happened, at all, since

she had jumped away like a startled fawn.

But this third kiss… It was a *kiss*. It was the sort of kiss a man and woman shared when they liked each other above all others.

It was the sort of kiss lovers stole before ripping off clothing.

The thought went straight to his groin.

He groaned.

"Nathaniel?" A rosy flush bloomed on her cheeks. "Did I do something wrong?"

"God, no." He scooped her up and settled her on his lap. "Do it again. Kiss me." There was a needy edge in his voice that he wasn't sure was altogether manly. He didn't care. He *was* needy.

God, how he needed this. Needed her. Wanted her.

Needed *her* to want him.

If she thought less of him for it, she didn't show it. She framed his face in her hands, holding his head still so she could press her lips to his forehead. He tried not to breathe as she dropped feathery kisses to his eyelids, cheeks, and nose. Each touch left him hungrier for more, and when she finally slanted her mouth over his, he was nigh starving.

She smelled like paradise and offered heaven with that sweet touch of her lips, but it was not enough. Not nearly enough. He needed more.

He reclined into the nook of the chaise, keeping one foot on the floor while propping his other knee up on the seat so that it gently nudged her forward. And forward she came. Her breasts flattened on his chest and their kiss deepened. Their tongues stroked together furiously. She wiggled against him, trying to get closer.

Sweet merciful heavens.

If his cock had been interested before, it was now downright fascinated.

He banded his arms tightly around her waist, holding her still. "Don't move," he choked out, panting against her ear.

She didn't listen, of course. She struggled in his arms, lifting herself on her elbows to better see his face. "Why not?"

He couldn't answer. Her position presented her breasts to his chin, her arched back causing them to strain against the ruffled neckline of her gown. If he tilted his head just a little, he could nuzzle against all that satiny flesh.

She gasped in surprise when he did just that.

With one arm still firmly anchoring her hips to his, he swept his other hand up her ribcage to cup a breast in his palm. He crooked a finger over the lacy edge and tugged. *So close.* Another tug. *Just a little more.* He tugged again. His efforts were rewarded. Out popped a pale pink nipple.

He ran his thumb over it, thrilling when it tightened to a hard bud. Later, he would wonder what had come over him, but at just that moment he had only one thought. He had to take her in his mouth, had to suck deep. His whole body throbbed with it.

And so, he did.

"Nathaniel," she cried on a gasp.

Too much.

Her breast was in his mouth, his name on her lips, and it was all simply too much. He had to move or he would disgrace himself. He sat up too quickly, and she tumbled from his lap.

"Oh!" she cried as she hit the floor.

He looked down at her in horror. Her hair was mussed, her limbs sprawled in a most unladylike fashion, her breast exposed, and her eyes full of shock. *Damn!* He hadn't disgraced himself—not in the way of a green boy, at least— but he would still like to take a flying leap out the stained glass window.

She had set her dress to rights by the time he found his words.

"Alice, I'm so terribly sorry. Please forgive me—" *For groping you? For dumping you on the floor?* "For everything."

"You have had your share of falling at my feet, Nathaniel." Her lips twitched. "I suppose it was only fair to take my turn."

And then she laughed.

Laughed!

That was when he knew.

There was no doubt in his mind.

She was the woman he wanted by his side, through the good times and the bad. He wanted to spend the rest of his life with Alice Bursnell.

Even if it meant never eating porridge again.

He caught her hand, turning it over to kiss the tender underside of her wrist. "Alice, may I have your permission to speak to your aunt? Naturally, I would prefer to speak to your father, but given the distance to Northumberland, I think I should speak to Lady Shaw first."

Alice stared up at him with baffled black eyes. "My aunt? My father? Whatever for?"

He laughed. "To ask for your hand. Have I bungled it so badly?" He pressed a hand to his forehead in mortification. "Deuce take it! Of course, I should have started with you, Alice."

Her mouth dropped open.

Happiness? Or shock…?

He went down on a knee to grasp her hand in his. "You *will* marry me, won't you, darling?"

Chapter Thirty-One

For one sweet, dazzling moment, Alice almost thought she could say yes.

Lord Abingdon's proposal hung in the air, as precious as diamonds strung on a gossamer thread. By God, how she wanted to kiss him and say, "Yes!" and then perhaps kiss him again, and again, and again. Her whole body throbbed with the joy of it. How lovely it would be to spend her nights in his bed and her days by his side. She had been so lonely since Adelaide—

She pulled herself up with a start.

"I can't marry you." She wrenched her hand free of his grasp with a desperate sob. "No! I can't possibly marry you." She looked around frantically for an escape.

Too late.

He caught her in his arms. "But you must marry me, darling. You let me kiss you. You let me touch you here." His palm slid over her breast. "I want you. You want me. That's what a kiss means. What sort of lady would you be if you accepted my kisses and touches but refused my offer of marriage?"

"A very bad one," she whispered in misery. "Because that's what I am."

He laughed and nuzzled her neck. "Nonsense."

Why wouldn't he listen? This was madness! The tip of his tongue flicked against her collarbone, and her knees weakened in response. *Dear heavens.* She must put a stop to this while her brain was still functioning. And her willpower.

There was only one way she could think of.

Confess all.

"You don't understand." She had to force the words from her lips. "I knew who you were before the chandelier fell."

He raised his head, wariness seeping into his eyes.

"But that is not the beginning," she rushed on before she could turn coward, averting her gaze. "I suppose the story begins much the same way my life began—with Adelaide. We are opposites in that, you and I. She was born first, and it was I who came minutes later." She chanced a look at his face, did not like what she found there, and looked away again.

She stepped back, out of his reach, and clasped her hands in front of her so they wouldn't shake so badly.

And told him everything.

Adelaide's seduction and demise, how Alice had discovered the portrait in the locket, the year she'd spent searching for the man pictured in it, and her initial mistake in identity.

"It was such a relief to discover you had a brother. You were so very different from what I expected. It had puzzled me greatly."

He flinched. "Yes, quite understandable. How could I seduce your sister when I could barely form a sentence without my tongue tying itself in knots?"

She shook her head. "I only meant that you did not strike me as an unprincipled rake."

She bit her lip. How naive she had been! She had thought seduction and betrayal were intimate bedpartners in a man. But now she understood the truth. Abingdon could seduce quite easily—her eager response to his kisses was evidence of that—but he could not betray. If he had seduced Adelaide, he would have married her.

His expression grew cool and flat. "We have seen quite a lot of each other in the past month, and here you are at my home. I must ask, why do you bother with my company when you know I am not Adelaide's lover?"

She did not like to answer that, but she must. She studied her hands, filled with guilt and shame. "I do not know how to track down Nicholas on my own. No one else seems to have any memory of him. You are my only means of finding him."

"I see." He pondered that, his expression unreadable, while she waited.

Would he understand?

Could anyone?

"Revenge is such a tricky thing," he said at length, "so dependent on the character and temperament of the receiver rather than the giver. I suppose when you believed I was your man, revenge was fairly straightforward. I would fall in love with you, and you would break my heart. A man such as myself makes a very easy mark when it comes to the affections of a lady like you. But you must realize, Nick is a different sort altogether. Heartbreak won't work on him."

Her own heart was beating very fast. Abingdon was being so very reasonable…and yet, she felt instinctively his cool words shielded an entire universe of hurt. She simply couldn't let him think—

"It's true I had hoped to gain your trust," she said contritely. "But it had not occurred to me to break your heart."

"Why not?" he asked with more curiosity than rancor.

She swallowed. "I did not believe I could."

"No?" he asked, far more gently than she deserved.

There was a painful burning in her lungs, as though every breath drew in a blaze of fire with it. She gazed at him mutely.

"Tell me, what will you do when Nicholas is found?" he asked abruptly. "You have now confessed your scheme to me. Does that mean you give up your revenge? Or do you mean to harm him still?"

She lifted her chin. "I loved my sister very much, my lord."

His expression shuttered even more. "So you do *not* give up. But you see," he said evenly, "I also love my brother very much."

She looked pointedly at the portraits behind him. "Even though he might be trying to kill you?"

"Yes," he admitted freely. "I love him unconditionally. I cannot allow you to harm my brother, Alice."

The whirl of her conflicting emotions roiled to a tight knot in her stomach. *Adelaide's honor must be avenged.* Alice couldn't live with herself if she didn't follow through. "Do you really think you can stop me?" she asked.

The gauntlet was thrown.

She saw the knowledge of it flicker in Abingdon's blue eyes.

"My father might be dying," he said.

She looked at him, startled. She reached out a hand to him, but he instantly stepped back.

"Do not touch me," he said.

And with those words, she recognized the rage and betrayal that lurked beneath his polite coldness.

She dropped her hand, cut to the quick. Not that she could ever blame him.

He looked away briefly, as though to compose himself. "Father gave me two directives to complete before his eventual demise," he continued as if there had been no interruption. "One, that I marry, and two, that I bring Nick home. Unfortunately, I don't know where my brother is any more than you do. But perhaps news of a wedding would rouse him. If he truly is behind the attempts on my life, he would be eager to kill me off before the threat of an heir became imminent." Abingdon shrugged. "Or, perhaps, he would think a wedding the proper place to heal the familial rift. Weddings are good for that, I've heard."

She couldn't breathe. The indifferent, cynical man before her was nothing like the shy, gentlemanly nobleman she had come to know.

"I feel obligated to point out the fatal error in your strategy," he said icily. "You should have accepted my proposal. Then Nick would have come home, and you could easily have gotten your revenge."

The disdain in his eyes threatened to choke her. The cold savagery of his rebuke reminded her of his brutal early ancestor.

She put her hand to her throat. "Nathaniel, please—"

"*Now* you choose to call me by my first name?" He smiled slightly, and it was the coldest thing she had ever seen. "Well, *Alice*, you can go straight to hell."

Chapter Thirty-Two

Nathaniel stared at the spot seconds earlier occupied by Alice. Her scent still hung in the air, taunting him. He wished he could set the air on fire, burn the fragrance of sweet lemons out of existence. Not just in this spot, but in the whole room. In the whole house. In all of England. He wanted to scrub his world clean of any trace of the traitorous woman.

It had not been real. None of it. She had not found him amusing, or interesting, or even likable. She had not enjoyed his kisses or caresses. It had all been a ruse, carefully crafted to trap a different man into her clutches. His brother.

Nathaniel was cursed.

His whole damned family was cursed.

He spun on his boot, ignoring the sharp twinge in his ankle, and came eye-to-eye with the first Earl of Wintham. He ground his teeth and bowed to the portrait. "Damn you, too."

He moved to the second portrait and bowed again. "And you."

He moved to the third and bowed. "And you."

And so on down the line, until he reached his father. There, he paused. He could not damn his father, no matter how unhappy he was with their family history. His father had made mistakes, but Nathaniel believed his heart was in the right place, which was more than he could say for the earls who had come before him.

Had Stephen any qualms before he poisoned Philip? Had Charles felt remorse when poor Morgan's drunken gurgles were at last silenced in the puddle? He very much doubted it. His father had wanted to keep both his sons in the land of the living. Was that so very terrible?

Yes.

It had been terrible for Nick, banished from his only family as a boy, and as a man, trapped behind enemy lines with no safe route home.

Home? Not that Nick had ever had a real home.

It had been terrible for Freesia, who loved Nick and refused to believe her brother capable of fratricide.

It had been terrible for their mother, who missed her second son every day, and had agonized over his well-being during the war with France.

It had been terrible for their father, who likely recognized that things would have been far better if Nick had been born first.

It was all very biblical, really.

Jacob have I loved, and Esau have I loved just a little bit less.

Nathaniel had always been less than Nick. A hairsbreadth shorter, a hairsbreadth thinner, and always, always far less charming and accomplished.

The family had sacrificed Nick, and for what? Nathaniel hadn't even done his duty to continue the family line. At this point, it was entirely possible that he would die without a wife and without an heir, leaving Nick or his progeny to inherit the title, anyway, rendering fratricide quite unnecessary. His family's entire sacrifice would be moot.

Nathaniel's own life was not enough. *He* was not enough. Not for his brother. Not for the earldom. Not for his family.

And, clearly, not for Miss Alice Bursnell.

Chapter Thirty-Three

Alice went, not to hell, but straight to the library. Thankfully, Aunt Bea and Eliza were both there.

"We must leave," she announced firmly. "At once."

Eliza's eyebrows went skyward, but her friend remained silent. She merely pushed her papers and pen aside and waited.

Aunt Bea looked up from her book, but kept one finger marking her spot. "You mean abandon the house party? Why, whatever is the matter, dear?"

"We must *leave*," Alice repeated. "Now."

"Oh, Alice, we cannot return to London just yet. The countess would take it as a terrible insult."

Likely the countess would find it a much deeper insult if they remained under her roof. After all, Alice had just refused to marry one of her sons and sworn vengeance upon the other.

She looked about the room desperately. If she did not depart of her own volition, she feared Lord Abingdon would have no qualms about physically booting her from his estate.

Aunt Bea must not be subjected to such a mortifying scene.

If there was ever a moment for hysterical dramatics, this was it.

Alice picked up a book and hurled it to the wall with all her strength and stamped a foot as loudly as she could. "I want to *go home*."

"Oh, *Alice!*" Aunt Bea said on a gasp.

Eliza rose to her feet. "You must feel wretched, indeed, to send Mrs. Edgeworth's laudable prose flying. Perhaps some air will do you good. Baroness Shaw, will you excuse us? I believe Alice and I will take a stroll about the garden."

Aunt Bea nodded gratefully, her eyes wide.

Alice followed Eliza out of the library. But she would *not* change her mind.

"Is this to do with Lord Abingdon?" Eliza demanded when they were outside and out of earshot of the house.

"No." Alice threw herself down on a garden bench and stared angrily at her fingertips. She could still feel the warm press of his lips against them.

She wanted to scream. Her own *body* was betraying her!

Eliza hiked an eyebrow.

"Fine," Alice snapped. "It *is* to do with Lord Abingdon. Everything is *always* to do with Lord Abingdon."

"Ah."

"Ten minutes ago, I refused his offer of marriage on the grounds that I am determined to destroy his brother."

Eliza sat in stunned silence before finally saying, "Oh, dear. Perhaps you had better start from the beginning."

Alice exhaled forcefully, but did as she was told. For the second time in as many hours, she found herself pouring out the story of Adelaide and Nicholas Eastwood, and Nicholas and Nathaniel, and, finally, Abingdon and herself.

"Well!" Eliza said when she had finished. Her friend glanced at the rosebushes helplessly. The rosebushes apparently offered no advice, so she pulled herself together. "You cannot return to London and leave poor Lord Abingdon to the mercy of his very bad luck, that much is obvious."

Alice frowned. She had rather thought her friend would understand that they must retreat posthaste. "Why not?" she demanded.

"Because you're in love with him," Eliza said matter-of-factly.

Alice's world came to a sudden, irrevocable halt.

In love with Lord Abingdon?

Heavens, no. Surely not.

She cared for him, certainly. She was always happy to see him. In fact, there was no one she would rather converse with or laugh with or...or indulge in sweet kisses with. But that was not love. That was friendship...perhaps with a healthy dose of lust.

Under different circumstances, that might possibly be a solid foundation for marriage. Even if, as Eliza had once pointed out, marriage might be better off without the burden of love.

Besides, the whole notion of love *or* marriage between Alice and Nathaniel Eastwood was impossible.

She could not love him. Her abiding love for Adelaide was what drove her need for revenge. Loving the brother of her sister's seducer would be in direct opposition to that. She could not love both. Where one gained in her affections, the other must falter.

She could not—no, she simply could *not!*—abandon her need for revenge. It was all she had left of her sister.

She watched Eliza stroke a glossy green rose leaf with one gloved fingertip. Soon, the buds would be blooms.

"I am *not* in love with Lord Abingdon," Alice stated resolutely.

"No?"

She lifted her head and met her friend's smirk with a glare. *"No."*

"And yet, your own actions suggest otherwise. It is very puzzling, I must say." Eliza turned abruptly from the rosebush with a swish of muslin skirts.

Alice faltered under the directness of those blue eyes. "You think I'm in love because of a few kisses? I assure you, that was all a ruse to gain information on his brother." The lie tasted like ash in her mouth.

Eliza gave her a pitying look. "Those were not the actions I was speaking of."

Alice furrowed her brow. "What, then?"

"Why, your refusal to marry him, of course." Eliza smiled. "He is a bumbling sort and painfully shy in society, but no woman hell-bent on revenge would let that stop her from accepting. You must have realized that such a marriage would make revenge *easier.*"

"Nonsense," Alice said sharply, despite the fact that Abingdon had said exactly the same thing, and well, it was no doubt true. "I simply do not wish to tie myself forever to a man under such disagreeable circumstances," she insisted. "I did not refuse out of regard for him. I refused out of regard for *myself.*"

More lies…

"But, Alice, you told him the *truth*," Eliza said gently.

Struck speechless, Alice opened and closed her mouth like a fish gasping for breath.

There was no arguing that.

For God's sake, why *had* she done such a rash, imprudent thing?

"He was kissing me," she said finally. "I couldn't think. He has this way of— Well. It's difficult to keep one's wits when he's doing that. You have no idea."

A smile lurked at the corner of Eliza's mouth. "Quite so."

"Oh, hush," Alice grumbled, the heat of her chaotic emotions dissipating a bit.

Eliza sat next to her on the bench and patted her hand sympathetically. "Sweeting," she said hesitantly, "are you quite sure it must be this way? I think you would be quite content with Lord Abingdon for a husband. Revenge is hardly the stuff of lasting happiness."

Happiness? Who said anything about happiness?

"Of course it must be this way," she said. "What other way could there possibly be?"

Eliza pursed her lips. Alice waited, a pitiful hope arising in her chest.

But in the end, her friend just shook her head. "Such a waste," she murmured regretfully. "Secrets, intrigue, love. I feel we are all characters in a Gothic romance."

Alice couldn't agree more.

And like any good Gothic tale, this one would end unhappily.

Chapter Thirty-Four

Alice felt slightly nauseous as she dressed for dinner. How on earth was she to keep Lord Abingdon from tossing her out on her ear? For, she had realized, Eliza was right—Alice could not, in all good conscience, leave for London just yet.

She was *not* in love with the viscount, but that did not mean she wished to see him murdered, either. More important—*much* more, she told herself sternly—she could not leave when it was so obvious that Nicholas Eastwood must be hiding somewhere close.

Lord Abingdon might live in denial, but Alice harbored no such illusions. Nicholas *must* be behind the attacks on his brother. Who else could it be? And if Nicholas was lurking about the estate, so must she.

Both for her sake, and for Nathaniel's.

Unfortunately, he would undoubtedly disagree. On all counts.

Bother.

She took special care with her appearance for dinner, allowing Mary to fuss over her curls until they were just so.

Alice's dress was a pale lilac color. Normally she detested pastels, but there was elegant embroidery of dark purple around the sleeves and along the neckline, and that saved it. The color even turned her eyes a smoky lavender, which was quite flattering.

If Abingdon sent her packing, at least she would do so in style.

Mary met her eyes in the mirror with obvious satisfaction. "You look gorgeous, miss."

"Thank you, Mary."

"He won't be able to resist you, if you don't mind me saying so."

Alice smiled faintly and gathered her courage. She swept out of the room, down the stairs, and into the library where Lady Wintham's guests had gathered for a pre-dinner aperitif.

She took a hesitant step forward, her gaze darting around the room. Where was Eliza?

She saw Aunt Bea standing with Lady Claire and her mother, and made her way toward them.

Suddenly, there was a strong hand on her elbow, and before she could even gasp, she found herself no longer in the library. Instead, she was in a small, dark space. She heard the sound of a match being struck, then a lantern on the wall glowed bright, illuminating the room.

"Lord Abingdon. How delightful," she managed past her suddenly dry throat.

"You're still here." His tone suggested that was a very bad idea on her part.

"Indeed." Her glove had slipped down slightly when he grabbed her elbow. She tugged it carefully back into place, then took in the cramped surroundings. "Speaking of which, where, exactly, are we?"

"One of the many hidden rooms in this house. We came by way of the wall panel next to the bookcase."

She examined the wall closer, curiosity overtaking her trepidation. "And I suppose this lever brings us back?"

"Yes."

She did not touch it. This was the first useful information she'd gotten since arriving. "How many hidden rooms are there at Haverly?"

"At least half a dozen that Nick or I or Freesia discovered. Possibly more that we haven't found."

Alice looked about. "It doesn't seem to lead anywhere. What was the purpose of such a room, I wonder?"

"I'm sure my ancestors had their reasons, nefarious or otherwise."

She grinned at that, in spite of herself.

He didn't smile back. "You're still here," he repeated.

"Yes. You never actually told me to leave. You told me to go to hell. I assumed you didn't mean literally."

He gave her an incredulous look. "In that case, let me make myself perfectly clear. You *will* leave at first light tomorrow morning, escorted by force, if necessary."

"Absolutely not. I intend to stay."

"Indeed?" His voice held a distinct warning, but she ignored it.

"It would be uncomfortable, would it not, if I were to tell the countess exactly *why* I am looking for Nicholas? I presume she would be most unhappy to hear of his contemptible treatment of Adelaide, and her unhappy fate. On the other hand, if I were to stay, I would naturally not wish to bother her with such a sordid tale. It would stay our little secret."

His eyes smoldered with barely leashed fury. "Blackmail? That is beneath you."

She lifted her chin and ignored the sick feeling in her belly. "Have our kisses taught you nothing, my lord? Nothing is beneath me."

But she found herself proved oh so wrong by six feet of

irate male.

He pushed her up the wall, her toes dangling helplessly a foot above the floor, unable to find purchase. She grasped his shoulders to steady herself as his hard thigh slid between her legs, pinning her between the wall and his body.

"Do not toy with me, Alice," he growled. "I am not your plaything."

She stared down at his furious face and, really, she couldn't help herself. She lowered her head—a mere fraction of an inch, no more—and rubbed her lips against his. For a moment, they both went completely still. It was so quiet she could hear her own heart pounding feverishly in her chest. Or was that his?

Then he made a hungry noise, his lips parted, and he devoured her kisses like a starving man unsure of his next meal. His tongue danced with hers, and he sucked it into his mouth. Pressure was building, first in her belly, then lower still. She writhed against his leg, trying to ease the ache. There was too much blasted fabric in her way!

"Please," she whispered. "Oh, please." She didn't know what she was asking for, but she knew instinctively that he was the only one who could give it to her. She writhed again.

He looked into her face, and whatever he saw there made his mouth twist in a grimace. Slowly, slowly, he released her, lowering her to the ground. He stepped backward.

She took in great gulps of air and tried to steady her shaking limbs. He would not? She was his for the taking, and he *would not take her*?

But why should he, when she had proved herself nothing more than a shameless wanton? A blackmailer with no soul? A— She lacked words for what she was.

A shudder wracked her body. Tears sprang to her eyes. She was so incredibly ashamed.

His arms immediately came back around her. "Hush,

now," he said softly. "Be still."

But she couldn't. It was all too humiliating.

Without thinking, she pushed him aside and grabbed the lever. Immediately, the door slid into a pocket in the wall, and she was blinking in the sudden bright light of the library.

And Lady Claire blinked right back.

Chapter Thirty-Five

Alice tried to imagine what Lady Claire must be thinking, which was an odd experience, to be sure. It had never occurred to her that Lady Claire had actual thoughts.

Alice knew her face was flushed from Nathaniel's kisses, her dress smudged from the dirty wall, and her hair askew. If ever there was a time that Lady Claire might truly have a thought, this was that inconvenient time.

There was a low murmur of voices from the hallway outside the library.

Oh, hell and blast.

Abingdon stepped forward quickly. Lady Claire just as quickly shoved him back into the secret room.

"Close the door!" she hissed. She whirled to Alice. "Faint!"

Without a second thought, Alice obligingly dropped to the floor.

Lady Claire immediately lowered herself in a graceful squat and proceeded to pat Alice on the cheek. "Miss Bursnell! *Oh*, Miss Bursnell, *please* wake up!" she called loudly.

A crowd of guests gathered round. Through her shut eyelids, Alice could see their shadows.

"What on earth?" Aunt Bea said on a gasp of alarm.

"We were going in to dinner when a mouse ran across her foot," Lady Claire explained. "Miss Bursnell fainted. Just dropped like a stone!"

There was a pause while the crowd digested this highly unlikely information.

Alice groaned inwardly.

"My niece *fainted*?" Aunt Bea said, the word tinged with disbelief. "Because of a *mouse*?"

"A mouse in *my* library?" Lady Wintham demanded, aghast.

"It was a very little mouse," Lady Claire said hastily, as if size was all that mattered.

Alice decided it was better for all concerned to stop thinking about mice immediately. She gave a delicate cough.

"I think she's coming to!" Lady Claire said excitedly. She patted Alice's cheek again, perhaps a bit more roughly than circumstances strictly demanded.

Alice swatted her hand away and opened her eyes. She did her best to look confused. "Aunt Bea? What am I doing on the floor?"

"You fainted!" Lady Claire said firmly.

Two strong hands grasped her arms. "Miss Bursnell, if I may?"

She looked up at Duke Wessex and nodded. "Thank you, Your Grace."

He hauled her to her feet. His eyes twinkled. Alice decided she did not like Wessex one bit. He was always amused at one's expense, but never at his own.

"Oh, dear," Lady Claire said innocently. "I'm afraid the fall has made your dress dirty. Your hair is mussed, as well."

Which, of course, she had to point out to everyone.

Wessex offered his arm, and she took it, allowing him to lead her in to dinner.

"Where is Nathaniel?" she heard the earl mutter to his wife. "Wasn't he here a minute ago?"

"Oh, he's somewhere close by, I'm sure," the countess returned, unperturbed.

Wessex smiled down at Alice. "I daresay that is correct, don't you?" he murmured in a hush that only she could hear. "I think it highly likely that Abingdon is holed up somewhere close by, indeed."

Alice pretended not to hear him.

But she cast a look over her shoulder at Lady Claire, who was tripping along on Dillingham's arm, listing for him all the shoes she had tried on that night. Hearing her silly conversation now, no one could have guessed that just moments ago she'd been the razor-sharp author of the deepest intrigue possible...and savior of Alice's badly wavering reputation.

She shook her head.

Really, the woman was quite frightening.

Chapter Thirty-Six

Nathaniel waited in the priest hole, ears straining, until the last muffled conversation had faded. When he was certain the library was empty, he pulled the lever. The room was, indeed, empty.

And he was late to dinner.

Damn.

He walked briskly to the dining room and paused in the doorway. "Apologies for my late arrival." He considered drumming up some plausible explanation, realized no one cared—in fact, they had barely noticed his absence—and took his seat between Lady Claire and her mother.

Lady Claire smiled at him and launched into a description of all the meat pies she had ever eaten in her life and who had shared them with her.

He gave an inward sigh. Such was his penance.

Across from him, Alice was engrossed in conversation with Colonel Kent. Watching them, Nathaniel's blood began to simmer. How dare she look at the man like that? Her eyes were gentle and kind, her smile sweet. She never looked at

Nathaniel like that. She was never sweet to him. She had no right to give such smiles to Kent, when only moments ago she had been in Nathaniel's arms, begging him to—

To…what?

Stop, most likely.

He frowned and took a swallow of wine. For one brief, exquisite moment, he had thought she was asking him to divest her of her virginity right there against the wall. Which was absolute nonsense, of course. The wall was dirty. One did not deflower even a chambermaid in such a manner—he assumed—much less a lady. He was cock-brained, that's what he was—which, unfortunately, seemed to be his usual state when it came to Alice.

Kent bent his head closer to Alice to say something. Her hair grazed his cheek.

Nathaniel wondered whether Kent's military career had really been as exemplary as everyone said. Perhaps the colonel had committed some grievous offense that would put him in front of a firing squad. Someone should investigate the matter.

"And then, Lord Abingdon, you will remember the time two years ago on the second Monday in June when Lady Albertson hosted a picnic. You gave me your mince pie because the horse had eaten mine."

Nathaniel came back to himself with a start. He looked askance at Lady Claire. No, he did not remember that. Why the devil did she think he would? Who cared about mince pie, anyway?

"Are you quite certain it was the second Monday in June?" he teased soberly.

"Quite," she said, unperturbed.

He did not know what to make of that. It was such an oddly specific memory that he would have believed the girl harbored a tendresse for him if he hadn't known better.

He should really thank Lady Claire for shoving him into the priest hole and protecting Alice from scandal. She would have been forced to marry him, and no amount of revenge could have stopped it. And *then* where would they be?

In bed, probably, and hating each other in between hours of hot, melting kisses.

Yes, he owed Lady Claire a debt of gratitude for saving him from such a terrible fate.

He scowled at her.

She smiled serenely and ate a piece of venison.

Alice had now turned her attention to Sir Bellamy. Her expression was one of polite interest, but something in the way she gripped her fork suggested she would like to stab him in the eye with it. Nathaniel tried not to smile.

But then Kent stole her attention back, and Nathaniel was miserable again.

This was madness! She was an avenging angel come to destroy his own brother. She would let nothing, including Nathaniel, stand in her way.

She did *not* care for him. She had told him as much right out. He was merely a pawn in her grand scheme for vengeance.

The trouble was, he was such a damned willing pawn. He could not seem to defend himself against her. He had told her to leave, she had outright refused, and then she had *kissed* him. And now, here she sat at his supper table, flirting with another man. The whole situation was utterly preposterous.

How was he to stop her quest for revenge? For stop her, he must. He could not let her win this game with his brother's life. It would tear his family even further apart. They would never be whole again.

It would likely kill his father.

Nathaniel's conscience bit at him. Because…hadn't Nick done exactly that to Alice? He had destroyed her sister. He had seduced a gently bred innocent and left her to suffer the consequences all alone. His behavior was an outrage. Such a thing could not be allowed, either.

Yes, Nick would have to be dealt with—but by Nathaniel, himself, not by Alice.

Perhaps a restitution could be paid. Easier said than done. What price did one put on a lady's—a sister's—life? Would fifty thousand pounds suffice?

He looked at Alice and knew the truth.

No.

She had lost her sister. No amount was great enough to make up for that.

Chapter Thirty-Seven

Where *was* Nicholas Eastwood hiding?

It was only just after dawn, and Alice stared up at the house, thinking, while her maid stood behind her, yawning.

Nicholas *must* be nearby, otherwise he would not have been able to set the traps for Nathaniel. Nicholas couldn't have known his brother's daily routine without watching him for a period of time. So, he must be close. Perhaps in town… although, he was more likely hiding in the woods somewhere to avoid being recognized.

Or perhaps he was much closer. Perhaps he had been hiding right under her nose the whole time. Now that she knew about the existence of secret rooms in the manor, she couldn't believe that Nicholas wouldn't take advantage of them.

She pressed her lips together in a tight line. She did not like to think of him being so close to Nathaniel. Still, Nicholas knew of the rooms, but so did Nathaniel. If Nicholas was hiding in one of them, Nathaniel could easily find him.

If he bothered to look.

Which he hadn't, because he didn't really believe Nicholas was trying to kill him. Or if he did, he had just accepted his fate.

Alice ground her teeth in frustration.

"I believe I shall take a walk, Mary," she said, turning abruptly.

Mary frowned. "You have not yet eaten breakfast, miss."

Alice waved her hand dismissively. "That can wait. My walk cannot."

Mary sighed and trotted after her. "To the daffodils, miss?"

Alice narrowed her eyes. "As it happens, yes."

"Perhaps your aunt would like to accompany us?" Mary suggested hopefully.

"*I* would not like that," Alice said.

Mary let out a second, much deeper sigh, to let Alice know exactly how she felt about *that*.

"Perhaps this afternoon we can go into town," Alice said. "I had a thought you might like some new hair ribbons."

Mary gave her an assessing look. "I suppose the baroness needn't be bothered every time you wish to take a walk," she allowed more cheerfully.

Alice grinned.

It was a misty morning. The ground was still slick with dew, and her slippers soon grew damp. This annoyed her greatly...until she caught sight of Nathaniel rounding the lake.

Mary let out a shriek. "Why, he's...*naked*!"

"He has on trousers." *But not a shirt, thank heavens.*

Lord, he was beautiful.

"Miss Alice, you mustn't be here!" Her maid's voice rose in panic. "Your aunt— The countess! Please, miss, we must—"

"Do be quiet, Mary. I'm trying to watch."

Mary let out an indignant squawk.

Nathaniel caught sight of them then, slowed, and halted. His hands went to his hips, and he scowled at them.

Alice dropped into a curtsy.

Mary groaned.

He stalked over, halting so close to Alice that she could feel the heat from his exercise radiating from his body like steam. She shivered. And not from dislike.

"To what do I owe this pleasure?" he asked sardonically.

Twice before, she had been confronted by this very same sight. But the first time she had been merely shocked, and the second time they had been in actual danger. Both times his shirt had been speedily replaced. This time, Alice looked her fill.

His chest and stomach were dusted with short, coppery hair, which she had noticed before. What truly fascinated her, however, were his nipples. Whatever were they for? Men did not nurse babes. A memory sprang to mind—his hot mouth on her breast, suckling. *That* had not felt maternal in the least. Would he like it if she did the same to him?

"Alice," he said roughly.

"Oh!" Her cheeks blazed.

Mary cleared her throat. "My lord, if you will excuse us—"

Alice interrupted, "Lord Abingdon and I have important matters to discuss. If you would be so good as to stand back fifty paces, Mary."

Mary did not move a step.

"*Hair ribbons*, Mary," Alice reminded her. When her maid remained stubbornly in place, she clamped her jaw. "And perhaps a new bonnet?"

Mary curtsied. "My lord will put his shirt on first, if you please."

Nathaniel gave a startled look to his bare chest. While

he remedied his nakedness, Alice sent an annoyed glare to her maid, who returned it with a smirk. She dipped another curtsy and was off. Alice counted as she stepped.

"She can still see us," said Nathaniel, now wearing his shirt.

"But she can't hear us, and that's the important thing," Alice said.

He tipped his head. "Of course."

She smoothed her skirts and gathered the precious few wits that hadn't deserted her at the sight of his naked chest. "Lord Abingdon," she began.

One corner of his lips curled upward.

She frowned. "Something amuses you?"

"As you've already intimated, I believe we're beyond such formality. We know each other's sins, and I have taken certain liberties with your body. You have been false with me three times. In this matter, at least, you will be honest. I am not Lord Abingdon to you, except in public. In private, you will call me Nate."

For a moment, she was torn between the desire to throw herself into his arms and beg his forgiveness, and the equally strong desire to kick him in the knee for his presumptuousness.

She did neither.

"Very well. Nate," she said, trying out the sound of it. It made her insides feel squishy. That wouldn't do at all. "No. Nathaniel," she said briskly. That was the name that had slipped out once before, and it felt far less…intimate. "I have a proposal to make."

His eyebrows shot up. "By all means, let's hear it."

"I need your help to find Nicholas. No one knows this house and property as well as you. If your brother is determined to remain hidden, I have little hope of finding him without your help."

"You cannot be serious."

"I assure you, Lord…Nathaniel, I have never been more so."

"And yet, if you find him, you will harm him. You're asking me to betray my own flesh and blood."

She wanted to shake him. Why was the man such a fool about his scapegrace of a brother? But she had prepared for his objections. "But I am not asking you to betray him. I am asking you to prove his innocence."

Abingdon—Nathaniel—crossed his arms over his chest. "Explain."

"If Nicholas is hidden here on the estate, he means to kill you," she said. "No one hides because his intent is benevolent. However, if we search the estate, leave no stone unturned, no secret room unsearched, we can likely assume it is someone else trying to murder you."

"A cheerful thought," he muttered.

"We would find the murderer, whoever he may be," she said firmly. "And you would be safe."

"But if we find Nicholas, *he* will not be safe," Nathaniel reminded her.

"You would be there with me. Would you rather I discover him on my own?"

Nathaniel's hands clenched into fists and his eyes turned stormy. "No."

"Then it would be wise for you to assist me in my search, if only to ensure I do not succeed."

His gaze narrowed. "You are playing with me again, like a cat with a mouse. I can't trust you."

"All the more reason to keep me close," she dared.

He moved like he meant to reach out and grasp her.

Her heart beat wildly, and she took a step toward him when she ought to have stepped back.

He halted, his hands raised to her shoulders but not touching them. "It's a dangerous game you're playing, Alice," he said quietly.

"It's not a game, my lord," she returned. His eyes flashed, and she hastily amended, "Nathaniel."

His arms dropped to his sides. "I cannot trust you," he said again.

"I have never lied to you, not even when it would serve my purposes to do so. I should never have spilled Adelaide's secret to you, nor my intentions for Nicholas. Even now, I am telling you the truth."

That gave him pause. He searched her face. "Why?"

She smiled slightly. "Because I know you cannot stop me. You will help me find Nicholas, and I will gain my revenge."

"No," he said slowly. "I meant, why did you tell me about Adelaide?"

Alice bit her lip. She knew what Eliza thought about that, but she wasn't willing or ready to concede she did it out of any tender feelings for this man.

She shrugged a shoulder. "I already told you. I need your help."

He continued to study her, his blue eyes thoughtful.

"Very well," he said finally. "We shall hunt for Nicholas together. But make no mistake, Alice. I *will* stop you from harming him in any way."

Chapter Thirty-Eight

Nathaniel decided not to escort Alice back to the house. It was ungentlemanly, but she could hardly complain about his behavior while she was in the midst of the unladylike pursuit of ruining his brother. He needed time to think, and that was something rarely accomplished in her presence.

Or never, actually.

This entire situation was madness, he told himself for perhaps the millionth time since the fateful night the chandelier fell. Absolute madness.

He hated her. He hated the way she looked at him as though hoping for his kiss, when in actuality, she wanted no such thing.

Most of all, he hated that he cared so much for her, when she did not care for him.

He was a fool, a *damned* fool, but he *did* care about her. So, he could not let her find Nicholas by herself. If Nick was capable of fratricide—which Nathaniel didn't want to believe, but he had to be realistic—who knew what a murderer could, or would, do to Alice?

There were any number of hiding places on the estate. Among those were half a dozen spots where he was quite certain Nick was *not* hiding. He would take her to those places first and let her investigate.

Once they eliminated possibilities that were too small, too risky, or too obvious, there were only three other places Nick was likely to be. Nathaniel had no intention of sharing those with her. He would inspect them on his own.

He laced his hands behind his neck and stared unhappily at the ground.

The trouble was, he could not keep his promise to his father without meeting Nick face-to-face. But if they *did* meet face-to-face, one of them could quite possibly end up dead. Then, not only would he have broken his promise to his father, but his father would have lost a son.

Not the ideal ending to a termite-infested family tree.

Nathaniel had hoped to put off the moment of truth for as long as possible—or at least until he had produced an heir of his own. If guilty, Nick might kill Nathaniel without much remorse, but he would doubtless feel a qualm or two at murdering an innocent babe.

But now Nathaniel had no choice but to bring about that dreaded meeting.

He *must* find Nick before Alice did.

And soon.

Chapter Thirty-Nine

Alice watched Nathaniel ride off with Duke Wessex and huffed in frustration. Had he enlisted the duke's help to find Nicholas? And left her out in the cold?

She needed to follow them.

But how? One couldn't be sneaky on horseback. No mount would tiptoe daintily through the woods and remain unseen.

She would have to force Nathaniel to confess to his subterfuge.

One way or another…

"One day," Eliza said, peering out the window over Alice's shoulder, "your face will freeze into that scowl permanently. You will be hideous, sweeting. Do you want to be hideous?"

Alice's scowl deepened. "If you tell me to smile, Eliza, so help me I'll break the nearest vase."

Eliza glanced around the room. There were at least a dozen to choose from. "There is no need for such violence, although I daresay it would be an improvement to the decor. I am merely suggesting that, just for today, you put aside all thoughts of revenge and dastardly deeds, and join me in a little fun."

"Fun!" Alice nearly choked on the word. "While Abingdon is ruining everything? Impossible."

Eliza patted her arm sympathetically. "Just like a man. But you cannot do anything about that right now, can you? So, in the meantime, why don't we explore the village? It's not raining, for once, and I could use the exercise."

Alice sighed. She *had* promised Mary hair ribbons and a new bonnet, and it would not do to renege on their agreement. Servitude was a funny thing. On one hand, a mistress wielded considerable power over her maid's well-being and daily happiness. On the other hand, a maid invariably knew where her mistress buried the bodies, so to speak. And Alice had buried a lot of bodies lately. A steady supply of frivolities was not too much to ask in return.

She summoned Mary, and the three of them set off on the road that led into the village. The day was lovely, a warm spring afternoon that was blessedly free of clouds. It had rained the evening before, so the road was not dusty, but it was not so wet that there was mud. Birds were singing, and the sweet smell of grass and blooming flowers filled the air.

Alice felt her sprits lighten ever so slightly. It was hard to feel dark and gloomy when everywhere she looked there were signs of new life and rebirth.

She breathed in a deep gulp of air and let it out slowly, feeling more unhappiness slip away with that release.

Eliza opened her parasol to give them shade and linked her arm through Alice's. "Isn't this better?"

Alice felt her smile blooming, stretching muscles that felt almost stiff with disuse. How disturbing. Had she really been so unhappy that she hadn't smiled for so long?

Except when she was with—

She stopped that thought in its tracks.

She would *not* yearn for something—someone—that could never be hers.

No matter how wonderful his lips made her feel.

"Much better," she admitted. "I had not realized how dark my mind was feeling."

They passed the blacksmith, where a man watched the smith shove a horseshoe into the flame, and the bakery, where they were surrounded by the most delectable of scents. Finally, they stopped at Mrs. Buffet's Sundries for Ladies, where Mary promptly went to work examining every last ribbon Mrs. Buffet could produce. She turned them this way and that, admiring some, and discarding others with a deprecating sniff of her nose.

Alice grinned. "Anything she wants," she told Mrs. Buffet. She handed the woman several coins. "We will return after tea."

Mrs. Buffet curtsied. "If you please, miss, the Bell and Spoon down the road a bit has a very pretty tea service."

"Wonderful!" Eliza exclaimed. "I am quite famished from our walk."

Alice nodded. "Please see that my maid does not starve until we return."

"Yes, miss," Mrs. Buffet said, beaming and curtsying once more. "Might I say, miss, you are that kind and generous, that you think of such things."

Alice and Eliza stepped out of the tidy shop and back into the sunshine. A man darted into the shop just as they left it. Alice halted, frowning.

"No, you don't," Eliza said. "I am hereby banning frowns, scowls, and glares from your face for the rest of the afternoon."

Alice shook her head and laughed. "As you command. Come, I am hungry, and a spot of tea is in order."

The Bell and Spoon was one of those coaching inns that

also served as the heart of a village. It was clean and neat, cheerfully decorated in tones of blue and yellow. She smiled at the innkeeper's wife, who introduced herself as Bess as she set down a tray of tea, sandwiches, and little cakes.

"Will you be requiring your room tonight, miss?" Bess asked.

Alice raised her eyebrows quizzically. "Pardon?"

Bess hesitated, her confused gaze darting between Alice and Eliza. "The room, miss?"

"Thank you, but we are staying at Haverly," Alice said.

"The inn is lovely," Eliza assured her with a smile. "We would be pleased to stay here if we hadn't made other arrangements."

Bess curtsied. "If there is anything else the ladies require, just let me know."

"Thank you." Eliza turned her attention to the tea. "Shall I pour?"

Alice nodded. Her attention caught on a man sitting in the corner behind Eliza. She couldn't see his face behind the newspaper. Nor had she seen his face as he leaned into the blacksmith shop, nor when he pushed past her into Mrs. Buffet's Sundries.

But it was the same man, she was certain of it.

She lifted the teacup to her lips to hide the words. "I do believe that man is following us— No, don't turn around. I would rather not alert him."

"Is it Nicholas?" Eliza calmly stirred a lump of sugar in her tea.

"I think not." Alice hadn't seen his face, but she had seen his hair—a pale brown color, utterly ordinary and not remotely similar to the red-gold of the Eastwoods.

She leaned slightly over the table, pretending to study the selection of sandwiches on display, and watched the man through her eyelashes. There was nothing remarkable in his clothing. He looked like neither a gentleman nor a laborer, neither rich nor poor. There was nothing in his physical appearance that proclaimed his place in society. He could be a gentleman who cared little for fashion, or a barrister, or a professor, or a farmer. He could be all of those things or none of them.

"Chicken and ham. Both look delicious." She chose chicken and took a bite. "It *is* good."

"What do you suppose he wants?" Eliza asked. She bit delicately into a white cake with pale pink frosting and licked her lips.

"Oh, the usual things," Alice said with a small smile. "Murder, mayhem, or money."

Eliza chuckled. "Well, if that's all…"

Alice rose from her chair. "I believe I shall casually stand in front of that bookcase and wait for him to tell me all about it."

Eliza anxiously bit her lip. "Do be careful."

Alice walked over and stood in front of the bookcase, hands clasped behind her back, perusing the volumes that lined the shelves. And waited.

She was not disappointed.

"There is nothing I enjoy more than a good book. Do you not feel the same, Miss Bursnell?" he asked.

She turned to look at the man. His face was averted as he studied a volume to his right. She suspected she would never fully see his features.

"I like history, but I have very little use for novels," she told him. "Have we been introduced?"

"Mr. Manning, at your service." He bowed his head, his hair falling in his face.

She pursed her lips. "What service is that? And why should I require it?"

"Ah." He sounded amused. "Perhaps it would be more

accurate to say we can be of service to each other."

She doubted that. Instinctively, she did not trust this man. Nothing about him seemed real. Even his voice was without accent—not English, Scottish, French, or Austrian, and yet it could be any of those. It was as if everything about him had been carefully curated to pass unnoticed wherever he wished.

"What can I do for you, Mr. Manning?" she asked briskly.

"You can tell me the location of Nicholas Eastwood."

She tried hard not to show her surprise. "I haven't the slightest idea."

"But you will." She could hear a distinct smile in his voice. "You have been searching for him, and I have no doubt you will find him, eventually. I have been watching you for quite some time, Miss Bursnell. You saw me today only because I wanted to be seen."

A chill trickled down her spine. Of that, she had little doubt.

"I'm afraid I have my own purpose for finding Mr. Eastwood," she said lightly. "I cannot oblige you."

He stooped to select a volume on the lower shelf. "Our purpose is the same, my dear. We both seek to punish him for his crimes. Let me assure you, it is not my intent to go beyond what the law requires. Prison, not death, will be our revenge." He put the book into her hands. "When you discover his whereabouts, write a note and leave it in this book. I will fetch it."

She looked down at the volume. *A Modest Proposal* by Jonathan Swift. "An odd choice," she murmured. She glanced up. "And if I refuse your request?"

He paused. "There is always the brother."

Fear flickered through her. She could not allow this dangerous man anywhere near Nathaniel.

"I—"

But he was already gone.

Chapter Forty

"It seems to me, the easiest solution to your problem is to simply marry Miss Bursnell and be done with it," Wessex said. Looking quite pleased with himself, Wessex nudged his chestnut gelding with his heels, urging him forward.

They had escaped from the house, saddled up their horses, and Nathaniel had poured out the story...with one or two exceptions. He hadn't betrayed Miss Bursnell's confidence regarding her sister, and he had left out the kissing.

And his overpowering desire to do it again.

"Yes, marry her immediately," Wessex continued. "She can't very well ruin your brother if you ship her off to Scotland, which you would be well within your rights to do. Marriage is ownership. She would have to submit to your will, and it is your will that she not ruin your brother. Problem solved."

Nathaniel considered this unique angle on the subject. The suggestion was not without a certain appeal, even if he suspected Wessex's assessment of the fetters of marriage was grossly exaggerated.

Besides, he'd already tried that strategy and been refused.

He shook his head. "It won't work. She will never agree to marry me."

Wessex considered. "She will take some persuasion, I suppose. But it can't hurt to try."

Nathaniel cast his friend a withering look.

"Oh, I see," Wessex murmured. "It's like that, is it?" He furrowed his brow thoughtfully. Suddenly, he brightened. "Seduce her, then."

Nathaniel wanted to groan. Seduction was what had landed him in this mess in the first place. And what had *that* solved for either his brother or himself?

"Pray, how would *you* seduce a gently bred virgin?" He had meant the question to be sardonic, but, to his disgust, he sounded intrigued.

"How the devil should I know?" Wessex demanded indignantly. "I've never despoiled an innocent."

"Hmm," Nathaniel said noncommittedly.

Wessex glared. "I haven't."

"You merely suggest others do so."

Wessex huffed. "It's not as though I am asking you to do something unethical. I am *not* advising you to steal the lady's virtue and leave her ruined, impoverished, and possibly with child. I am *merely suggesting*, as you put it, that no good can come of Miss Bursnell's antics, not for you, and certainly not for her."

"I don't necessarily disagree, but—"

"If you truly care for Miss Bursnell, you would save her from herself." Wessex tapped his crop on his thigh. "When you look objectively at the situation, I am only asking you to do the honorable thing."

Well, that was rather turning the matter on its head. "It's such a pity you were born a duke. You would have made an excellent barrister."

"And earn my keep through employment?" Wessex

shuddered. "Never."

There was, unfortunately, one fatal flaw in the duke's plan. Alice could not be seduced. Not by Nathaniel, at any rate. Three times he had kissed her. The first had gotten his foot stamped upon. The second led to a spurned marriage proposal. And the third? *God.* He shuddered.

It was enough to make a man wonder if maybe he was rubbish at this kissing business.

And other things.

Things he very much wanted to do with Alice. Despite his better judgment.

He groaned inwardly in frustration. Why did she have to be so damn desirable?

"I won't force myself on her," he said. "She doesn't want me, and I don't know how to make her want me."

God, now he was whining.

Wessex brought his horse to an abrupt halt. "Nate, I'm going to ask you a question, and I must insist on an honest answer. Are you a virgin?"

Nathaniel hesitated, and went with the truth, as embarrassing as it was to admit. "I am not…as experienced as you."

"No one is as experienced as me. So, you're not untried in the ways of *amour.* Thank God." Wessex signaled the horse to move forward again.

"Not entirely untried, no. I tried— That is—"

"What?" Again, Wessex halted.

Nathaniel couldn't meet his eyes. "I came close, once. It was that ballerina when we were at Oxford. I went to her room, and she tried to stab me with a knife. I barely escaped with my life."

"Good God!"

"She wasn't defending herself," he quickly added. "I did not force myself on her. Likely, someone had paid her to do it." He did not have to say who. "I didn't care to repeat the experience. So…I didn't."

Wessex's jaw ticked. "You haven't been with a woman *ever*?" He blew out a breath. "But surely— Didn't you— How could you—" He let out a great hoot of laughter.

"I'm glad you find this so amusing."

"You're a green boy!"

Oh, God. It was his school years all over again. *Shy, awkward, hopeless.*

"And here, I thought you were merely discreet." Wessex leaned on the horse's neck for support as he shook with another laugh. "Good…Lord." He leaned farther still, and over he went, tumbling to the ground, where he continued to chuckle.

Nathaniel wondered if he could convince his mount to step on the duke. Perhaps the horse found Wessex as annoying as he did.

"Confiding in you was a mistake. You will be of no help to me, I can see that now."

Wessex sat up with a wide grin.

Nathaniel rolled his eyes. "Do get up and stop being such a jackass."

Wessex got up, but Nathaniel doubted he would ever stop being a jackass.

The duke brushed himself off and swung back into the saddle. "Confiding in me was just the thing to do," he said. "Your problem is solidly within my realm of expertise— women."

Nathaniel shook his head. "That's not—"

"It all makes sense now," Wessex cut him off. "I thought you were playing some sort of game with her, but you simply didn't know any better. Never fear. Luckily for you, I have information regarding Miss Bursnell that you, poor man, do *not* have."

What was Wessex implying? Was he speaking of women in general, or Alice in particular?

Had Wessex *kissed* her?

Nathaniel felt a hot flash of rage and briefly contemplated murder. Then he came to his senses. Wessex might be a confirmed rake, but he would never betray a friend.

Still, Nathaniel wanted to hear the words. "Just what are you saying?"

"I'm saying that you are mistaken, because she *does* want you," Wessex said bluntly. "Anyone can see that."

"*I* can't," Nathaniel grumbled.

"That is merely due to your unfortunate lack of experience."

Quite possibly.

"Explain."

"I saw her come out of that secret room, before she pretended to faint. I assume that was one of the times you kissed her. I noticed her lips had that swollen, red look of a mouth that had been kissed quite passionately. Her brain was clearly muddled from the experience, because she left it to Lady Claire, of all people, to save the day."

Nathaniel waved a hand dismissively. "She doesn't kiss me because she wants me. She kisses me because she wants to tempt me into helping her find my brother. And it's working, more's the pity. I am sorely tempted."

Wessex shook his head. "Trust me. She wants *you*. A lady can't fake that sort of thing."

Nathaniel gave a snort, unconvinced. She had *told* him she did not want him, both by refusing his offer of marriage and in as many words in the hidden room.

Have my kisses taught you nothing?

"Does she push you away? Demand that you stop?" Wessex asked.

Nathaniel furrowed his brow. The first time, at the

theater, she had done both. But before that, she had kissed him back. In the Great Hall, she had kissed him willingly, and even let him do…other delicious things. Even now, the thought of what she had permitted heated his blood.

But the last time they kissed, in the hidden room…and *she* had kissed *him*… What had *that* been about?

"Well, she often says 'please.'" Nathaniel frowned. "I believe she means 'please stop.'"

Wessex stared at him for a moment and then gave yet another bark of laughter. Thankfully, only one. "Poor fool. Poor bloody, innocent fool."

Nathaniel held his breath and counted to ten. He had never punched a friend in the nose before, but there was a first time for everything…

"Why is it so hard for you to believe she wants you?" Wessex demanded before Nathaniel could make a move.

"Because no one ever has," he said flatly.

Pity slashed across the duke's face but was quickly buried. "I suggest the next time you find yourself kissing Miss Bursnell, you keep your wits about you and pay attention. You will understand quickly enough that she truly desires you."

The next time? There wouldn't be a next time. She had already kissed him into agreeing she could stay in the house and that he would help her find Nick. Another touch of her lips would have him swearing to avenge her sister's honor himself.

Hell and damnation.

He was in such serious trouble.

Chapter Forty-One

"You don't really mean to tell that man where Nicholas is?" Eliza asked in disbelief.

Alice was mildly surprised at the astonishment in her friend's voice.

They were walking together along the road back to Haverly, with Mary following several steps behind them, happily swinging her new bonnet.

"I don't know where Nicholas is," Alice reminded Eliza. "But when I find him, of course I shall. It is not for me to save him from prison. We are a civilized nation. He has committed crimes and must bear the lawful consequences of that, whether he is the son of an earl or no. Who am I to stand in the way of justice?"

"What crimes?" Eliza asked suspiciously.

"Mr. Manning didn't say," Alice admitted after an uncomfortably telling pause. "It hardly matters, does it? It is not as if Nicholas will be hanged. Perhaps he will be sent to Australia. I hear the climate there is very pleasant."

"Do not be flippant with your soul, Alice." Eliza halted

them both and grabbed her by the shoulders. "Are you quite *certain* he will not be hanged, or shot, or otherwise disposed of without lawful authority?"

Again, Alice paused. Well...truthfully...

Eliza gave her shoulders a rough shake. "You are *not* certain! Admit it. You trust Mr. Manning no more than I do. But you *want* to believe him, so you have fooled yourself into thinking everything will turn out all right. Be very careful, Alice, that you do not do something unforgivable."

Alice closed her eyes for a brief moment. "If you are thinking to salvage my friendship with Lord Abingdon, you needn't bother. He loathes me, and I deserve it. Nothing can change that now."

Eliza shook her head, making her curls bounce. "It is not Lord Abingdon I am concerned about. Have you considered what happens when all of this is over? When your revenge is fulfilled, but you still have no sister? What then? Will you be able to forgive *yourself*?"

Alice shivered as a stiff breeze tugged a lock of her hair from its pins.

What then, indeed?

Back at the house, they parted ways. Eliza headed for the library, proposing to catch up on her correspondence, and Alice went in search of hidden rooms. Nathaniel was nowhere to be found, and she had no intention of sitting around waiting idly for his help.

The second drawing room held promise. The walls were covered in thick panels and tapestries, just the sort of thing one might use to disguise a hidden door.

She lifted one tapestry—a unicorn resting its head in the lap of a golden-haired maiden—and felt underneath. The wall was smooth and seamless. She moved to the next one, this time a knight riding to rescue a lady in a tower. Another blond innocent, Alice noted ruefully.

"Looking for something?"

She spun around, and there was Nathaniel leaning casually against the doorframe, arms crossed over his chest and a scowl darkening his face. A shiver of unhappiness ran through her. The look in his eyes was almost cruel. Oh, how he hated her!

"Just hidden rooms, secret passageways, that sort of thing." She waved him off with a flick of her wrist. "You know, the ones you promised to help me search for clues, my lord."

He growled. "Nathaniel."

She deliberately turned her back to him. "I was certain something would be here. Do tell me if I'm wasting my time, my lord."

He was beside her in an instant. "You seem to have forgotten we are on more intimate terms." His hand went to the back of her neck, and he applied gentle pressure, turning her to face him. "Perhaps I should remind you? A kiss might do the trick."

She licked her lips, and his eyes lowered to her mouth.

"Would you like me to kiss you now, Alice?"

"No." Her heart was beating very fast.

"Liar," he whispered, then dropped his hand and stepped back. "There is a secret room that connects to this one, but the entry is not located behind the tapestry."

Tapestry? Who cared about a blasted tapestry? Why was he not kissing her? Had he not just said he would?

Ah, yes. Because she had told him no.

He tipped his head, waiting for her response to…to what? Were they still talking of kissing? His lips looked so warm, and she could almost feel their heat against her mouth.

"Alice?" he prompted. "Do you want to know where the entry is?"

She nodded.

He walked over to a large cuckoo clock hanging level to his chest and pushed the center dial. Immediately the clock swung forward, revealing a dark hole, no more than two feet square.

"Oh!" Alice stood on her tiptoes, her hand on his shoulder for support, and peered into the hole. "I can't see anything."

"Well, it's dark, and you're small." He looked down at her and smirked. "If you want to explore, I'll have to boost you up. There are stairs on the other side to help you down."

She hesitated nervously. This was not the kind of entry she had expected.

"Or I can just go myself," he suggested. "I'll let you know what I find."

"I think not," she said drily. "Here, help me up." She faced the wall and lifted her arms.

For a moment there was nothing, and then his hands were on her waist and he lifted her into the air, directing her to the hole. She squirmed until she was halfway through the tight passageway and looked around.

"Alice," he said in a strangled voice. "You must hurry."

"I'm trying!" She wiggled her bottom a few more times, trying to get leverage to reach the stairs, and tumbled all the way through, bypassing the stairs altogether. *"Oomph!"*

"Alice! Are you all right?" He stuck his head in the opening. He appeared worried. About *her.*

She smiled inwardly. "Just fine, thank you."

"Move aside. I'm coming in."

He struggled to fit his wide shoulders through the small passage, and she swallowed a giggle. But he managed to free himself, and suddenly he fell in, just as she had, landing on top of her with a *thunk*.

"Ow!"

"Oh, God, Alice, I'm so sorry."

"Move."

He rolled at the same time she did, and they collided again.

"Damn," he muttered.

"Lord Abingdon!" She fell against him, giggling helplessly.

And then she wasn't giggling, at all, because his lips found hers in the darkness.

"Nathaniel," she whispered into his mouth.

"There it is," he said in a tone of deep satisfaction. His mouth left hers.

She wouldn't cry. Or hit him.

She *wouldn't*.

"Where are we?" She sat up and looked around. The room they'd landed in was surprisingly large.

He hadn't shut the clock behind them, so it was dim in the space, but not pitch dark. She could make out faint shapes. He lit a lantern on the wall and closed the entry door.

"Freesia was the one who discovered this room. She declared it hers—no brothers allowed. Sometimes she would hide here from her governess." He smiled slightly. "We never told."

We, including Nicholas. Alice tried to imagine it—the twins and the sister, before the tree incident had cut short their innocent childhood. Had they wrestled and fought, the way boys do, and protected their sister, as they ought? Who had Nicholas been, before he became the villain he was now? Once, he was just a boy. Once, there had been mischief and laughter, not bloodshed and tears.

She felt a pang in her chest, like an arrow to the heart, for the boy he once was.

Good Lord. Sympathy…for Nicholas?

Her brain must be addled from the tumble down the stairs.

"It's lovely in here," she said, now that she could see her

surroundings more clearly.

It was a girl's playroom. The floor was covered by thick carpet. Along one wall was an oddly vibrant purple sofa. Against the other wall was a writing desk.

"She must have loved coming here." Alice trailed a finger over the desk. It came back dusty, and she wiped it on her skirt. "It's a nice little escape."

"Everyone should have a space of one's own," Nathaniel said. "It was her great misfortune that, as a girl, she was given much less privacy than we as boys. Her room could be invaded at any time by her governess, her nurse, or her maid."

Alice turned and looked at him curiously. "And where was your own hideaway? Or did you share everything with Nicholas?"

Nathaniel laughed. "I never liked to share. Nick and I had separate sleeping rooms in the nursery, and of course I claimed a secret room of my own, as did Nick."

"Hmm."

"He's not there," Nathaniel said, clearly guessing which direction her mind had turned. "It would be too obvious. He would know I'd look for him there. Still, I will show you, for your own peace of mind."

"And yours?"

He shook his head. "No. We won't find him at all. Nick isn't trying to kill me."

"Then we will find out who is," she said determinedly. "That can't be a bad thing."

He smiled. "Do you know, I feel quite safe with you. It's the oddest thing."

Her belly fluttered.

"We shouldn't be here," she said, "since it is Freesia's domain. I imagine a brother is a brother, no matter his age, and she would be most displeased to find you here."

"I suppose you are right." Nevertheless, he sat down on

the sofa and looked at her. "I should not be sitting while a lady stands. Perhaps you would remedy that offense on my behalf?"

She laughed and sat next to him. Her elbow was aching from her fall, and she rubbed it. It would be blue tomorrow, no doubt.

"We shouldn't be here," she repeated. Although, it felt singularly wonderful to be sitting so close to him.

"We are not here. We are figments of our own imaginations."

She laughed again, rather breathlessly this time.

He took her arm, gently pushed up the sleeve, and touched the small bruise. "Does it hurt?"

She nodded.

He pressed his lips to the spot. "I'm so sorry, darling."

"It's all right." She tried to pull her arm back, but he held on. "Nothing is broken."

"Were you hurt anywhere else?" His eyes glinted in the light of the lantern.

Just her heart.

She shook her head. She would be damned before she let him kiss her *there*.

"I'm afraid I was hurt," he said. "It's only fair that you should return the favor and kiss it better. No other salve will do."

She rolled her eyes. That was a line she would expect from a two-year-old boy or an experienced rake. Clearly, Nathaniel had been spending too much time with Wessex.

And yet, there was an impish look in his eyes that she couldn't resist. "Oh, very well." She held out her hand. "Your arm, was it?"

He started unbuttoning his shirt.

"What are you doing?" she demanded, taken aback.

"Showing you my injury." His fingers moved quickly, and

then his shirt was open.

"I am *not* going to kiss your chest."

Although…she might actually like that.

Would he?

"Of course not." He gave her a scandalized look. "It's my ribs."

"Your…ribs?" Without her permission, her eyes trailed down his lean, muscled torso.

"Right here." He indicated the area with his finger, then bent over to examine himself closer. He frowned. "I think it was from your knee, when I fell through the opening."

She narrowed her eyes. "When you nearly crushed me, you mean?"

He grinned. "Yes, then."

"You got what you deserved."

"But it hurts. Won't you kiss it better, darling?" he coaxed. "Please."

What was he about? Scarcely ten minutes ago he was looking at her as if she was the embodiment of everything wrong with the world, and now he was playful and teasing. His moods made her head spin.

Not that she cared terribly. As long as he didn't stay angry with her.

She took in the sight of him. His skin glowed like warm marble under the lantern's light. She had never touched a man intimately, in a place hidden by clothing. Not with her fingers, and certainly not with her mouth.

He had touched her in such a way, both with his hands and his lips at her breast. Why should she deny herself the same pleasure?

She pushed gently at his shoulders, and he let himself be urged down across the sofa, his body spread before her like a scrumptious feast. She hesitated, unsure of how to proceed, and glanced at his face. He slung an arm across his eyes, but the rosy flags on his cheeks betrayed him. That hint of shyness was comforting. She relaxed slightly.

Cautiously, she ran her hands over his stomach. The square boxes of muscle were so different from her own softness. He spasmed, folding nearly in half, and grabbed her wrists. She rocked back on her heels and stared at him with wide eyes, startled.

"I'm sorry!" she gasped at the same time he said, "That tickled."

They looked at each other.

"Would you rather I didn't…?" She trailed off uncertainly.

He leaned back and covered his face again. "Alice," he said gruffly. "For God's sake, kiss it better."

She touched him on the ribs again, firmer this time, so as not to startle him. He trembled under her hand, and his lips were parted, taking in slow breaths of air. Satisfied, she leaned closer to where a reddish-purple mark was blooming close to his side.

Oh, dear. She really had hurt him.

She counted his ribs with her finger as she went. One, two, three, four. How strange that the same bones inside her were also inside him, and yet they were not the same, at all. His were ever so much more interesting.

"Here?" she asked. "This is where it hurts?"

"Yes," he said on a deep exhale.

She kissed the mark softly, gently.

He made a sound. It was a nice sound, somewhere between a sigh and a moan. She wanted to hear it again. She lowered her mouth to his warm skin. He didn't make a noise, but his fingers clenched.

As were places in her own body. It felt…good.

She trailed her lips higher, exploring the ribs she had counted. He was taking quick, shallow breaths, judging from the way his chest rose and fell beneath her mouth. She paused at his nipple. It was not pink and puckered like her own. Instead, it was flat and reminded her of a copper penny. She ran her tongue experimentally over the tip. It hardened slightly, and he made that noise again, slightly deeper this time.

There was an answering tug, deep in her belly. It made her want all sorts of things that she couldn't put words to.

She moved to his other nipple and licked.

His hips jerked, and he groaned. "Alice, you will drive me mad."

"Hmm," she said. She would enjoy that. There were so many places to kiss—his shoulders, his neck, his stomach, and perhaps the bulge in his breeches she was so very curious about. She could feel it against her stomach, and she was quite certain it was growing.

Suddenly, he flipped them both so she was beneath him, her legs trapped between his. For one brief moment, she saw the look in his eyes, and it was not hate. He wanted to devour her, much as she wanted to him.

Then his mouth was on hers, and his hot tongue plunged into her. It was not a gentle kiss. It was rough, almost punishing in its need, demanding that she give him everything.

She drank him in, allowing him to taste her lips, her tongue, anything he wanted. He pulled back to take a breath, and then his lips were at her ear. He caught the lobe in his mouth and grazed it lightly with his teeth. She ran her hands over his shoulders, taking his shirt with them. She loved feeling the muscles ripple beneath her palms.

Feeling brazen, she pulled the tie from his hair and let the red-gold waves fall free. She sank both hands into them, enjoying the thick silkiness. "I love your hair," she murmured, pulling his face back to hers.

"Do you?" She felt his smile against her mouth. This time, he was gentle. He fed her sweet, teasing kisses. "I have quite a lot of it, you know. On my head." He bit her lower lip gently, making her gasp. "On my chest." He nibbled along her jaw line. "And lower."

"So do I," she said, too drugged from his mouth to know what she was saying.

He paused. "Well, you can't mean your breasts, because I've seen those. They're lovely and hairless. Do you mean here?" His hand crept up her thigh until it reached the juncture of her legs. When she nodded slowly, his eyes turned dark. "Will you let me see?"

She should say no. A lady would not even speak of such a private part, much less show a man. Even when one was married and used those parts with her husband, the deed was done in the dark, under the covers. No one *saw* anything.

That was what she'd always been told.

"If you want to," she whispered, her brazenness increasing.

In a flash he had her on her feet and her dress off, tugging it down her body and past her hips. "Thank God you're not wearing a corset," he muttered.

He knelt before her and gently dragged her drawers down to her ankles. She leaned on his shoulders and stepped clear of them. Then he rocked back on his heels and simply gazed at her, his eyes on the curly thatch level with his face.

Her legs trembled. She had been damp before, but now she was aware of a strange gush of moisture in that very same place. "Please stop looking at me. It makes me feel…odd."

"You're so beautiful," he said reverently. His hands were shaking as he grasped her hips. He leaned forward and placed a kiss just above the curly hair. "Can I touch you?"

She bit her lip and whispered, "Yes."

His hands spanned her, and he used his thumbs to separate her midnight curls. She was exposed to him now, and completely vulnerable. Even she had never seen this part of her open like this. Perhaps she should feel embarrassed, but instead she felt powerful.

Worshipped.

One finger slid between her mysteriously slick folds, touching a spot that made her shudder and press against his hand. He stroked again, and she couldn't keep a moan from passing her lips.

"Do you like that?" he asked, his voice thick.

"Yes," she said. It was indecent how much she liked it.

He continued his exploration, sliding his finger even lower. "There is a sweet little passage just here," he said. "That is where I would enter you. Like this." His finger pressed slowly inside.

She cried out, her inner muscles resisting the intrusion. She grabbed his shoulders for fear she would fall over.

"You're so small." He sounded like he was choking. "How will I..." He retreated, eased his finger in slow and deep, and retreated again.

It felt so odd being filled by him. But without him, she felt strangely empty. "Again," she said.

His finger entered her again, and it was easier this time. This time, when she clenched around him, it was from pleasure. With his finger sliding in and out, his thumb circled that very sensitive spot. Suddenly, she was panting, her hips rocking to a rhythm she couldn't control.

"Please," she gasped.

He froze. "Shall I stop?"

"No!" She dug her fingertips into his shoulders. She might die if he stopped. Certainly *he* would, because she would have no choice but to kill him. "Don't stop."

His fingers moved again, stroking and swirling, until she thought she would go mad from it. Pleasure was pulling her under, into some dark, secret place where there was nothing but the feel of his hands, the smell of his skin and her damp flesh, the sounds of heartbeats and his voice whispering words of praise and adoration.

Her body tightened like a coil, then released in an explosion of pleasure. She shuddered, her legs gave way, and she fell forward with a small cry.

He caught her, bundling her into his arms, and laid her down on the sofa next to him. She pressed her face into his chest, her heart beating madly.

She wondered if she was well and truly ruined.

But decided she didn't care.

Chapter Forty-Two

This, Nathaniel decided, was going to kill him.

He lay back on the sofa, Alice's naked body pressed against his side, his cock harder than it had ever been in his entire life. So hard his whole body ached with it. Every part of him was roaring to strip off his breeches and take her.

But she was so small.

And her sister… His brother…

And, no. Alice deserved a marital bed.

His marital bed. If only he could figure out how to make that happen.

Until then, he would simply suffer. Hopefully his cock wouldn't fall off. Could that happen? It was his favorite body part, and he would not like to be without it.

Slowly, he became aware of her fingers drifting in his chest hair. That felt so good.

Too good.

Oh, God.

She was actually going to kill him.

"Can I touch you?" she whispered. "The way you touched

me?"

He was going to hell. He had to accept that, because there was no way for him to say no. He needed her touch, or his cock truly would fall off.

"Yes." He dropped kisses on the crown of her head.

She reached for him. He went completely still as her trembling fingers undid his buttons. He sprang free, jutting toward her, and she gave a small cry of surprise. For a moment he wanted to laugh, but then those fingers touched him, stroking softly around the velvet tip and the bead of moisture there, then down his shaft. Her touch was a tease, and anticipation drove him nearly to the brink of insanity.

He groaned, and her eyes lifted questioningly. "How should I touch you?" she whispered.

He may not have much experience with being touched by a woman, but he knew how he touched himself. "Wrap your hand around me. Yes, like that. Stroke up and down. Harder."

Her hand tightened. "Like that?"

"Harder."

"I won't hurt you?"

Again, he struggled not to laugh. "You won't hurt me, darling. *Please*, Alice. I need—"

And there it was. Suddenly, he understood why Wessex had called him a fool.

"Please" didn't mean stop.

Not remotely.

She gripped him tighter, her motions firm and rhythmic. He groaned again, and his hips thrust against her, his forehead dropping to rest on the top of her head. When he felt a tingling at the base of his spine, he knew he didn't have much time left.

"Alice, you must stop. Something is going to happen. You won't like it," he said urgently.

But it was too late. Pleasure exploded, and he rolled her quickly, releasing against her soft, bare stomach with a rough groan.

She shrieked in surprise as he spent, warm and wet and sticky.

Damnation. He had made a lady *sticky.*

"Don't move," he said. He grabbed his cravat and wiped her clean. He could feel her watching him, but he was too ashamed to meet her eyes.

"Was that supposed to happen?" she asked cautiously.

"Yes. Although, optimally, it would happen inside you, not on your belly. It's my seed."

"Oh." She thought about that, appearing relieved. "Yes, that makes sense."

He choked back a laugh.

"And it means there is no risk of a child from this," she pointed out, ever practical.

He shook his head. "None."

She looked at him, waiting nervously.

His pulse sped even faster. Did she expect him to offer?

He *should* offer for her. Only the worst kind of scoundrel would not, after what he had just done to her. True, she could not be with child, and no one would ever know of this interlude. But she was his, just the same. She would *not* share with another man what they had just shared here, together. He wouldn't allow it.

But he could not offer for her—not yet, so soon after the first time he'd gotten down on one knee. He had asked her once already, and her answer had been a resounding no.

If he asked her now, he would never feel sure of her true feelings. She had given him her body, willingly and joyfully... but that was not enough.

He wanted her heart.

Chapter Forty-Three

There was nothing more excruciating than watching the woman one had just held so intimately flirt with another man.

Nathaniel came to this unpleasant conclusion that same evening after suffering through drinks, where Alice had stayed close to Miss Benton and Lady Claire, and dinner, where he was once again seated nowhere near Alice, and now, finally, through parlor games, where she happily paired off with Colonel Kent for whist.

It was intolerable. He had been *inside* her. Not the part of him that he most wanted there, but still. A part of him had been in a part of her. That made her *his*. Colonel Kent would simply have to find another whist partner.

He glared at Colonel Kent.

Colonel Kent ignored him.

Alice turned to the colonel, showing Nathaniel only her profile, the glimmer of a smile tugging at the corner of her lips. She whispered something to his rival, who threw back his head with a great shout of laughter.

Nathaniel's gut twisted.

"For the love of God, Nate, have some pride," Wessex muttered. "Do not stand there gawking like a lovesick idiot."

The trouble was, Nathaniel *was* a lovesick idiot, which made it remarkably difficult not to gawk like one. One day, Wessex would find himself brutally in love with a lady who laughed and flirted with another man, and then he would understand. The thought made Nathaniel feel a minuscule bit better.

"Turn around and walk with me to the far corner by the window," Wessex said quietly. "We will pretend to talk of books or some other nonsense."

"But then I won't be able to see her," Nathaniel protested.

"You are making a spectacle of yourself. Do as I say," Wessex commanded. "I will see her for you, and I promise my eyes make a better interpreter of her behavior than yours could. You are too blind with lust."

Nathaniel ground his teeth and followed Wessex on a slow tour around the parlor.

As they passed by Miss Benton, Lady Claire, and the marchioness, Wessex said loudly, "I cannot agree with you. *Glenarvon* is the best literature of our time, and I won't hear a word against it."

Miss Benton glanced up and rolled her beautiful blue eyes.

"Why are you baiting Miss Benton again?" Nathaniel asked when they were safely past. "*Glenarvon* was dreadful."

Wessex shrugged his shoulders. "Haven't read it. But since Lady Caroline Lamb was banned from Almack's for the tale, I must surmise that it is quite good."

"It was scandalous. That's not the same thing as good."

"Don't be absurd. They are exactly the same. Literature is meant to entertain, not to lecture." He frowned. "Good lord. Now we are *actually* speaking of books instead of merely pretending to discuss them. How tedious."

Nathaniel had his back to Alice, and it was driving him mad. The urge to turn and drink her in was too much. "What is she doing now?"

"She won the trick." Wessex watched silently for a moment over Nathaniel's shoulder. "She's quite good, I think."

"She would be," Nathaniel muttered.

"It's a matter of having a deep understanding of how one's partner would play, don't you think? She does very well with Kent. They understand each other through only a look."

Nathaniel gave Wessex a look that threatened murder.

"Right." Wessex glanced again. "She is not completely absorbed by the game, however. She is looking around the room a bit. But not at you, not at all. That's interesting." He paused, watching. "I think she might be angry with you."

Nathaniel studied his glass of port, endeavoring to remain expressionless. Apparently, a futile task.

Wessex narrowed his eyes. "Nate, what did you do?"

Placed his fingers where his fingers did not belong. Made her touch him like she was a common wench instead of the daughter of a viscount. Spilled his seed onto her belly. Really, it could have been any of those things. How was he to know?

"I know you did not seduce her, because you would be announcing your engagement as we speak," Wessex said with a distinct edge to his voice. "And you are not."

Or, yes, it could have been that.

Nathaniel kept that thought to himself.

"Abingdon," Wessex said. *"What did you do?"*

Nathaniel winced. Wessex only referred to him by his title when things were very serious. Since Wessex never took *anything* seriously, this had only happened twice in their entire friendship—once when his father had died, and now…this.

"I will offer for her when the moment is right," Nathaniel said.

"Will that be before or after the babe is born?" Wessex snapped. "Good God, Nate, you can't mean to—"

"Enough," Nathaniel growled. "Do you think *so* poorly

of me? She is *not* with child. Things did not go so far as that."

Wessex calmed down. His eyes glinted with curiosity. "How far *did* things go, then?"

Nathaniel hesitated. He had questions, and Wessex, being a man of great experience, likely had answers to those questions. Such as, how did the act itself actually work? His finger barely fit inside her, and his cock was much larger than a finger. But he couldn't ask that without telling Wessex where his finger had been. And that, he simply would not do.

It wasn't that Wessex would be shocked. Nathaniel was… untried, but he wasn't innocent, by any means. He had heard Wessex and other men speak in great detail of their physical exploits in the bedchamber, of which the explorations of fingers were the least shocking. So, he had a general idea about what went where. And that it must work, because not one of the gentlemen had ever complained of a woman being too small. Quite the opposite, in fact… Despite everything, he was fairly certain he had brought Alice to orgasm, and the thought still made him hard.

He wasn't going to share *that* with Wessex, either.

He wasn't going to share any of it with anyone but Alice. The fragrance of her skin, the sound of her moans, the sweet taste of her mouth, the exquisite feel of her muscles in the deepest part of her—that was all *his* alone.

"It was more than a kiss, and that is all you will get from me. I am not a scoundrel. I offered for her once, you know that. I will offer for her again, when she—" He broke off.

Wessex waited. Nathaniel said nothing.

"When she what?" Wessex finally asked impatiently.

"When she loves me," Nathaniel admitted.

Wessex looked to where the lady was again provoking Colonel Kent to laughter. "Dare to dream, my friend," he said evenly. "But don't wait too long, or you will find someone else has gotten there first."

Chapter Forty-Four

Alice was keenly aware that Nathaniel was not looking at her. Not as much as a glance.

How *dare* he ignore her?

He had touched her more intimately than she had even touched herself, and now he stood chatting with Duke Wessex as though it had never happened. It was unbelievable, unforgivable, and…and…unpleasant. Yes, that was exactly the word for this slightly sick feeling in her stomach. It was vastly unpleasant.

He had not offered her marriage, the beastly man.

She had expected he would, as that was the natural order of things. If a man kissed a lady—much less removed her clothing—that man *must* marry her.

She would have refused him, of course. What happened had changed nothing of substance between them. Very likely he knew that. Which, no doubt, explained his outrageously inexcusable behavior toward her ever since.

Even so! He should have at least done her the courtesy of *pretending* to follow society's rules. Was she a lady, or was she not?

Perhaps he thought not.

A true lady would never have behaved in such a wanton fashion. She had thrust herself against his hand, over and over again, begging him with her body if not her words—although she rather thought she had done that, too.

Oh, dear. *Not acceptable.*

A hot flush crept up her neck.

"Are you well, Miss Bursnell?" Colonel Kent asked. "You look overheated."

"The room is very warm." She fanned herself, nearly scattering the cards. She gathered her wits and placed her card, winning both the trick and the game. "There."

She stood, and the colonel quickly stood, as well.

"Will you accompany me to the garden?" he asked. "Perhaps the cool evening air will do you some good. Your aunt will, naturally, accompany us."

Alice looked to her aunt, who nodded her agreement. "Thank you, yes." Alice could not stay in the parlor for a moment longer. The room was simply too small for both Nathaniel and herself.

The colonel offered his arm, and Aunt Bea followed them out. As she swept by Nathaniel and Wessex, she could feel a burning sensation on the back of her skull, as if he were branding her with his glare. She raised her chin a notch. If it bothered him to see her on the arm of another man, then he could have damn well spoken even a single word to her at *some* point during the evening. Lord knew, she had given him plenty of opportunities.

As they stepped outside, Aunt Bea plopped herself down on a stone bench and arranged her shawl. "I shall rest here, I believe. My dear niece may accompany you to that wall over there and not a step farther," she told the colonel sternly.

Colonel Kent bowed. "That is very gracious of you, my

lady. I shall keep Miss Bursnell safely within your view."

Well, that was sweet. Alice felt a sharp pang of guilt. Aunt Bea had done her best to keep Alice's virtue intact, but if she had succeeded, it was only on a technicality.

Colonel Kent bowed his head to Alice. "Shall we?"

She nodded and stepped with him into the garden. The sun had set but the moon was full, lending a silvery glow to their surroundings. The wind blew, rustling the leaves on the rosebush and the lace on her dress. She shivered.

"May I offer you my jacket?" Colonel Kent gallantly asked. "I should have thought to bring your shawl."

"Oh, no." She smiled. "I was overheated, remember? I'm quite enjoying the chill now. It's invigorating."

He hesitated, then moved his arm—the one she held— closer to his side, thus tucking her into the warmth of his body. "Miss Bursnell…"

They stopped, and she released his arm, turning to face him. "Yes, Colonel?"

"There is a matter that I very much wish to discuss with you. It has been on my mind for some time now, and I cannot think it will be a surprise to you, nor, I hope, unwelcome."

Oh, no.

She glanced over her shoulder. Aunt Bea was still on the bench and appeared completely occupied with folding and unfolding her shawl into neat little squares.

Clearly, she would be of no help.

Alice turned stoically back to Colonel Kent. "Oh?"

"My days in the army are numbered, I am happy to report. I intend to resign my commission, now that France is no longer an immediate threat. I have given a great deal of thought to what I shall do next. Idleness does not suit me."

"No, indeed." The colonel was perhaps ten years older than herself, but even war had not dimmed his obvious vitality.

He grinned back at her, his white teeth flashing in the moonlight. "I'm so glad you agree."

"So, what are your plans for yourself, if I may ask?" She subtly emphasized the word "yourself."

"Twofold." He clasped his hands behind his back and studied the ground at their feet. "First, I intend to buy a small estate in Hampshire, not so far from here. The war was terrible for humanity, but it was good for my investments. Second, I plan to enter political life, to the extent the people of England want me to. Since I am not a member of the peerage, this would require my election to the House of Commons."

She touched his sleeve, impressed with his ambition. "You will have no difficulty with that. I believe Lord Abingdon, in particular, would be happy to back you. You are of a similar mind on so many things."

"Yes." Kent gave a rueful smile. "And therein lies the problem."

She blushed. She couldn't pretend not to understand him.

When she said nothing, Kent continued, "Every day, I expected an announcement to be made. But I must admit, I found myself relieved beyond measure when no such announcement came. Please forgive the boldness of my question. Is there no understanding between you and Lord Abingdon?"

"Oh." Uncomfortable and uncertain of how to answer that, she found herself fascinated by the pattern of a roseleaf. "I think it is safe to say Lord Abingdon and I understand each other perfectly. Which is why we are *not* engaged."

"I see."

She hoped with every fiber of her being that he did *not* see.

"Miss Bursnell, I am going to do a very foolish thing." He took her gloved hands in his. "I am going to ask permission to court you, and then I am going to kiss you."

She jerked her head up in surprise.

"Or perhaps," he said thoughtfully, glancing to where their chaperone was not paying the least bit of attention, "we can dispense with the talking portion and let the kiss speak for itself."

His mouth descended before she could formulate a reply.

For a moment, she allowed it. His kiss was gentle but firm. It didn't make her erupt with passion and need, the way she did with Nathaniel's kisses, but it was hardly the worst thing to ever happen to a girl. She might not feel overpowering lust, but she did feel fondness for the man who stood with his lips pressing hers. She might have been quite taken if she hadn't had Nathaniel's kiss to compare it to…

But she had.

Oh, yes. She was surely and completely ruined.

Not by society's rules—no, it was much worse than that. She was ruined for all other men.

For any man save Nathaniel Eastwood.

A deep yearning swelled in her breast. It was like homesickness, except tenfold stronger. Instead of missing the mountain crags and foamy seas, it was a longing for Nathaniel's teasing smile and his arms about her and— Oh, heavens. It was simply *him*—all of him, from the awkward red hair on his head down to his delightfully ungainly feet.

She made a noise of despair, and stepped back, breaking the kiss. "I—"

"Don't." The colonel touched her cheek softly with the back of his hand. "Don't say anything just yet. Let things settle. Hastiness has resulted in many a miserable marriage. All I ask is that you consider me as a suitor. That is all. Just consider." His eyes searched her face. "Will you do that?"

After a brief hesitation, she nodded. What else could she do? The man was a true gentleman. And very…pleasant.

He took her hand, turning it over to press a kiss to her

palm. "I am grateful."

Guilt shot through her like an arrow. He was a good, kind man. He would make an excellent husband. He was brave and honorable and true.

But he wasn't Nathaniel.

Chapter Forty-Five

It was not yet dawn when Nathaniel left the house. All was silent. The guests were still sleeping, and even the maids had not come downstairs. He was dressed head to foot in black, and rather than saddle his horse, he chose to walk. It would not do to alert anyone to his presence, should there be anyone to alert where he was going.

Ages ago, he and Nick had stumbled across an old gamekeeper's cottage. By the time they found it, it had not been used for at least a century. To say it was in disrepair would be a colossal understatement. Thick vines had covered it from foundation to roof, making it almost impossible to tell it was there. They had left the vines but repaired the inside. They had plugged holes in the roof, replaced the termite-eaten door, added a support beam here and there to stop the whole building from falling in on them. And slowly, sneakily, they had added furniture and other comforts. A chair, a pillow, blankets. Plates and bowls and forks, along with a jug to fetch water from the nearby stream.

It had remained their secret. They had told no one, not

even Freesia.

Perhaps now it wasn't even Nathaniel's secret anymore, because he couldn't find the blasted thing. A chipmunk darted across his path, startling him. He turned around, and around again. There was a familiar mark notched on a tree—a few feet higher than originally. They had made slashes at eye-level, back when they were boys, to mark the correct path. But now the trees and vines were so thick he began to think they had devoured the old home, furniture, blankets, and all.

He stumbled over a root, barely catching himself before he hit the ground. He cursed, groping wildly for purchase among the branches. His hand hit stone, and he stopped.

He felt about, pushing at the vines. Some clung firmly, but others shifted easily, as though they had been moved before. Recently.

He pressed deeper there, and found the door. He turned the knob, and it swung open.

He hesitated on the threshold.

Perhaps it would be better not to know…

"Do not be a coward," he growled out loud.

And stepped inside.

It was pitch black. He could make out nothing more than shadowy shapes. He went perfectly still, every sense heightened, and listened. There was his heartbeat. Outside, the wind rustled amongst the trees. Other than that, there was nothing. He was alone.

Obviously. Or he would be dead.

Filled with relief, he struck a match, using the light to find a candle. Once lit, he surveyed the room. It looked much the same as the last time he saw it.

Except—

The hairs on the back of his neck stood on end.

Someone had definitely been here.

The room was not dusty.

It did not smell of stale air.

Furthermore, most damning of all, a blue pelisse was folded neatly over the chair. It was Alice's. He was sure of it. The one she had left behind after rescuing him from the ridiculous hole. Whoever had set the trap must have found it and brought it here.

And that someone was Nick.

Who else could it be? Who else would have been at that deadfall but the person who dug it? Who else knew of this old cottage but himself and Nick?

No one.

A wave of nausea gripped Nathaniel, and he stumbled for the door.

It couldn't be true.

There must be some other explanation. Nick was his brother. His *brother*. They shared flesh and blood and a birthday. Before they were forcibly separated, they had always been together, since before birth. Nick had even saved Nathaniel's life, once. The river had swollen to twice its normal size from rain, and he had fallen in. The current nearly swept him away. He would have drowned if Nick hadn't waded in and hauled him back to the bank.

Was he regretting that decision now?

Because Nick obviously wanted him dead, or he wouldn't be here.

It was unthinkable.

It was unbearable.

All the evidence was crystal clear before him, and still his heart refused to accept the truth. His own brother could not be guilty.

Probably, poor Philip Eastwood had felt much the same way, until he felt the first stab of poison twisting his gut.

Nathaniel gulped in air, letting the cool air calm his heated face. He wiped the sweat from his forehead with his sleeve.

Damnation.

What was he to do now?

Should he wait for Nick to return? No, he was unarmed. That couldn't end well for him.

And Alice—

Oh, God. Alice.

He had hoped, somehow, that she was mistaken, that Nick hadn't seduced Adelaide any more than he had tried to kill Nathaniel. Now he appeared to be guilty of the latter, and Alice had evidence of the former.

Whoever Nick had been as a boy, as a man he was a villain. He had to be stopped.

But how?

Nathaniel's heart was breaking for what he must do. How could he possibly confess the truth to Alice?

But confess he must.

Chapter Forty-Six

Alice had watched Nathaniel leave the house, counted to ten, and followed him. He had not been going for his morning run. She'd known that because he was wearing boots and he'd been heading away from the lake rather than toward it.

He'd walked quickly, his stride sure, and she'd done her best to follow as quietly as possible. When her foot had snapped a twig, she'd darted behind a tree and held her breath. Would she be found out? But, no. He had not turned around, nor even hesitated. His mind had been occupied fully by other matters.

He'd been looking for Nicholas. Without her. As she had known he would.

Would he find him? By God, she'd hoped not. It had surprised her how strong the feeling had been. Which had not made sense. Wasn't finding Nicholas exactly what she'd *wanted*? One couldn't make a man and his reputation suffer without first knowing where he was and what he was up to. And yet, she had hoped that he would *not* be found anywhere near Haverly. If he were found close by, it would mean she had been right, and Nicholas was trying to kill Nathaniel.

It had suddenly been of utmost importance that Nicholas was not guilty of *that* particular offense, no matter what other crimes he had committed.

In her entire life, she had never hoped so strongly to be wrong.

Hopeful, but not stupid.

She had come prepared with a dagger hidden in her skirt. *Someone* had to carry a weapon, just in case, and she'd known it wouldn't be Nathaniel. It would never have occurred to him to defend himself against his brother, much less with a weapon. Until that point, his plan had been to avoid the kill-or-be-killed scenario at all costs. That was sweet, really. It was a shame his brother most likely did not return his tender feelings.

Which was why she'd brought the knife.

The air had turned even colder as they'd moved deeper into the forest. Then Nathaniel had stopped, and she had ducked behind a thicket, startling a chipmunk. It had scurried past him and disappeared into the trees. She'd breathed quietly and tried not to move as she'd watched Nathaniel turn in circles, examining this tree and that, muttering to himself.

She had begun to think they were lost.

Brilliant.

Then he'd stumbled. She'd gasped and quickly covered her mouth with a hand. Had he heard her? No, he'd started feeling amongst the vines, pushing them aside.

Oh, honestly. How could he *not* have heard her? The man paid so little attention to the world around him. How was it even possible that he was still alive? Nicholas should have found it easy enough to kill him and make off with the earldom long ago.

And then Nathaniel had simply vanished into the vines.

Good lord.

Which was where she stood now, caught in a web of dilemma.

Should she go after him and risk coming nose-to-nose if he'd merely stumbled into a thicket? Or face-to-face with his would-be assassin? Or just wait to see what happened…

Perhaps a bit closer examination.

She reached into her skirt pocket for the knife and darted to where he had disappeared.

It was a door! Well hidden and ancient, to be sure, but definitely a door.

She froze at the vine-covered entrance, listening. There were no scuffling noises, no cries of pain, or shrieks of murder, thank goodness. Just the muffled sound of footsteps on a dirt floor, then silence, then footsteps again coming back toward the door.

She looked about and quickly hid behind a tree. A moment later, Nathaniel stepped through the vines. His face…

Oh, dear heavens, *his face.*

It was gruesome to witness so much pain. She took a step toward him, remembered where she was, and quickly hid again. She pressed the heel of her palm to her mouth and bit, hard, at the flesh of her thumb, to keep the tears at bay.

As she watched, he covered his eyes with his hands then threw back his head and howled. The sound of his anguish and heartbreak ricocheted off the trees. She felt his pain as if it were her own.

He stood there for a long time before angrily swiping his sleeve across his eyes. Then he stormed away.

She waited, clenching and unclenching her fists, the sharp crescents of her nails leaving deep marks against her palms.

When she was certain he was gone, she pushed through the vines as she had seen him do. She opened the door and stepped into a room.

She saw a chair, a desk…and her blue pelisse. Understanding instantly what its presence here meant, she moved to the desk and found a bit of paper and pencil.

She scrawled a note, the pencil biting and ripping at the paper with her fury. She placed the note against a wooden beam, removed the knife from her pocket, and stabbed it through the paper, holding it impaled on the beam.

She thought that made her point rather nicely.

Chapter Forty-Seven

Alice prepared herself carefully for meeting Nicholas. Mary braided her hair in tight coils so that it resembled a crown about her head. She wore a dress of deep red—the same dress she'd worn the night she'd first met Nathaniel. As a final touch, she swiped red rose balm on her lips and a bit of crème on her cheeks. She rarely used such things, but tonight she made an exception.

Men wore armor into battle.

Women wore rouge.

"That will be all, Mary," she said, dismissing her maid.

Mary didn't budge. She clasped her hands as though in prayer and stared at her mistress in the mirror. "Please, Miss Alice, don't do it."

Alice paused. "Don't do what?" she asked cautiously.

"Whatever you are about to do. I have been with you these seven years, and I know when you are up to something dreadful. Please, Miss Alice. I beg you."

Well. It was nice to know that Mary held *some* affection for her, even if she did consider Alice to be something of a hoyden.

"All will be well, Mary. You needn't have any fear." She gave the girl's hand an affectionate pat. "Now, if you will please look the other way so I can make my escape…"

Mary groaned, but she did as she was told.

It was ridiculously easy to leave the house without notice. The men were playing billiards in one room, and the ladies were taking tea in another. Alice merely walked by both rooms without pause and slipped out the door.

She felt slightly ridiculous marching through the fields in a ball gown the color of blood, but no matter. One could not wear one's afternoon dress to meet an enemy on the battlefield.

When she came to the lake, she paused. Here was the spot she had assigned as their meeting place. The hole had since been covered, but he would know its former location. He had dug the damn thing, after all.

The wind rustled. The daffodils bobbed their golden heads, and the hair stood on the back of her neck. She turned slowly.

And there he was.

Nicholas Eastwood looked exactly like Nathaniel…only not. They shared the same red hair and crystalline blue eyes, and they were both sleekly built like lions. But something about this man struck her as dangerous. He was tightly coiled, as if ready to attack, and his face had a gaunt, menacing look to it. One glance told her he knew what it felt like to kill a man.

Suddenly, Adelaide's fall from grace made sense. *This* was a brooding hero, if ever there was one.

Her heart hammered in her chest. She wanted to flee and at the same time hurl herself at him and scratch his eyes out.

"Adelaide," he said, and stepped toward her.

She lifted the gun from her skirts.

He froze.

"I'm sure you understand why such drastic measures are necessary," she said conversationally. "You are a dangerous man, and I have no wish to be murdered. We must talk."

He studied her closely. "You are not Adelaide," he said finally.

"I am her sister, Alice. Did she never mention me?"

He shook his head.

Alice frowned. "I wonder that she did not. We were very close, my sister and I."

"Did she ever mention me to you?" he asked. When she shook her head, he said, "Then perhaps you were not as close as you thought."

Alice glared. Insufferable man.

"So," he continued. "You are not Adelaide, and yet you believe we need to talk. What do you wish to speak of? The health of our prince regent? Apple tarts, perhaps?"

Alice gritted her teeth. "I would like to discuss Nathaniel. Particularly, your attempts to murder him."

For a moment Nicholas looked truly surprised before he wiped all expression from his face. Again, he studied her. She had the odd sensation that she was watching a master chess player shift pieces around on a board.

"If you wish to discuss my dear brother, Nathaniel, the future Earl of Wintham, I would be delighted." He bowed gallantly. "But before we delve into such a tedious topic, I request that we come to an understanding on Adelaide. Specifically, where is she?"

"Dead," Alice said through clenched lips.

Again, that careful study behind a facade of indifference. "Do you think so?" he asked curiously.

"I know so," Alice spat out. "She died in childbirth, taking your child with her."

In an instant, the gun was twisted from her hands and her

arms gripped in a bruising vise. She gasped from the pain but did not cry out.

"Are you certain she was with child? Answer me!" He gave her a firm shake.

"I saw her belly increasing with my own eyes," Alice said. "She was sent to a convent in France to hide her condition. A month later, we received word that neither my sister nor her child survived. Your picture was in her locket. Do you deny you were the father?"

"No." He released her, his hands dropping to his sides. "I don't deny it."

He returned her gun.

She stared, startled, at the lethal object in her hand. Was this a trick?

"You seem more comfortable with it," he explained. "I don't wish you to feel unsafe in my presence."

Her mouth dropped open in astonishment.

"This has been a truly enlightening conversation, but I must take my leave. There is a matter that requires my immediate attention. If you will excuse me, Miss Bursnell." He bowed.

Alice recovered her tongue. "No, I will *not* excuse you. We have not yet discussed the issue at hand."

"Oh, yes. Nate." He waved his hand dismissively. "That matter is of no consequence to me."

Fury rushed through her veins like blood. "It is of consequence to *me*."

"Very well." He gestured for her to continue.

She drew herself up to her full height—which, granted, wasn't very tall, but at least he wouldn't see her as weak and shrinking. "I have a proposal to make you, Mr. Eastwood."

His eyes glimmered with amusement. She did not like that.

She also did not like his tone when he said, "Do tell. I am

all eagerness."

"You needn't be an ass," she said crossly. "You are extremely unlikable."

"My apologies," he said, clearly meaning no such thing. "How can I be of assistance?"

She narrowed her eyes and studied him. She considered herself to be an excellent judge of character, but she could not get a sense of Nicholas at all. The man's face was like granite and gave nothing away.

"While in town yesterday, I met a gentleman who called himself Mr. Manning," she said. "I don't believe that was his true name, so I don't expect you to know him. But he knows *you*. You belong in prison, according to Mr. Manning, and he requested my assistance in putting you there."

"And what did I do to deserve such a fate, pray tell?"

"He didn't say, and quite truthfully, I find it unimportant." She shrugged. "You are already guilty of the seduction and betrayal of my sister, and attempted fratricide. I am hard pressed to consider any crimes greater than those."

"Truly heinous crimes, indeed," he said. "So, it is your intention to turn me over to this Mr. Manning?"

"I considered it. But after giving the matter careful thought, I came to the conclusion that Mr. Manning wishes you dead, not imprisoned."

"Ah." Nicholas nodded. "You did not want blood on your hands to keep you from a peaceful night's sleep."

She arched her eyebrows. "Oh, I think I should have slept quite well, sir. But Nathaniel wouldn't like it. Until this morning, when he discovered your hiding place, he did not truly believe you could be trying to kill him. You broke his heart today, but even so, he wouldn't like to see you dead."

There was the smallest twitch of movement by Nicholas's left eye. "Nate thinks I am trying to kill him?"

What an odd thing to say. She tilted her head and

considered the man with more care. "He *knows* so, Mr. Eastwood." Who else could it be, after all?

He leaned back against the trunk of an oak tree and crossed his arms over his chest, a gesture so like his brother. "What do you suggest we do now, Miss Bursnell?"

"Mr. Manning has searched high and low for you without success. He requested that once I find you, I write him a note and deliver it to a secret place, and he would take care of the matter from there." She laced her gloved fingers together. "I am prepared to write whatever you wish."

"You are all kindness," he said, presumably for no other reason than to irritate her.

"I want something in return," she said.

"Of course you do. Name your price."

She smiled. "There is a boat departing for India in a week. I want you on it."

"Very well. I accept the terms of your proposal," he said after a moment's consideration.

That was rather easier than she'd expected.

"I have business there," he said. "You are not sending me to my doom, to your eternal regret, I am sure."

How irksome that he seemed able to read her mind so clearly when his remained a dark pit.

He proceeded to tell her what the note must say. He repeated it so that she would not forget the exact details. She shot him daggers with her eyes. Then he repeated it once more for good measure, and she considered kicking his knee.

He bowed.

She did not return the courtesy.

She was sure she felt his gaze as she stormed across the field, but when she turned to look back, he was gone.

Chapter Forty-Eight

The note was written. All that was left was for Alice to deliver it. She folded and sealed it carefully, and dismissed the actual message from her mind. What Nicholas had planned for Mr. Manning was of no concern to her. One had to accept certain risks when one associated with nefarious men. Surely, Mr. Manning was aware of that.

What mattered was that in a week's time, Mr. Nicholas Eastwood would be bound for India, and Nathaniel would finally be safe. All she had to do was wait.

And deliver that letter.

She tiptoed down the stairs, hoping to go unnoticed by Aunt Bea and Nathaniel, specifically, and everyone else, in general. She had cleared the parlor door when she heard a throat clearing behind her.

She turned slowly. "Eliza."

"Where are you going?"

"Into town," Alice said evasively.

Eliza was not so easily evaded. "Why?" she asked bluntly.

Alice pursed her lips. "You know why." She hadn't told

Eliza about meeting Nicholas, nor about their agreement. She thought that might be a bit much for her friend to keep quiet, and keeping quiet was so deeply important.

Eliza rapidly took several steps forward. She reached out, touching Alice's sleeve. "Please don't do this, Alice."

"I must, Eliza." Alice took her hand and clasped it tightly in her own. "I *must*."

Eliza sighed. "Very well. Let me accompany you. No, don't argue. You know as well as I do that Mr. Manning cannot be trusted. Likely, he is there at the inn, hiding, watching, and waiting for you to slip your note into the book as arranged. It is too dangerous for you to go alone."

Alice opened her mouth to protest, but closed it quickly. Eliza was right. Mr. Manning had been so careful to conceal his face. Perhaps he would welcome an opportunity to make Alice disappear, as well, just in case. It would be better to take Eliza along.

They had the use of Aunt Bea's carriage, since she had not yet risen. When they arrived at the inn, Alice quickly looked about. Mr. Manning was nowhere to be seen—not that she had expected otherwise. Still, she instinctively knew Eliza was right. He was here, somewhere, waiting for the letter.

She went directly to the appointed bookshelf, removed *A Modest Proposal*, and pressed the note inside the cover. She moved to put it back just as Eliza lifted her arm to straighten her bonnet, and the book was knocked from her hand.

Alice gasped. "Oh!"

Eliza stooped to retrieve it, giving Alice a reassuring smile. "You're just nervous." She handed her the book. "We should leave as quickly as possible."

Alice peeked under the cover. The note was still there. For a moment, she had thought it had slipped out—she'd glimpsed a white corner between Eliza's fingertips. But no, here it was. Alice carefully slid the book to its proper place.

"Shall we return to Haverly?" she asked.

"Or perhaps we could visit Winchester Cathedral?" Eliza suggested, linking their arms as they hurried out of the inn. "The drive is no more than a half hour. I know you have a fondness for all things old and dusty, and I have reasons of my own to make the pilgrimage."

"What sort of reasons?" Alice asked curiously, ignoring the fact that a great deal of her delight at the abbey had been because of their unexpected company... She accepted the footman's help into the carriage.

"Oh, the dull sort." Eliza followed her in. "Dillingham is plaguing the life out of me. I cannot bear another sermon on cravats."

Alice laughed and breathed a sigh of deep relief as she settled against the cushion. It was done. The letter was delivered. She had done her part, and now it was on Nicholas to hold up his end of the bargain. She could relax for the moment, perhaps even enjoy these last few days at Haverly before she parted from Nathaniel forever.

"In that case, by all means, let us go to Winchester. You are correct, of course. I find musty old cathedrals positively thrilling. The older and mustier the better." She rubbed her hands together gleefully. "Do you know that King Harthaknut was buried there in 1042? Well, not exactly—it was Old Minster then. England hasn't had a Scandinavian king since. Doesn't the name just roll off the tongue? Hartha-knut. Harth-a-knut."

"Fascinating," Eliza said drily.

"It *is*," Alice insisted. "All history is. Consider this, then. A hundred years from now, our great-great grandchildren will stand on those very stones and wonder the very same questions. How can that *not* be fascinating?"

"Well," Eliza mused, "if the choice of conversation is between ancient bones and the perfect cravat knot, I must choose the bones. I may not share your passion, but I daresay I shall not be bored."

Alice repressed a sigh. She loved old buildings, so she would not be bored, either. And she enjoyed Eliza's company. But she could not help longing for Nathaniel.

Chapter Forty-Nine

"But why? Why are you dragging me to God-knows-where, when it is obviously going to rain?" Nathaniel asked. Wessex was being obnoxious to the extreme.

His friend tugged on his gloves. "It is not going to rain."

Nathaniel shot a dubious glance heavenward. He pointed meaningfully at the heavy gray clouds.

"It always looks like that," Wessex said dismissively.

"That's because it's always raining, or just about to," Nathaniel shot back. "This is England. If I am to spend an afternoon soggy and cold, I demand at least an explanation."

"I'm investigating a theory," Wessex said vaguely.

Ridiculous. Wessex didn't have theories. He tried not to think too much, at all, if he could help it.

Nathaniel didn't have time for this nonsense. He had a brother bent on murder and a lady bent on revenge, and never the twain should meet…if he could only manage it.

"I would much rather stay home," he said bluntly. "Go without me."

"I can't go alone." Wessex's expression was one of horror.

"She'll suspect—" He snapped his mouth shut abruptly.

Nathaniel was immediately suspicious—not that he had ever believed Wessex's motives to be pure. Wessex's motives were never pure. "*Who* will suspect? *What* will she suspect?"

Wessex pushed him toward the waiting carriage. "Your mother. Your mother will suspect that your ankle is broken, not merely sprained, and lock you in your room for the remainder of the fortnight. And if you are locked up, who will protect Miss Bursnell from the constant overtures of Colonel Kent? More important, who will assist me in my schemes?"

Nathaniel halted by the carriage door and turned slowly to face his friend. "Let us get one thing straight right now. I will not be party to any of your schemes, particularly the ones involving Miss Benton. Do I make myself clear?"

"Of course."

Nathaniel peered deeply into his eyes. Wessex did not so much as blink.

"You are full of shite."

"Quite so." Wessex rapped his knuckles on the driver's box to get the man's attention. "Follow the ladies' carriage, but for God's sake, stay out of sight."

Nathaniel bit back a growl and climbed into the carriage. Of *course* Wessex would drag him into every blasted scheme, and of *course* they would all involve Miss Benton. And wherever Miss Benton was, there Alice would be, as well. She was using Miss Benton as a shield, to protect her from *him*.

It had been two days since he had touched her so intimately, two days since he should have offered and didn't. She had not spoken a single word to him during those two days. It had been the worst kind of torture, knowing she was under his roof and hating him so much that she couldn't bear to speak to him.

Although, to be fair, he hadn't spoken to her, either. Mainly because she had such a dreadful way of ferreting the truth out of a man. It would be a matter of moments before she knew Nick's exact location. Nathaniel swallowed a silent groan. Hell, all she had to do was *kiss* him, and he would escort her there himself.

No. It would be better to avoid Alice altogether until he had solved the issue of Nick. He could not marry Alice with Nick standing between them.

The coach made a sudden swing to the right and came to a halt. Wessex pushed the curtain aside and stuck his head out the window. "Where is she, Smeet?"

"Around the corner, Your Grace. They went into the inn."

Wessex pulled his head back inside, looking puzzled. "Wait here." He exited the carriage. A moment later he came dashing back. "They're on the move again. Winchester Cathedral, Smeet."

Nathaniel groaned again, this time out loud. "No more of this! Leave Miss Benton alone, for God's sake."

Wessex crossed his arms. "Why are you whining? The cathedral is ancient and boring. Hundreds of bones have decayed there. Isn't that just the sort of thing that interests you?"

"Generally speaking, I should love nothing better than to spend an afternoon surrounded by centuries of England's history. But you forget that I have lived here my whole life. I've been to Winchester dozens of times. I would much rather go home and spare myself Alice's wrath."

Wessex laughed. "Coward. You do realize she spent half an hour in the garden with Colonel Kent? If they are not already engaged to be married, they will be soon. Your only option is to be a man and finish the job you started. Seduce the lady and, for the love of all things holy, *ask her to marry you* instead of slinking off like a scoundrel."

Nathaniel glared. He did not like thinking of Kent in the

garden with Alice. It made him want to roar and tear things apart with his bare hands. "Is that your scheme for Miss Benton, then?"

"Don't be absurd. Our situations are entirely different. You actually *want* to get married. I don't want anything of the kind. I don't want to marry Miss Benton. I just want her to want to marry *me*."

"What?" Wessex had him truly flummoxed this time. "If you do not wish to marry, why does it matter whether Miss Benton wants to marry you?"

"It's damned bothersome, that's why." He scowled out the window. "Every other woman wants to marry me. Why won't she fall in line? It irks me."

Nathaniel rolled his eyes. "Heaven forbid."

The carriage pulled up to the cathedral. They paused at the entrance. It didn't matter how many times he visited, the building always captured his awe and admiration.

"Look at that." He waved an arm, gesturing broadly at the whole structure. "Just look at it. Look at those arches. *That* is perfect symmetry. Symmetry that has survived seven hundred years of renovations and even a change of religion."

"Terribly fascinating," Wessex said in a tone that suggested the complete opposite. They entered the cathedral, and he cast a sharp look about. "Let's start in the south transept." When Nathaniel nodded and followed him dutifully, he said, "Aren't you going to ask why?"

"No."

"Why not?"

"Because when Miss Bursnell asks—and she *will* ask, make no mistake about that—what the devil you're up to, I want to be able to say in all honesty that I haven't the slightest idea."

Wessex considered this. "Good thinking."

"Yes, I thought so."

They turned the corner. Nathaniel found himself confronted by exactly what he expected—and exactly what he feared. There was Miss Benton. And next to her stood Alice.

Their backs were to them. Was it too late to flee? Perhaps the women were not yet aware of his presence.

It would help if he could move his legs. But they kept him firmly rooted, refusing to budge even a millimeter away from Alice. It was all he could do to keep his arms from reaching for her. His heart pounded in his chest. *Mine*, it thumped. *Mine, mine, mine.*

"Good heavens. Izaak Walton was buried here?" Miss Benton was saying.

"Indeed. Because writing a book about the art of fishing exalts him above other, mere mortal writers, such as Shakespeare, for instance," Alice said dryly.

Miss Benton chuckled. "Well, I suppose they had to find someone appropriate to bury in here," she conceded, glancing around at the small chapel dedicated to St John the Evangelist and the Fisherman Apostles. "I suppose we can take comfort in that."

"Why must we take comfort?" Wessex asked.

Miss Benton clutched Alice's sleeve. "I believe I heard a donkey bray. Did you?" she whispered loudly.

"Come now!" Wessex protested. "One doesn't cut a duke. Not even you, Miss Benton."

The ladies turned in unison and dropped curtsies. "Your Grace," Miss Benton murmured. "Lord Abingdon, it is always a pleasure."

Nathaniel doubted that.

From the sideways glance Alice sent Miss Benton, he thought it a safe bet that she felt the same.

Look at me, he willed her silently. If she would only look at him, his eyes would tell her the truth. *Blame Wessex. It's all his fault.* But she kept her eyes stubbornly on the stone floor.

"I must say, I'm terribly relieved to find you ladies here," Wessex drawled. "You have saved me from Lord Abingdon's lecture on the symmetry of old rocks. I thought a brandy in the library was better suited for today's weather, but he would have none of it."

Oh, wonderful. Now Alice would think the outing was his idea, with the purpose of following her, naturally. Nathaniel immediately wished himself buried six feet under the cathedral—or, better yet, he wished *Wessex* buried six feet deep. With a heap of old rocks stacked on top, just to be safe. If any a man were ever to turn vampire, it would be Wessex.

Alice was still refusing even to glance in Nathaniel's direction, but Miss Benton's eyes twinkled at him. "Did he also tell you about King Have-a-nut?" she asked Wessex. "That was the lecture I received from Miss Bursnell."

"Harthaknut," Alice muttered.

"Ah!" Wessex's expression was one of deep sadness. "Then you understand how I have suffered."

Miss Benton laughed. Alice glared at them both...*and stepped closer to him.* Nathaniel willed every muscle in his body to freeze, lest the slightest twitch scare her away.

"If we hadn't stumbled upon you ladies, he would ramble on about who was buried where and how they took their tea," Wessex continued.

"That is just like Alice!" Miss Benton exclaimed. "She always wants to discuss the daily minutiae of the long-ago departed."

Alice growled low so low only he could hear it, and stepped even closer. "Insufferable creatures," she murmured.

Nathaniel blinked. *Us against them.* That's what Wessex had done. When they had first entered the room, the pairings were obviously males against females. But Wessex had shifted the teams. He had given Alice a reason to side with Nathaniel.

The man was a genius. Annoying, perhaps, but a genius, nonetheless.

A sudden clap of thunder ricocheted like a gunshot through the cathedral, echoing off the stone walls and halls.

Sending Alice flying straight into his arms.

Chapter Fifty

Alice couldn't help herself. Truly. At her parents' estate in Northumberland, she had often heard the French and English trading cannonballs from across the channel. When the teeth-rattling boom of thunder now filled the small chapel, she launched herself at the closest safe harbor.

Perhaps she clung to him longer than was strictly proper, but how could she deny herself the pleasure? Since the moment he had screamed in anguish in the forest, she had longed to comfort him, to hold him through the storm of his disappointment until he reached equanimity on the other side.

He touched her back gently. "It's all right."

"Of course it's all right. It's thunder, not war." She released him in embarrassment and stepped back.

"Shall we hunker down here and wait for the storm to pass or brave the rain?" Wessex asked.

"We can't drive in the rain—at least, Miss Bursnell and I can't," Eliza said. "We came by open curricle, and we would get soaked through."

Another clap of thunder shook the windows.

"I doubt the rain will let up soon," Nathaniel said. "If we wait much longer, the roads will be impassable."

"You can come with us in my carriage," Wessex said. "We can leave the curricle in the stable here and arrange for its return this afternoon. That is, if you ladies don't mind driving backward. I get terribly sick, so Lord Abingdon and I must claim the forward seats."

"Oh, dear. I have the same malady, so I must beg Lord Abingdon to allow me his seat," Eliza said. She eyed Wessex suspiciously. "I was not aware that you get carriage sick, Your Grace. How odd."

Alice gritted her teeth, instantly realizing the implications.

Wessex declined to answer. He led them back to the cathedral entrance, where his footmen dashed out to meet them with umbrellas. Before she could protest, Alice found herself in the carriage with Nathaniel seated beside her.

But, really, what could she say? She did not want poor Eliza to cast up her accounts. Alice doubted Wessex was in any similar danger, but one simply did not call out a duke, no matter how much the duke deserved it.

Everything would be all right, she told herself. She and Nathaniel weren't alone together—Eliza and Wessex were right there, practically toe-to-toe with them. The carriage was spacious, as befitted a peer of Wessex's standing. It was not as if she and Nathaniel would be forced to *touch*.

Yet, touching was all she could think about. *Her hands in his hair. His hands tugging down her bodice. His mouth on her breast.*

She shivered. He silently removed his cloak and draped it over her lap. It was still warm from the heat of his body.

Her resistance sank a little lower.

She tilted her lips in a small smile. "Thank you, Lord Abingdon."

He nodded and turned to look out the window. The rain had colored his red-gold waves a slick, dark bronze. As if he could feel her eyes on him, he ran his hand over his damp hair, brushing water droplets onto his ear and neck.

She was overcome with a sudden longing to kiss those beads from his skin…and…and to *nuzzle*, to warm her body with his own. She wanted to take care of him and let him take care of her.

This was a problem.

If he wanted anything more than her body, he would have said as much after their…encounter…in the hidden room. He'd had her in the palm of his hand, quite literally, and still he had let her traipse through a darkened garden with Colonel Kent.

It was *humiliating*.

She frowned at the cloak on her lap. There would be no nuzzling. But she found herself shifting almost imperceptibly closer to him.

The rain had not slowed upon their arrival at Haverly. Great sheets of water dumped from the sky like a waterfall. Wessex jumped out of the coach, helped Eliza down, and ushered her inside the house. Nathaniel followed his lead, offering his hand to Alice. He took the umbrella and dismissed the footman and the driver to see to the horses.

Under the shelter of the umbrella, she looked up at Nathaniel. And her heart clenched. Once Nicholas was gone, she would be, too.

She tried to memorize the curve of his jaw, the exact blue of his eyes, the way his copper lashes started as dark brown before fading to shimmering gold at the tips. The way his mouth—

Oh, heavens, that mouth.

She stood on tiptoe and pressed a soft, quick kiss to his lips. "Good-bye," she whispered against his ear. Then she darted out into the rain.

She didn't make it far. She heard his footsteps behind her then felt his hand on her arm, pulling her back against him.

"No," he said furiously, just before his lips came crashing down on hers.

The umbrella fell to the ground, splattering mud as it landed. She didn't care. She was soaked to the bone, as was he, but his heat kept her warm as their tongues clashed together. She twined her fingers in his hair, pulling him closer. It was not nearly enough. The ache low in her belly told her nothing short of complete and utter ruin would ever be enough.

He pulled back with a low growl. "Go into the house. Straight up to your room, do you understand?"

No, not really.

She stared mutely at him through rain-soaked eyelashes. He couldn't mean…

Could he?

"Alice." He gave her a small shake. *Do you understand?*

"Yes," she whispered.

He pressed his mouth hard against hers and then released her with a tiny push. "Go."

She did not stop to think. She just went.

Chapter Fifty-One

Nathaniel entered the house just in time to hear Alice tell her aunt that she was soaked to the bone and needed a change of clothes.

"I'm feeling rather tired after our morning, Auntie. I believe I shall spend the afternoon resting in my room. Please make my apologies to Lady Wintham."

He turned and made for the south staircase, thanking God that he was a man. No one would question his disappearance. They would assume he was playing pool or drinking brandy or tending to estate matters in his office— some manly pursuit or other that did not include ravishing a lady in her bedchamber.

He took the stairs two at a time. Once at his own room, he speedily stripped off his damp clothes and replaced them with dry ones. He didn't bother with a cravat or other niceties. He fully intended to be naked again in mere moments.

He had known the moment Alice said good-bye at the carriage and touched her lips to his that she meant to leave him forever and return to London or, God forbid, Northumberland.

The thought was unbearable. He would ruin her first, bind her to him in a way that left her no choice in the matter.

He walked softly down the hall, carrying his boots in one arm. There was no one to see him in his state of half dress, for which he was profusely grateful. For once, it seemed that luck was on his side. He knocked quietly on her door and turned the knob. It was unlocked.

"Alice," he said, then stopped.

Good God.

She was standing in the middle of the room shivering violently, and her lips had a faint bluish tinge to them. He locked the door and was next to her in an instant. She was still wearing her wet clothes, every cold fiber clinging to her delicate skin.

"I dismissed my maid," she said through chattering teeth. "I thought…"

He swore softly. What an ass he was! It hadn't occurred to him that she could not undress without help. While he had been caring for himself, Alice had been rapidly freezing to death.

He turned her around and stared at the row of buttons down her back. They were so tiny and there were so damned many. The wet fabric made the task even more difficult. He struggled with the first one for a full minute before it finally slipped through the hole. He moved on to the next.

She made a small, rueful laugh. "I can't feel anything. I think I'm numb." Her teeth clacked together with every word.

He swore again and gathered a fistful of fabric in each hand. With one hard tug, the tiny pearls popped from their moorings and scattered to the floor, the sound of their demise muffled by the plush rug. He wrestled the dress, heavy with water, off her body and pulled her shift over her head.

She was now naked in his arms, but he couldn't enjoy it. Not when it was his fault she was near death from cold. He scooped her up and deposited her under the thick covers. After removing his own clothes for the second time, he joined her.

"I'm still cold," she whispered. Her icy hands went to his chest.

He flinched and pulled her in closer so their thighs and bellies melded together. She wrapped her arms around his waist and burrowed in, taking his heat for her own. He gave it freely. She could have all the warmth his body possessed, even if he turned into a man-size icicle, if it meant she would stop shivering.

He lifted one leg over hers, tangling their limbs together. He ran his hands briskly down her arms and back, trying to warm her skin.

"Nathaniel." She laughed against his throat. "If you rub me any harder, my skin will start to smoke."

He dropped fervent little kisses on the crown of her head. Damn it! Even her hair was cold. "I'm so sorry I made you wait, Alice. Forgive me?"

"Of course." She kissed the underside of his jaw. "Silly man."

She wiggled against him. His cock, which had repentantly stood down during the crisis, now perked back up. Alice, he suddenly realized, was naked in his arms—and now he *could* enjoy it. She was in his arms, and she was going to let him kiss her and touch her and do all manner of things. Things he longed to do, things he had dreamed of. Things—

Things he didn't actually know how to do.

Dear God.

Should he tell her? Most men over the age of nineteen had bedded a woman at least once. By thirty, an earl-to-be should have had dozens of partners. Surely, she expected him to be no different.

But what would he say? *Well, darling, it turns out that neither of us knows what we're doing, so say a prayer and hope for the best.*

No.

He started to shake.

"Oh, no. I've made you cold now, haven't I?" She stroked her hands over his chest and back as he had done for her.

But he wasn't cold. His blood was on fire. Her lips burned a path up his throat, and he groaned. It didn't matter that he had never done this before. Millions of men since Adam had figured it out and lived to tell the tale over frothy pints of beer. He would, too. He thought of the moment in the secret room where she had come apart in his hands, and that gave him courage.

She reached between them to where he was nestled against her soft belly. Her fingertips brushed against the velvet tip, and his cock jerked eagerly. *Christ.* He would spend like a schoolboy before he ever breached her maidenhead.

He gave a strangled laugh and arched his hips away from her touch, holding her wrist still with one hand. "No, darling, not this time."

"I can't touch you?"

She sounded oddly deflated. Could it be that she wanted to explore him as much as he wanted to explore her? That was…unexpected. And yet, she didn't seem frightened or disgusted, which was what he expected after the way he had spent himself on her belly. True ladies, he had always heard, were ill equipped to handle the more animalistic aspects of sexual desire. They preferred to lie there, eyes squeezed closed, and think of England.

But Alice was a true lady, and she had just reached for his cock.

Which meant…

Which meant…

Well, it meant that men were idiots when it came to ladies. Hardly new information, that.

He took her hand and pressed it to his lips. "You can

touch me here." He moved it to his chest. "And here." Her fingers instantly played with the hair there, and he smiled. "You can touch me anywhere except where I want your touch the most. It will all be over far too soon if you touch me there."

She wound her arms around his neck. "Can I kiss you?"

Sweet merciful heavens. He had heard of women doing such things if one paid them enough, but ladies? Never. He pulled back and regarded her uncertainly.

Ah.

No.

She meant a proper kiss. On the lips.

Although, perhaps someday...

He took her mouth before his addled brain could finish the thought. Her lips parted, granting him entry, and he slipped his tongue inside. They tasted each other, tongues gliding and searching.

With gentle pressure, he rolled them so she was on her back and he was on top of her. Her legs fell open without protest, and he settled in the cradle of her thighs. He felt her nipples against his chest and lowered his head to lick the hardened peaks. She arched, thrusting herself deeper into his hot mouth.

Desperate little sounds escaped her, urging him on. Her hands tangled in his hair, holding his mouth where she wanted it, and he was only too happy to oblige. He lavished attention on first one breast and then the other, licking and sucking and grazing lightly with his teeth. Her hips bucked against him, and he thought he would go mad with desire.

Kiss her everywhere, Wessex had suggested. *See what she likes.*

He hadn't the time. His cock throbbed painfully. There would be, he hoped, many such encounters in their future. He could kiss her and touch her to his heart's content then, but just now, he was in danger of exploding.

He slid his hand between them, seeking. *Please, please*

be ready. Thanks to the bragging of his friends, he knew that her body would help him fit, but only if he first helped her. He touched her. She was damp, but perhaps not quite enough. The vivid descriptions he'd heard made him seek out a certain place between her folds, and he easily found the small pearl that was said to give the greatest pleasure. He pressed his thumb against it and swirled. She cried out, and he gave a low growl of satisfaction. After a short time, his finger glided easily inside her. She was ready.

He took his hand away and smoothed the hair from her forehead. He nudged the tip of him against her entrance, and hesitated. He should give her a chance to change her mind, to take what was left of her virginity and flee.

Like hell he would.

"Alice," he said. "You are *mine*."

He pushed inside.

But only an inch.

She clenched around him, keeping him from fully inserting himself.

"Darling," he pleaded with a groan. He kissed her trembling lips. She relaxed slightly, and he gained another inch. "Let me in, sweetheart."

"Slowly. Please?" Her eyes were wide and anxious.

Now would be the time to tell her he didn't have as much control over his body as she believed. But no. Why terrify her further?

"Does it hurt?" he asked and immediately wished he hadn't. Of course it did.

"A bit."

He hated that he must hurt her. He nuzzled her breast again. That, at least, she seemed to like. She whimpered, and her inner muscles stretched a little more, allowing him to sink deeper into her.

Sweat broke out on his brow. Nothing about his hand-induced releases had prepared him for her tight, wet heat. Good Lord. She was so small.

Again, he slipped his hand between them, teasing her nub, distracting her from the pain as he went deeper still. He was buried almost to the hilt when he realized she'd had no maidenhead. He remembered, then, the rumors he had heard about ladies who rode horses.

Thank God, thank God, thank God.

There would be no more pain. No more than she was already experiencing, at any rate.

She was panting now, her breath coming in erratic puffs against his neck. Her fingertips dug into his back. He started to ease out but her nails dug deeper.

"Nathaniel," she whispered. "Do you think… Could you hold still? Just for a moment."

He said a very bad word. "I have to move, darling. I think I might die if I don't." He shuddered, clinging to his control by the thinnest of threads. "*Please*, Alice."

She looked up at him. Something shifted and softened in her face. It was sweet, so sweet that he was dizzy from it.

"It's all right," she said.

Her hands ran down his back to the hard muscles of his buttocks. She pressed him down, urging him deeper inside, raining kisses against his neck and shoulder. Her touch dissolved the last threads of his restraint. He thrust into her hard and fast, once, twice, three times.

The force of his release caused his body to shudder hard against her.

He buried his face in her neck as she stroked his hair gently. He sighed and relaxed farther into her embrace.

There was something he needed to tell her, something important, but his brain had turned to mush, and whatever it was, it slipped further and further away. Until…his thoughts ceased completely.

Chapter Fifty-Two

Love, Alice thought as her fingers idly stroked Nathaniel's red-gold mane, was extremely inconvenient.

It wasn't the sort of thing one could pin down. Love couldn't be locked in a jar or shoved into some dark corner until life was less messy. It refused to be safely contained, and instead grew and grew until it pushed against the walls around her heart, cracking the bricks she had worked so hard to build there.

Yes, love was damnably inconvenient.

Especially now, because Nathaniel had fallen asleep on top of her.

Her arm was tingling as though a thousand pins were stabbing at it, but she wouldn't wake him for the world. He was so beautiful. Sleep softened the lines of his forehead that grew deeper when he was particularly anxious. He looked peaceful and content, nestled there against her shoulder. His bronze eyelashes fanned against his cheek, where here and there was a charming freckle, the sole remnants of a childhood likely plagued by them.

God, she loved him.

It was a deeply uncomfortable feeling, almost as if she were holding something large and bulky deep inside her chest, and it didn't quite fit. Either it was too big or she was too small—it was hard to say which. It made her feel so many contrary things. Strong and weak, brave and fearful, whole and torn. Love wasn't just one feeling, but rather the sum of a hundred swirling emotions.

Including guilt.

Oh, heavens, the guilt.

Nathaniel wanted, more than anything in the world, to end his feud with Nicholas and mend the rift that had torn his family apart. Even attempted fratricide could not sway him from his goal. She knew this. His brother was the thing most dear to his heart…and she had taken that from him. To keep Nathaniel safe, yes, but also for her own selfish purposes. She had sent Nicholas away to India because she knew she and he could not coexist in Nathaniel's world here in England.

She had sent Nicholas away because she wanted Nathaniel for herself.

That was not an act of love.

She had met Nicholas in secret, delivered her ultimatum, and secured his promise. Nathaniel had been given no choice in the matter.

And what would *his* choice have been? He could have either Nicholas for a true brother or Alice for a wife. To have both was an impossibility that even love could not overcome. Which would he have chosen? The thought was like a chill wind blowing across her heart.

She held him just a little tighter. Because she knew.

You are mine, he had said as he entered her. But if he had truly intended to make her his, would he not have asked her the question that would have done so?

And yet, he had not asked.

Which tore her heart in a thousand small pieces.

But, ultimately, it made up her mind.

She had to tell him what she'd done, before it was too late. He could not lose his brother on her account. It would shatter her heart completely, but so be it.

With that thought, she closed her eyes.

When she opened them again, she was alone.

Chapter Fifty-Three

An hour earlier, Nathaniel had opened his eyes, looked at Alice, and known immediately what he had to do. Now, he looked down at the letter he had written.

To Mr. Nicholas Eastwood:
Dear Sir,
It appears you are returned to England. Since you did not notify our family of your arrival, I assume you do not wish me to, either. I also assume you have your reasons for your behavior, even if those reasons are very bad.
It has come to my attention that approximately two years ago, you met a young lady by the name of Adelaide Bursnell. According to Miss Adelaide's sister, you treated her with utmost disrespect and used her terribly, causing her and her family the deepest grief.
Please confirm or deny.
Lord Nathaniel Eastwood, Viscount Abingdon

Nathaniel took the letter to Nick's hiding place and left it propped on the table.

After luncheon, Jimmy, the footman, knocked on the library door and silently handed him a missive, written on a blank calling card. It was painfully short.

To Lord Nathaniel Eastwood, Viscount Abingdon:
Nate,
Confirmed.
Nick

The crack in Nathaniel's heart deepened. Until this moment, he had held out hope that Nick hadn't really done what Alice accused him of. Attempted fratricide, Nathaniel had almost come to terms with, but seduction and betrayal of Alice's sister? It was too much.

"Is there a response, my lord?" Jimmy asked.

"Yes. Wait a moment, please."

Sir,
I hereby demand satisfaction on behalf of the egregiously wronged lady. Please name your second, the day and time, etc.
Abingdon

Nick must have been loitering close by, because Jimmy arrived with a response within minutes.

Nate,
Oh, for God's sake.
Nick

Typical.

As much as Nathaniel wanted to reconcile with his brother, this could not be deflected, nor swept under the rug. If for no other reason, Alice would never let it go. Not until she'd avenged her sister. And it was best for all if it was Nathaniel who provided that revenge.

With an unbearable heaviness in his chest, he took up his pen.

> *Sir,*
> *The insult to Miss Adelaide cannot stand. Name your second and choose the place.*
> *Abingdon*

Again, a response came within minutes.

> *Nate,*
> *How can Miss Adelaide feel the insult if she is presumed dead?*
> *Let us meet at the oak tree. You know why.*
> *Nick*

His brother was clearly an unfeeling monster. It made Nathaniel feel slightly better about what he must do.

> *Sir,*
> *Alice feels the insult enough for both of them, I assure you. Your second?*
> *Abingdon*

This time the response took longer. After half an hour, Nathaniel desperately wanted to storm outside, find the blackguard in his hiding place, and smack him soundly across the cheek with his glove, just to drive home his point. But honestly, he could not face the man without strangling him, so he restrained himself.

He paced impatiently before the fireplace, waiting for the footman's return. Two hours later, Jimmy dashed into the room, slightly breathless, and held out the card with a small bow.

Nathaniel did not reach for it. He looked at the small white paper with a surge of distaste. "Leave it on the table."

After Jimmy bowed and left, Nathaniel hesitated, then strode over to peer down at the note.

Nate,
Colonel Kent will stand as my second. Be so good as
to inform him, as I do not personally know the man.
He will be of some comfort to Miss Alice, should the
need arise.
Nick

For a moment, Nathaniel saw red. *Colonel Kent?* Nick was baiting him. Worse, it was working. Clearly, Nick had been watching their comings and goings long enough to realize the colonel was Nathaniel's rival for Alice's affections.

Damn his brother! He was a blackguard *and* an ass.

He ground his jaw.

Nick,
Weapons?
Nate

When the reply came, Nathaniel stared down at the back of the card that had been placed on his desk, loathe to turn it over. He squeezed his eyes shut to battle the flood of conflicting emotions that coursed through his entire being.

This moment was inevitable, it seemed. Foreordained by their bloody ancestors over the past two hundred years. He had tried—by God, he had tried so damned hard to avoid this very scenario, but here it was, at last. One couldn't avoid one's fate. At least it was on his own terms.

He couldn't bring himself to care enough about a title and bit of land to take his brother's life, and he would happily run away to save his own. But Alice? Yes, she was worth fighting for. Even if the fight was with his own twin.

How would it end? Gun shot? Rapier wound? He would rather not know, quite frankly, but ignorance wasn't an option.

He opened his eyes, took a steadying breath, and picked up the card. He turned it over and scanned the contents. He stared for a moment in shock, rubbed his eyes, and stared again.

And then, very slowly, he smiled.

Chapter Fifty-Four

Alice paced in front of the fire. The storm had not abated, and every fireplace in the house was roaring with flames. It was the perfect evening to curl up with a book and a cup of tea. Instead, she was practicing a speech in her head.

Nicholas has agreed to leave for India. I have every hope that he will drown en route.

No. That wouldn't do. Better to leave the suggestion of death out of it.

I followed you before dawn, found where Nicholas was staying, and arranged a secret meeting.

No, no, no. That made everything sound so...deceptive. She had only wanted to keep Nathaniel safe! That was where the focus should be.

I love you. Please forgive me.

Better.

"Alice, you will wear a hole in the carpet with your pacing," Eliza said from her cozy wingback chair. "What has you so worried?"

Alice threw herself on the purple settee with a groan.

"Do you remember the letter I left for Mr. Manning?"

"Of course." Eliza arched an eyebrow. "That is not the sort of escapade one easily forgets."

"There's a problem. A rather recent development, actually."

"With the letter?"

"Yes."

"Oh."

Eliza studied her nails, almost as if she was hiding something.

Alice stared at her friend. Eliza obstinately pushed back a cuticle.

Alice narrowed her eyes. "Eliza."

Eliza sighed. "I suppose it was too much to hope it would go undiscovered. I knew you would find out, eventually. You're so clever, and it would be obvious soon enough what had happened—or not happened, as the case may be."

In her mind's eye, Alice saw the white corner of paper between Eliza's fingers. She gasped. "You took the letter."

"Yes," Eliza whispered. "I took the letter."

Alice gazed at her friend in bewilderment. "But...why?"

"Because I love you." Eliza stood up and faced the fire. "My parents are dead. My brother is a good man in that he leaves me alone. We are not close. I have found myself quite lonely these past two years, with neither family nor close friends. Other young ladies don't seem to favor my company, with the exception of Lady Claire." Eliza smiled wryly. "They warm up a bit after they marry, and I'm no longer a threat."

"But I *am* your friend, Eliza."

"And I am yours. That's why I couldn't let you hand Nicholas over to that horrid Mr. Manning. If you had allowed Nicholas to be captured, Lord Abingdon would have been lost to you forever. He would never have forgiven you, Alice. You must know that."

She did know that. Alice hadn't intended Mr. Manning to capture Nicholas, but *Eliza didn't know that.*

Which meant…

Oh, heavens.

She sucked in a sharp breath of air.

"If you are going to protest, I must stop you right there." Eliza held up both hands. "You love him, Alice. I know you do. You can deny it all you wish, but it won't change the truth of the matter. Grief has addled your brain somewhat, and perhaps you are scared to love again, and you think it can only end in pain. But you *do* love him, and you cannot have his brother murdered."

"But, Eliza—"

"I betrayed you. You are not the kind to easily forgive such a thing. I knew when I replaced your card with a blank one that it must be this way. I shall be lonely without your friendship, but I hope that one day you will forgive me." She caught a tear with one gloved finger and wiped it away.

"For God's sake, Eliza!" Alice shouted. She jumped to her feet and gave her friend a rough shake of the shoulders. "The card was a trap for *Mr. Manning*, not Nicholas!"

Eliza's mouth fell open in a perfectly round circle. "Oh. Oh, dear."

"Oh, dear, indeed." *This was a disaster.* "I found out where Nicholas was hiding and arranged to meet with him. We struck a deal. I would write whatever he wished on the card to Mr. Manning, and after the matter was taken care of, Nicholas would be on the next ship to India."

She bit her lip wistfully. It had been such a marvelous plan. So neat and tidy, with no loose ends to tie up… If only she hadn't fallen in love with Nathaniel and Eliza hadn't stolen the letter.

As if reading her thoughts, Eliza asked shrewdly, "What did Lord Abingdon think of this plan?"

"He doesn't know." Alice buried her face in her hands and groaned. "I haven't told him."

"Ah." Eliza frowned.

"Oh, hush. I intended to tell him this very evening. Only, now…" Alice sank helplessly on the settee. Words failed her.

"Only, now I've botched everything," Eliza said almost cheerfully. "So, there is nothing you have to tell him, after all."

That didn't seem quite right. Nathaniel deserved the full measure of truth from her. But perhaps it mattered less now? Surely, her transgression was forgivable, now that it didn't end with Nicholas in India…

Nicholas, however, would not be pleased.

She raised her eyes to Eliza and saw her own sudden horror staring back at her. The same thought had occurred to them both.

"What about Nicholas?" Eliza asked. "Will he…?"

"Kill Nathaniel? I don't know. I don't know!" Alice wailed. She clenched her hands into fists, her nails digging her palms. "Mr. Manning must already have seen the card and likely thinks I'm playing him a trick. Or that I'm abominably stupid. Let's hope it's the latter. I must find him. I will tell him it was an error and give him the real letter."

"Alice, you can't!" Eliza protested. "It was dangerous the first time, and it will be doubly so now."

"But I must." A gnawing dread took up residence in the pit of Alice's belly. "I cannot let Nathaniel be harmed."

Eliza bit her lip. She crossed the room and sat next to Alice on the settee, taking her hand. "Tell him everything. Give Lord Abingdon the information he needs to protect himself."

If Alice told him the truth, then what? Nathaniel would seek out Mr. Manning, himself, to protect her, and Nicholas, too. What if Mr. Manning mistook Nathaniel for Nicholas?

He would be captured and perhaps killed.

She pressed a fist to her mouth and shook her head. No, she couldn't.

Eliza regarded her somberly. "Why do you have so little confidence in Lord Abingdon? He strikes me as a strong, capable man. Certainly, he's one of the more intelligent men of our acquaintance." She paused, considering. "Granted, he does not have much competition there."

Alice laughed through a sob. "It's not that I think him a dunce. It's that people in my life have such a terrible habit of dying. First my fiancé, and then my sister. I can't bear to lose Nathaniel, too."

"Oh, Alice." Eliza put her arm around her soothingly. "It will be all right."

But she didn't say how.

And Alice didn't see how it possibly could be.

Why, oh, why had she been so bent on revenge?

Chapter Fifty-Five

Alice dressed for dinner that evening with trepidation. She had not seen Nathaniel since he had left her room earlier—when he had most decidedly *not* offered marriage...which was worrying, but could wait to be dealt with until she was sure he would be alive to follow through. She rushed Mary through her toilet and hair, anxious to find him downstairs before the other guests made their appearance.

Mary was unhappy with the final result, but Alice waved her away. She treaded lightly down the stairs and into the library. To her great disappointment, the room was empty save for Colonel Kent, who was nursing a brandy and frowning at the window.

Well. This was awkward.

And why was he imbibing such strong liquor right before dinner?

He turned as she entered. "Ah, Miss Bursnell."

She was sore between her legs where Nathaniel had filled her only hours before. She felt it keenly as she stepped forward, and wondered if Colonel Kent could tell. He had asked her to consider him as a suitor, and now, not two days later, she had already fully given herself to another man.

Awkward, indeed.

"Miss Bursnell, I find myself in an unusually complicated and mystifying circumstance. Perhaps you can shed some light on the matter." He placed his glass on a table and stood, hands clasped behind his back.

"I shall do my best, Colonel," Alice said, feeling somewhat mystified herself.

"Lord Abingdon sought me out an hour ago. He requested my presence at a duel tomorrow morning. It seems I am to stand as a second." He gave her a perplexed look. "Not as Lord Abingdon's second, mind you, but as his brother's. It is odd, yes? I do not even know the man! Were you aware that Lord Abingdon has a brother, Miss Bursnell?"

The room bucked and rolled as if caught by a stormy sea.

"Miss Bursnell!"

She pitched forward and found herself supported by Colonel Kent. She clung to his forearms for balance. "There is to be a *duel*? Between Lord Abingdon and his brother?"

"Please sit down. You are not well." He tried to guide her to the sofa, but she gripped him tighter, holding him still. "Please, Miss Bursnell. You are so pale."

"You must tell me! Mr. Eastwood challenged Lord Abingdon to a duel?" She forced the words through frozen lips. *Oh, this was all her fault.* Nicholas had found out about the letter, and he was furious.

"As preposterous as it sounds, I believe—" The colonel straightened, his eyes flicking over her shoulder. "Ah. Here is Lord Abingdon now. He can explain."

She turned, startled. Were her eyes playing tricks on her? Surely, the man prowling toward her was Nicholas. This could not be Nathaniel. He looked…dangerous. Lethal, even. His eyes narrowed on Colonel Kent, and he moved like a lion stalking his prey. But the hand that grasped her around the waist was gentle.

"I have her," he said.

Colonel Kent did not miss his meaning. "Of course you do." He bowed. "Please excuse me, Miss Bursnell. Lord Abingdon, we shall discuss arrangements later."

"We shall."

He waited until Colonel Kent had left the room before he turned her to face him. "Alice."

He was furious, she realized.

Well, he had every right to be.

"There's been a terrible misunderstanding," she rushed to say. His eyebrow quirked but she hurried on. "A week ago, I met a man in town." She told him how she had discovered where Nicholas was hiding and met with him secretly. Without giving him a chance to interrupt, she explained about the note and the trap for Mr. Manning, and Eliza's well-meaning interference. "So, Mr. Manning never saw the note, which means that Nicholas failed. He thinks I tricked him, and that's why he challenged you to a duel!" she concluded breathlessly.

Nathaniel tilted her chin up with his finger. His expression hadn't changed an iota. "None of that explains why you were in Colonel Kent's arms just now."

She huffed. Frustrating man!

"Did you hear what I *said*?" She grabbed fistfuls of his waist coat. "Nicholas is going to *kill* you!"

"What I heard you say was that you have been keeping dangerous secrets with dangerous men. What were you thinking, Alice? Whoever this Mr. Manning is, he obviously cannot be trusted. And my brother? I should have thought you, of all people, would know better than to meet Nick without a chaperone. But apparently not. And then I enter my own library only to find you embracing Colonel Kent!"

She pulled back and peered up at him. He looked like

a sulky thundercloud. She would have laughed if the matter weren't so very serious. "Please, Nathaniel. Don't go through with the duel."

"But I must. The challenge has been given and accepted. It's a matter of honor."

"Honor?" she repeated. "Piffle. That's nothing but a silly concept invented by men to feel better about doing stupid things."

"Alice," he murmured, but he no longer looked like a thundercloud. Rather, he looked amused.

She gazed at him helplessly. Why, why, *why* wouldn't he listen? Didn't he understand that death was a permanent condition? She stretched up on her tiptoes and wound her arms around his neck. "Please," she said, putting all her feelings of anguish into the word.

Before he could respond, she pressed her lips to his. It was a desperate ploy, and she poured everything she had into it. She couldn't bear to lose him. *She couldn't.*

Her tongue slipped past his lips, hungry and needy, begging him to understand. When he groaned, she clung more tightly and intensified the kiss.

Don't leave me. Don't trade your life for nothing.

His arms wrapped around her waist, at last, and he hauled her up against the hard ridge emanating below his belly. He tore his mouth from hers with a low rumble and buried his face against her neck.

"Alice." His voice was raw and gravelly.

"Don't go to the duel tomorrow," she begged. "Go to Scotland instead," she suggested hopefully. "Or Italy. I hear it's lovely in the spring."

He laughed. Actually laughed! As if life and death and duels and fratricide were mere children's games.

Why were men such bloody *fools*?

Chapter Fifty-Six

That night in the wee hours, the mattress dipped and Alice rolled sleepily down the slope, startling awake when she landed against something solid and warm. She opened her mouth and found it quickly silenced by a large hand.

"Hush," he whispered. "It's me."

She lightly nipped the pad of his finger, and the hand retreated. "I wasn't going to scream. I knew it was you by your smell."

"Is it terrible?" He nuzzled her neck. "You smell much better."

"You smell delicious." Edible. Not like a dessert, sweet and vanilla. No, Nathaniel was the main course. Savory, warm, and satisfying.

He lifted the covers and slid in beside her. He was in a wonderful state of undress—a shirt unbuttoned at the collar, trousers, and bare feet.

Within her heart, joy battled with despair. She knew why he'd come. He was here tonight because he might not be here tomorrow. Seconds after her desperate kiss in the library before dinner, the others had arrived and ended their conversation. She had been unable to get him alone after that to continue pleading her case.

She shivered and snuggled closer, her heart aching. She skimmed her hands over his shoulders to the muscled contours of his chest.

"I didn't come here for lovemaking." His eyes searched her face. "You must still be tender. I only want to hold you."

"I want more than that." She traced his jaw with the backs of her fingers. It was smooth from when he had shaved for dinner. "You wouldn't let me touch you last time. Let me touch you now."

For a moment, there was nothing but the sound of heartbeats.

"Nathaniel?" she whispered.

"I—" He cleared his throat. "Yes, please."

Warmth spread through her. *Yes, please.* Oh, this man! Every moment spent with him, another fissure appeared in the wall around her heart. The pressure in her chest was almost unbearable, like a dam about to break through.

She nuzzled his throat, kissing the tendons and muscles usually concealed by a cravat. She flicked open the top button of his shirt, and then the next, following her fingers with her mouth. As the third button slipped from its anchor, she pressed a kiss to his chest.

"Alice," he murmured. "Where are you going?"

She paused to rub her cheek on the short copper hair that teased her lips. "Everywhere."

His heart was beating so hard she could feel it against her jawbone. *She* did that to him.

Just to test her power, she swirled her tongue over his nipple while keeping one hand pressed gently on his chest. She smiled when the heartbeats moved quicker. Her own nipples, hidden behind the thin cotton night rail, hardened into peaks.

The hair on his chest disappeared at the fourth button as she kissed down the ridged boxes of his abdomen. He quivered at her touch, the muscles tensing and releasing. The hair reappeared below his navel, albeit darker, in an unwavering line that disappeared into his trousers.

She followed it.

It was so much easier to remove a man's clothing than a woman's. It was almost as though his clothing had been created with anticipation of freedom, while hers had only considered containment.

He groaned as he lifted his hips, helping her to ease his trousers off. "Alice, I have to tell you. Tomorrow—"

No. She didn't want to hear it. She *couldn't* hear it without howling and sobbing. In desperation, she pressed kisses everywhere her lips could reach. His belly, his hip, his thigh…his staff.

He stopped talking.

She looked up at him. His eyes were closed, his hands fisted in the bedsheets. Encouraged, she kissed him again, her mouth open this time. His manhood jerked, and she started in surprise. Did that mean he liked it? Or was he… ticklish? *Could* a man be ticklish there?

"What shall I do?" she asked.

"Anything you want," he said between clenched teeth.

Well. That wasn't very enlightening.

"I've never—" he choked out. "That is, no one's ever…" He reached for her, stabbing his fingers through her hair. "There's only ever been you."

Her eyes widened at the words. "Only me?"

He jerked a nod.

A wave of possessiveness swept over her, so sweet it rocked her to her core. "For…everything?"

"Everything." He groaned. "Your mouth feels so good, Alice. Please touch me again, however you like."

Why, yes. She would like that.

She lowered her head and licked him from root to crown with one firm stroke of her tongue.

He arched off the bed. *"Holy mother of God."*

The tip was velvety soft. It reminded her of sponge cake. She kissed him there, darting her tongue out to taste.

He muttered a string of incoherent nonsense. That made her smile.

She parted her lips slightly, allowing more of him to slip into her mouth. But what now?

She thought of the way he had taught her to touch him with her hand. She thought of the way he had moved when inside her. Stroking, it seemed, was key. So, she stroked him with her mouth, gliding up and down, slowly at first, then a little faster.

He moaned, and his hands plunged deeper into her hair. They showed her a new rhythm.

Then, suddenly, she found herself gripped under her arms and pulled up his body. He rolled, pinning her to the bed. She felt a sharp tug of fabric followed by a ripping sound and a rush of cool air.

She felt his mouth against her breast and then her belly. Before she could get her bearings, he had settled between her legs, holding her thighs wide open with his shoulders.

"Oh!" She struggled to sit up, but he pushed her gently down. "Wait."

"I'm going to kiss you," he said, and she heard the wonder of it in his voice.

"I don't think—"

"Then don't think." His breath stirred her intimate curls. "Just let me kiss you the way you kissed me. Please."

She squirmed beneath him, somewhat scandalized.

But more excited.

"I have a duel tomorrow," he reminded her, his eyes

glinting up at her from between her thighs.

Unfair!

She could deny him nothing.

She had kissed him, yes, but it wasn't the same thing. This was altogether more embarrassing. Only, he didn't seem to think it was embarrassing. He seemed to think it was delicious. That *she* was delicious.

He kissed the core of her the way he kissed her mouth, open and with languid strokes of his tongue. He explored every part of her slick folds, and the aching pleasure point they had discovered together that first time. When his tongue glided inside her, she gasped.

Surely, this was indecent!

But she was beyond caring. She arched up, spinning higher and higher toward that blissful precipice. This time, she knew what was on the other side. She raced to claim it, but then paused, helpless, teetering on the edge. Just when she thought the throbbing torture would snap her in twain, his lips covered her need and he sucked it hard.

She cried out, her hips lifting shamelessly toward his mouth, as wave after wave of pleasure wracked her whole body.

When she came back to herself, she was tucked in his arms, his lips curved against her temple.

"Thank you," he said. "That was marvelous."

She laughed and felt his hardness stir eagerly against her belly. He was not yet sated, she realized. But neither was she. It felt greedy—needing more of him after he had already given her so much. So be it.

She hitched a leg over his hip so his staff nestled against her wet heat and rubbed herself against him, seeking.

"No, darling." His fingers dug into the flesh of her hip. "I'll hurt you. You're sore, and I can't be gentle. Not now."

"I don't care," she whispered. *She needed to be filled by*

him.

His eyes were wild with desire. "Are you sure?"

"God, yes," she said.

His arm wrapped around her waist, holding her steady, and he thrust inside her, hard enough that the bed moved. She gasped and clung to his shoulders. His powerful hips rocked against hers, joining them together. Her sore innermost muscles ached, but she ignored it. She wanted the pain, wanted the proof that he had been there inside her, long after he had gone.

He groaned. "I can't—"

And he didn't. Or rather, he did, thrusting deep into her and shouting his release into the pillow to muffle the sound. Then he collapsed against her, his hand tangled in her hair.

Oh, yes.

This was truly marvelous.

Chapter Fifty-Seven

The midmorning sunlight streamed through the window. Alice smiled dreamily and stretched out an arm but found only empty sheets next to her.

She bolted upright. Good God! What time was it? Had Nathaniel already left to meet Nicholas?

She swung her legs off the bed and rang for Mary. A moment later, her door opened. Mary bustled through, and with her came the sounds of distant shouting.

"What is happening, Mary?" Alice stood, wincing at the soreness between her legs.

Mary eyed her sharply. "Oh, the house is in uproar, miss. It's complete chaos. Would you like your green muslin?"

Alice shook her head. "The white."

"But you never wear white." Her hands faltered. "The fields will make you dirty."

"Today I will wear white," Alice said firmly. She had met Nicholas before as an avenging queen. Today she would be humble, virginal.

Well—Mary's gaze slid sideways to the rumpled, torn

night rail on the floor—she would be humble, at any rate.

"What is the uproar about?" she asked as her maid slid the dress over her head.

"Why, the duel, of course." Mary tsked. "Apparently Mr. Eastwood sent word to his sister. Lady Freesia arrived before dawn this morning, bringing their aunt, the Dowager Marchioness Breesfield, with her. Lady Freesia seems an all right sort, but the marchioness is none too happy about traveling all night, I can assure you. She has all the maids coming and going and crying and fussing."

By the time Mary finished relaying the gossip, Alice was dressed. She rushed down the stairs and into the breakfast room, where she nearly collided with Lady Freesia.

"Oh, Miss Bursnell!" Lady Freesia beamed. "How lovely to see you again, even under these rather inauspicious circumstances."

"Lady Freesia, I hope you are well."

"Quite." Lady Freesia cocked her head to the side, listening, as the dowager marchioness shouted something about the temperature of her tea. "Would you care for some eggs? Or perhaps some toast? The bacon—"

"I am not hungry, thank you," Alice interrupted rather desperately. "Did you speak to your brother this morning?"

Lady Freesia heaped scrambled eggs on her plate. "Which one?"

"Either." It didn't matter which brother came to his senses, so long as one of them did.

"As it happens, I spoke to both."

When she didn't continue, Alice tamped back her frustration. "And?" she prodded.

"They will meet at the oak tree in…" She glanced at the clock. "One hour. Goodness, we should hurry." She sat down without seeming the least bit in a rush.

Alice was at a loss. Lady Freesia was a beautiful girl,

dressed in a deep blue frock that exactly matched her eyes. She certainly didn't *look* heartless. Perhaps she was in shock.

"They have not called it off, then?" Alice asked. She clasped her hands in silent prayer. *Please, please let this be a mistake.*

Lady Freesia wrinkled her brow. "Of course not."

A small, desperate sob escaped Alice.

Instantly, Lady Freesia was on her feet. "Oh, you poor thing. This must be terrible for you, but it must be done. Surely, you understand that."

No, Alice did not understand any such thing.

"But *why*? Why must they do this?" she asked.

For a moment Lady Freesia looked mystified, but then her expression brightened. She had the answer. "Because they are boys."

Lady Freesia sat back down, spread a bit of honey on a slice of toast, and handed it to Alice. "Do try to eat something, Miss Bursnell. You'll need your strength." She eyed Alice with sudden wariness. "You don't swoon at the sight of blood, do you?"

Oh, heavens!

Alice looked at the toast in her hand. There was nothing to do but eat it. Clearly, Lady Freesia would not let them leave until both their stomachs were full. She took a bite and chewed. It was rather like chewing sawdust.

When she swallowed the last bite, she looked expectantly at Lady Freesia.

The girl glanced longingly at her teacup, but stood again with a sigh. "Very well. We'll be off. Nimbly will have the carriage pulled round."

"The carriage?" Alice asked, baffled. "It's a short walk."

"Well, yes. But I told the surgeon we would fetch him. He is in town."

Alice thought she might be sick.

Surgeons always attended duels, at the request of the participants. He would do his best to keep a wound from being fatal, but even if death wasn't instant, a gunshot or sword wound could fester. The only time a duel ended well was when the opponents shot into the air instead of aiming for each other.

Somehow, she doubted that was what Nicholas had in mind.

He had been waiting too long for this moment.

When they arrived at the appointed place, surgeon in tow, Alice looked about for Nathaniel. He was nowhere to be seen. Her heart gave a joyful leap of hope. Perhaps he had decided to flee to Scotland, after all.

Her hope faded as she caught sight of Colonel Kent and Duke Wessex. No, Nathaniel had not fled. He would never leave Wessex to face Nicholas alone.

She watched Colonel Kent approach the duke and bow. Together, they moved away from the oak tree to a flat, open area. They scuffed their feet in the grass.

"Ah, they're checking for dew," Lady Freesia explained. "Slippery grass would make everything more difficult."

That must mean the duel would be fought with swords rather than pistols. Alice wasn't sure if that was better or worse, but she thought it might be the latter. Gentlemen often shot into the air rather than at their opponents. How would one do that with a sword?

It was an intimate affair, if you could call it that. The only witnesses were Lady Freesia and herself, the surgeon, and Duke Wessex and Colonel Kent as the seconds. Lady Breesfield and Lord and Lady Wintham were not present, thank goodness. No parent would want to see the bloodshed of either son. Plus, a large crowd would mean Nicholas would be hanged for murder—unless he fled to the Continent.

Alice rather wondered at Lady Freesia being here, when

it came to that.

"I must stop this madness," Alice said through frozen lips. *It could not be allowed to happen.*

Lady Freesia turned to her with blazing eyes and red cheeks. "Don't you dare! Nick was banished from our home when he was ten. Ten! Can you imagine how terrifying that was for a little boy? Since then, I have waited nearly two decades for his return. This moment will finally heal everything. They should have done this years ago. Now, sit down and let them do what they must."

This moment would heal everything?

Was the lady *insane*?

"You are a horrid girl, and I hope your hair falls out," Alice cried.

Lady Freesia gaped, but Alice did not wait. She lifted her skirts and marched across the field. If Nathaniel refused to be reasonable and Lady Freesia refused to be sane, then she would deal directly with Nicholas.

"Colonel Kent, take me to Mr. Eastwood," she snapped.

He turned, startled. "Miss Bursnell—"

"*Now.*"

He nodded and took her arm, leading her behind the oak tree.

And there was Nicholas, leaning against the trunk, looking bored as sin and lethal as a snake.

He lifted his chin in acknowledgment. "Ah, Miss Bursnell. So good of you to join us this morning."

"I have come to apologize, sir," Alice said.

His eyes widened expressively. "Indeed?"

"Yes, sir." She twisted her hands together to steady them. "There seems to have been a…misadventure with the letter. I wrote the note per your instructions, but it never reached its intended audience. A good friend, thinking to save me from myself, replaced it with a blank card instead. Your message was never received."

Nicholas's face was scrupulously blank. "I did wonder. And you say a friend did this?"

She nodded.

"Heaven preserve me from such friendships."

She narrowed her eyes at him. Perhaps Eliza had made a mistake, but she had done so with the purest intent, sacrificing even her own interests to protect Alice.

She glanced over at Kent and at Wessex, both here at Nathaniel's request. Nicholas had no one but Lady Freesia, and she was clearly insane. He was all alone.

"You needn't call upon heaven," Alice said quietly. "You have preserved yourself, sir."

Something flickered in those icy eyes before it was extinguished. "Quite."

Enough of this. She gathered herself. "There is no need for a duel. I can fix this. I can still deliver Manning to you. I won't even request you depart for India. All I ask is that you leave Nathaniel alone."

He nodded slowly. "If I wanted my brother dead, that would make sense. I had my own need for Mr. Manning, and I was willing to agree to your scheme to further my personal goal. But now the plot is foiled, you believe I would immediately set my sights on the earldom. But you are mistaken on three counts, Miss Bursnell. The first being, I had no intention of going to India."

She straightened her spine. "But you said—"

"I lied," he said evenly.

Of course he had. Why had that not occurred to her? The blackguard was no gentleman.

"The second is that *I* did not challenge Nate to this duel. He challenged *me*."

"No," she said with a firm shake of her head. "That cannot be true. Nathaniel loves you, for all you don't deserve it. He has spent years running away to avoid this very situation. I don't believe it. And why should I? You just proclaimed yourself a liar."

"I assure you, I am speaking the truth about this. Nate challenged me to a duel." Nicholas seemed to find the matter almost as surprising as she did.

"On what grounds?" she demanded. "The earldom isn't enough reason. Not for Nathaniel."

"No, it isn't," Nicholas said thoughtfully. "Why does anyone fight a duel? In this case, because I caused the worst kind of grief to someone he cares deeply about."

A breeze blew, rustling the leaves of the oak tree and loosening her tight braids. Her lips parted. Twenty yards away, Nathaniel was in conversation with Lady Freesia. His back was to Alice, but it seemed as if he was comforting his sister.

He had done this.

Nathaniel had challenged Nicholas to a duel.

For years, he had run from their conflict, not for his own sake, but for Nicholas. He felt guilt over how Nicholas was treated.

He was banished for me, and I did nothing to save him.

Nathaniel's greatest desire was to mend the gaping wound in his family.

And yet, he had still done this.

For her.

To avenge Adelaide's honor and heal Alice's grief. Apparently, he thought those things worth fighting for.

Once upon a time, she would have agreed.

But now?

Something shifted inside her, and the pressure in her chest increased to the breaking point. The dam burst, and love came flooding through. And, oh, heavens, there was so much of it! It was like a tidal storm, sweeping aside everything in its wake.

She turned back to Nicholas.

A year ago, she had sworn revenge. Her hatred for this man had consumed her, eating away at her soul until there was nearly nothing left. She had devoted her life to destroying his.

She still missed Adelaide with an ache that would never fully dissipate. He had ruined her and indirectly caused her untimely death, and for that, Alice hated him still.

But it was such a small thing now, that hatred. It did not consume her. How could it, when her heart was so full of Nathaniel? There simply wasn't room for hatred and revenge.

Revenge wouldn't help Adelaide. It wasn't worth wasting Alice's life, and it certainly wasn't worth ending Nathaniel's.

Revenge was nothing.

Nicholas was nothing.

But Nathaniel…Nathaniel was *everything*.

She went to her knees.

Colonel Kent stepped forward. "Miss Bursnell, I say!"

But she kept her eyes trained on Nicholas. "Please, don't kill him. I couldn't bear it."

"Get up, Miss Bursnell," he said harshly. "This is beneath you."

No. Nothing was beneath her. Not when it came to those she loved.

She remembered saying those very words to Nathaniel, back when he'd accused her of blackmail, but she hadn't meant them then.

She meant them now.

She would do anything, *anything*, to keep Nathaniel alive.

"Please," she said again.

For a moment, the mask slipped, and Nicholas looked well and truly baffled. "You blame me for Adelaide's death, and yet you kneel before me?"

"I love him." It was the simple truth.

"Get up, Miss Bursnell. For the love of God. This is embarrassing."

"No." The damp earth sank through her skirt. "Not until you promise me you won't kill him."

Nicholas looked at her with an unreadable emotion tucked into the corners of his mouth. She might have called it compassion if she thought him capable of it. But his next words proved he was not.

"Adelaide's locket. Give it to me."

The locket was all she had left of Adelaide. Could she really give it to this odious man?

Yes, she could.

She unclasped it from around her neck with trembling fingers, kissed it once, and dropped it into his waiting palm. His hand closed into a fist around it.

"Nate is safe. You have my word."

Was that enough assurance?

It had to be.

Chapter Fifty-Eight

Nathaniel watched his brother approach him with a strange feeling of calm. Nathaniel was not a prideful man, by any means, but he knew his own strengths. He had trained in self-protection nearly his whole life with the intensity of a man who knew death was coming for him. He had boxed and fenced and run until his muscles screamed and grew stronger. In nearly any match, he was assured of holding his own.

Except now.

He knew, beyond any shadow of a doubt, that he was outrivaled. The man walking toward him was lethal, and Nathaniel understood that down to the very marrow of his bones.

But Nick would not win. He could not. A man could not destroy a woman's life without consequences. Nathaniel had right on his side, and right always triumphed.

He could not fail Alice.

He should have done this a week ago, when she had first told him of Nick's connection to Adelaide. Would she have clung to her revenge so desperately if he had called out Nick immediately? He hoped not.

No, he should have confronted his brother even before then, when the accidents had first begun. All this might have been avoided had Nathaniel taken control of his own life rather than being helplessly tossed about by fate. He had let his fear unman him.

Fate did not exist. All that existed were choice and consequence.

And love.

"You did not tell Miss Bursnell," Wessex said next to him.

Nathaniel felt a sliver of guilt, but it was a very tiny sliver. "I was distracted."

"You will be fortunate if she does not strangle you."

Nathaniel waved that off. "I will make it right."

They walked ten paces to a flat, open area. It was just outside the shade of the oak tree. There was something fitting about that, he reckoned. He removed his jacket and handed it to Wessex. He followed that with his shirt and cravat. He didn't want to muss the white linen with blood.

Nearby, Nick was doing the same thing, handing his garments to Kent.

Finally, the moment had come.

Nathaniel faced Nick, and Nick faced him, square on, for the first time in years. Nathaniel looked at his mirror image, and something twisted in his gut.

"Nick." Nathaniel stretched his hand to his brother. "It is good to see you again."

"Is it? I've heard otherwise."

Again, the knife twist in the belly. "You should have heard it from me, long ago. I should not have doubted you, but if I could not help being irrational, then I should have at least confronted you."

"What would you have said?" Nick asked curiously.

"I would have asked whether you wanted the earldom

more than you wanted a brother." A leaf blew onto his arm, and he brushed it off. "What would you have said in return?"

"Words would have failed me. I would have knocked you in the nose." Nick spread his hands expansively. "Thus, here we are."

"No, we are here for Adelaide," Nathaniel said sharply. "Or have you forgotten?"

The briefest glimpse of unease touched Nick's eyes. His hand went to the locket at his throat before dropping again. "I have not forgotten."

"Well? What have you to say about it?" *Say you were almost mortally wounded. Say she left first and you didn't know how to reach her.*

"I did not know she was with child. If she wrote to me, the letter was lost." He paused. When he spoke again, it was as though each word was forced from his lips. "But I caused Alice a great deal of grief, and for that please accept my sincere apologies."

It was something, but not enough. Adelaide should never have had to write that letter, except as a wife writes to a husband.

"Had it not occurred to you that would be the case? You were a soldier, Nick. Your *life* was not guaranteed, much less the mail."

Again, Nick touched the locket, his face blank. "Shall we begin?" he asked, and Nathaniel wondered if he only imagined the slight tremor in his voice.

"We shall."

They circled each other.

"Do you know, I have been quite looking forward to this," Nick said. He threw the first punch, more as a question than to cause injury. Nathaniel easily evaded and Nick grinned. "Perhaps this will even be fun."

"I believe that," Nathaniel said. "I can't say I blame you,

after the shabby way I treated you."

Annoyance flickered across his brother's face. "You are my *brother*. How could you let them send me away?"

Nathaniel flinched and then immediately flinched again when he felt a blow land solidly on his cheekbone. He stumbled back, but didn't fall.

He glared at Nick. "How could you seduce a lady and refuse to marry her?"

"I would have married her! I didn't get the damned letter!" Nick roared.

Oh, for God's sake. Did he truly not understand?

"Fuck the letter, Nick!" Nathaniel exploded. "You should never have left her to begin with! The stakes were too high, the risks too great. A man does *not*—"

He didn't finish. They clashed together, grappling like lions for territory, like warriors for Rome, or like two brothers who didn't know what else to do with each other. For a moment, Nathaniel's consciousness was consumed with pain, feeling it and causing it. And then, out of the corner of his eye, he saw Nick turn his head and startle as if he had seen a ghost.

It was Nathaniel's chance, and he took it.

He pulled back and delivered a blow so hard that his own teeth rattled in his skull. Nick's eyelids fluttered just before his body went slack, crumbling to the ground in a heap.

There. It was done.

Chapter Fifty-Nine

What Nathaniel wanted more than anything was to find Alice and collapse into her arms. He was exhausted. He also suspected he was hurt, but luckily, he didn't feel a thing. *Yet.* Later, after the exhilaration wore off, he would feel plenty.

But he couldn't go to Alice just yet because his brother was unconscious. Nathaniel nudged him with his boot, turning him onto his back. He squatted down and examined his brother's face. Thankfully, Nick had insisted a surgeon be present. His cuts would have to be stitched up with care to prevent scarring. Nathaniel got the impression that Nick wanted to blend in. Scars would make him stand out. It was something Nathaniel intended to give some thought to, once more important matters had been put to rest.

He finished his examination and stood, only to be bowled over again by a soft, warm cannonball that smelled deliciously of lemon verbena. He went back on one foot, steadying them both as his arms went around her.

"Vile, teasing man," Alice said her voice hitching. "Why didn't you tell me your life was not at stake?"

He turned his face in her neck and inhaled deeply. "Didn't I?"

She pulled back and gazed at him disapprovingly. "No."

"Hmm. It must have slipped my mind."

"I shall hate you tomorrow for frightening me so," she said. "But just now, all I feel is—"

Love. Please say love.

"Relief." She finally smiled at him, her eyes glowing.

He tried not to look disappointed.

Nick groaned at their feet, and they both glanced down.

Nathaniel mentally scratched two items off his list as complete. *Stay alive*, and *Bring Nick home*.

"Was it enough?" he asked. "Nick is not dead, as you can see. But thoroughly humiliated. Do you require further vengeance, or is it finished?"

"This was enough." She held his face in her hands and kissed him tenderly. "Thank you."

Thank God.

Enough to satisfy her sense of honor.

But was it enough to win her heart?

Chapter Sixty

Alice was utterly finished with the man.

It had been three days since the duel, and four days since Nathaniel had made love to her—for the *second* time. But had he offered marriage even once during those four days?

No, he had not.

He had scarcely even been in the same room with her, and never when she was alone. Sometimes she caught him watching her, his expression inscrutable. But the moment she moved toward him, he bowed and retreated.

Well, not always.

Sometimes he didn't bother to bow.

Now it was Sunday, and Alice had reached the limit of her patience. She did not care if it was the Lord's day. Surely, the Lord understood that she might be with child, and that trumped all else.

Then again, perhaps she was not. She had heard that children rarely resulted from the first encounter. However, she had seen many bouncing babes make their appearances a scant seven or eight months after the wedding, so she had her doubts.

Regardless of whether or not there was a child, he *had* ruined her. She could not marry another man, even if she wanted to.

Not when she knew what it was like to love Nathaniel. It would be preposterous. He knew that. He had told her as much. *Mine*, he had said, and she had agreed...even if the words were left unspoken. She was his, body and heart.

But...perhaps now that he had claimed her body, he no longer wanted her heart?

He had never said he loved her. It had been implied in every look, every kiss, every word between them. Or so she had thought. He had fought a *duel* for her, for God's sake.

Filled with irritation precariously close to hurt, she marched into the library. Because she wanted a book, but also because she wanted to see a certain person who could often be found in the library.

She was not disappointed. The library was full of books, and Nathaniel and Duke Wessex were seated in the comfortable leather chairs.

"Your Grace." She curtsied. "Lord Abingdon."

They stood and bowed.

"Excuse me," Nathaniel said, and promptly left the room.

She stared helplessly after him, her mouth hanging open in a quite stupid fashion. He had left her alone with Duke Wessex. Unchaperoned! Did the man truly care so little for her that he would risk her marriage to his closest friend?

"I— I—" She did not know how to begin or end, so she left those stuttered words hanging in the air.

"Sit down, Miss Bursnell," the duke said.

"I would rather not," she said, and edged toward the door.

His eyes twinkled. "I assume you mean you would rather not be forced to marry me. I ought to be quite insulted. But the door is open, and this is a house party, not Almack's. You are quite safe."

She hesitated.

"Sit down, Miss Bursnell," he repeated in the tone of a man used to getting his way.

She sat.

"I've always liked you, Miss Bursnell. Yes, from the very moment you pushed Abingdon out of the way of that falling chandelier and left me to save my own life, I've liked you. And he has also been rather fond of you."

She ignored the last part of his declaration. "I suppose I like you, as well, Your Grace, although I haven't truly given the matter much thought."

He laughed. "You are too kind."

What on earth did he mean by that?

"Do you know," the duke continued, "when Nate fell off his horse and you stood there laughing at him, I thought to myself, that lady will either be the death of him or the life of him."

She felt a queer burning in her chest.

"Everyone hoped it would be a love match. But what is love, really? I find myself asking that question repeatedly."

"Do you, Your Grace?" she asked in deep disbelief.

His lips tipped up in a wry smile. "One hears such conflicting reports. Is love desire, easily spent and replaced? Is love rage, something to kill and die for?" He paused and tapped his chin thoughtfully with his index finger. "I believe none of those things are love. I think, in the end, love is quite simple. It's holding someone else dearer than yourself."

He leaned forward suddenly, the smile vanishing from his face. For the first time in their acquaintance, the Duke of Wessex went completely serious. "Do you know how I came to this remarkable conclusion, Miss Bursnell?"

She shook her head warily.

"It was when I saw a lady sink to her knees before the one

man on earth who was most abhorrent to her, the man who had taken so much from her, and beg this man to spare the life of another. Only one thing under heaven can overcome such hatred. *That*, Miss Bursnell, is true love."

The silence ticked on for several moments.

Then she admitted quietly, "I would do anything for him."

"Yes, I believe you would." The duke sipped his tea. "Such a pity he does not know that."

She sat like a woman turned to stone.

He did not know?

How was it possible that he did not know? She had given him every indication...

She had given him *everything*.

"Another man, perhaps, would have understood your feelings," the duke said as though reading her mind, "without you putting them in words. In his defense, you did refuse his offer of marriage, and that mucked things up quite a bit. In his mind, at least."

She leapt to her feet, pinning Wessex with her gaze like a specimen on a board.

"Ah, enlightenment dawns," he murmured. He rose from his chair.

"I must—" She paused.

It was not enough to simply tell Nathaniel she loved him. He deserved so much more.

She took a cleansing breath. "Say nothing of this to him."

"I wouldn't dream of it."

She curtsied and moved swiftly to the door. There, she paused and looked back curiously. "Have you ever been in love, Your Grace?"

"Absolutely not! I have set the bar too high." He grinned. "You see, I hold myself very dear."

Chapter Sixty-One

Last Monday, Nathaniel believed there could be nothing more dismal than a marriage of unrequited love. How terrible it would be to see Alice at the breakfast table every morning calmly eating her eggs, while his soul died by inches.

On Thursday, he'd run five kilometers more than usual, but it had done nothing to quiet the hunger quivering in his every aching muscle.

On Sunday, he decided he was being a fool. So what if she did not love him? He would take her any way he could have her. Since she seemed not averse to him physically, he would simply keep her in his bed until her belly was swollen with his child. Unless she was already with child, in which case he would marry her tomorrow.

His hands clenched into fists. Surely, she would tell him if that were the case?

He felt a moment of anguish at the thought that she might *not* tell him.

Good God. He must speak to her. At once.

After searching the house and finding no sign of her, he

stepped outside. It was not yet midmorning, but the air was already warm, hinting at an unusually hot day. He started in the direction of the garden, but halted at the sound of low voices.

"I purchased the special license on behalf of Miss Bursnell just yesterday," Wessex was saying. "I expect the wedding will be immediate."

Colonel Kent spoke with his back to Nathaniel. "Thank you, Your Grace. This was...kind of you."

Nathaniel's stomach swallowed his heart. That was the only explanation for the gaping, wounded emptiness in his chest.

Chapter Sixty-Two

Alice was thinking.

About Nicholas Eastwood, of all things.

There was nothing more she wanted than to make Nathaniel hers, but perhaps he would be more willing if she first made peace with his brother. There was nothing else for it. She must see him before she spoke to Nathaniel. Since Nicholas was presently staying at the town inn rather than Haverly, thither she went. She did not mind the walk. Spring was about to turn to summer. Everything was lovely and just as it ought to be. The sun shining, the birds singing…the man with a pistol.

She halted.

"A moment of your time, please, Miss Bursnell," he said.

She did not think it boded well for her that he, at last, showed her his face. "Certainly, Mr. Manning."

He kept the pistol aimed squarely at her heart and stepped forward. "We had a bargain, Miss Bursnell, and you broke it."

"I did, indeed."

"You have made things very difficult for me. But no matter; I have a plan. Take me to Abingdon."

Fear rose in her throat like bile. "You mean Nicholas. Certainly. I will take you to him directly."

He laughed. "I would never survive such an encounter. Mr. Eastwood is a man of great physical prowess, and I, as you can see, am not. No, I prefer a game of the mind, for that is where I will have the upper hand."

She eyed the man speculatively. He was, as he had noted himself, slight of build, and only barely taller than herself. If he thought to win with his wits, he greatly underestimated Nicholas's mind. However, she would certainly not enlighten him.

"I will not take you to Abingdon," she said. "But I am on my way to visit Mr. Eastwood, and you are welcome to join me."

He stared at her. "You must do as I say. I will shoot you if you do not."

"You will shoot me if I do. You are an assassin, and I have seen your face," she said pragmatically. "I see no reason for Abingdon to die, as well."

He pushed his spectacles farther on his nose and glared. "You are trying my patience, Miss Bursnell."

"I do have that effect on people, yes," she said agreeably, despite the weakness in her knees.

"There are worse things than being killed, Miss Bursnell. Would you like to experience them?"

"No, I would not."

"How fortunate, then, that I happen to be here," said a voice she knew, and then he stepped out from the shadow of a tree. "I am Abingdon."

"Ah." Manning adjusted his spectacles again. "Quite fortunate, indeed."

"Nathaniel, no—" she protested, but he simply moved

her behind him.

There was a sudden flurry of movement. Arms reached around her, dragging her backward. She had one horrifying glimpse of Manning's arm twisted in a way an arm ought never to be twisted, and then she was turned into Nathaniel's broad chest. There was a scream, a thud, and then silence.

She clung to Nathaniel, trembling, breathing in his comforting scent.

"Shh," he said softly. "Everything is all right."

"Everything is *not* all right," Nicholas said from a few yards away. "I should have killed him. Now what am I to do with the man? He must be taken to London, but there are matters here I must—" He broke off abruptly. "Never mind that. It pains me to say this, but I owe you my thanks, Miss Bursnell."

She raised her head and looked first at Nathaniel, who frowned down at her with frightening ferocity. She swallowed hard and tried to free herself from his arms, but they might as well have been made of iron. She settled for craning her neck to look over at Nicholas.

"How did you know I was here?" she asked, flummoxed by the presence of both brothers.

"I knew Manning would come for you," said Nicholas. "I couldn't follow him, since I had no idea what he looked like, so I followed you instead. I've been following you for days."

Oh, heavens. She'd never noticed. Her mind had been too cluttered with frustration and hurt over Nathaniel ignoring her.

"When Nate discovered you had ventured out on your own without telling anyone," Nicholas continued, "he understandably had a bad feeling about it and came to find you. Fortunately, I managed to stop him from walking straight into Manning, and we had time to strategize whilst you were goading him into killing you."

Nathaniel's arms vibrated and tightened around her.

Out of the corner of her eye, she could see Manning's broken—but still breathing—body. Really, he had been right not to seek out Nicholas without careful planning aforethought. It had been ridiculously easy for Nicholas to overpower him. Which explained why Manning had tried to kill him with the blasted hole, rather than in a face-to-face confrontation.

Too bad he'd nearly killed the wrong brother. Several times.

For an assassin, he was rather careless, she thought.

"What *were* you doing out here, Miss Bursnell?" Nicholas asked. "You oughtn't to walk alone, you know."

"Yes, I know, but—" Again she tried to step from Nathaniel's arms, and again he would not let her budge. She sighed, and looked up at him. "Please, Nathaniel. You may let go now."

He made a low, unhappy sound in his throat, but did as she asked.

She felt Nicholas's watchful, alert gaze on her as she lifted her skirts to step over Manning's prostrate form.

"Nicholas, I—" She glanced up. "Oh, dear. May I call you that?"

He tilted his head and glanced between her and Nathaniel. "Of course. Under the circumstances, formality would be a bit absurd."

She paused, uncertain exactly what he meant by that, but continued frankly, "I do not like you, Nicholas. Your behavior toward my sister was abhorrent, and I can only suppose there were other ladies you treated just as shamefully. But Nathaniel loves you, and—" She broke off and cleared her throat, deciding to hold off on that train of thought. "In spite of everything, I find...I find I no longer wish you harm, Mr. Eastwood. In fact, I wish you happiness."

He studied her. "You really mean that."

She was somewhat astonished to find that she did. "Yes."

For a moment, his face was filled with such emotion that she blinked in surprise. And then it was gone.

"Call me Nick," he said. He turned back to Manning and nudged him with his toe. When there was no response, he smiled. "Take her home, Nate. I'll deal with Manning."

Alice wondered how, exactly, he would do so. But it was better not to ask.

"You'll come later, then?" Nathaniel asked, and she heard the thread of hope in the question.

Nicholas must have heard it, too, for there was affection in his voice when he said, "Soon."

Nathaniel nodded. He put his hand to her waist, guiding her past Manning's body. She glanced up at him, and the agony of the past week closed in on her once again. Would he go back to ignoring her?

No. Not if she could help it.

She thought about the advice Duke Wessex had given her earlier. And straightened her spine.

Time to gather up every last ounce of courage.

And do what should have been done days ago.

Chapter Sixty-Three

Nathaniel watched his brother stride away with mixed feelings. He wanted to call him back and insist he return with them to Haverly at once, to fulfill their father's dearest wish without delay.

But Nathaniel had his own dearest wish to deal with.

And unfinished business with Alice.

He turned to her, and instantly his mind surged back to that distressing conversation he'd overheard earlier between Wessex and Colonel Kent in the garden.

He needed to set Alice straight. The notion that she should even *consider* marrying another man was completely unacceptable.

He felt a soft touch on his arm. She was there, smiling up at him.

She looked happy, he thought bleakly. She looked like a woman in love.

His heart sank to his feet, reminding him of the huge gaping hole that overheard conversation had left in his chest.

She probably shouldn't be out here with him,

uncháperoned, as another man's betrothed, but since he had no intention of allowing any such marriage to take place, that fact rested lightly on his conscience.

"Shall we walk?" she asked. Her voice trembled slightly. No doubt she was still upset over nearly being kidnapped and murdered.

He held out his arm. She took it and led him, surprisingly, not toward the house at Haverly but across a field toward the lake. Their lake, as he had come to think of it.

For several minutes, he struggled with what to say. How to convince her to pick him. How to beg for another chance after he'd been such an idiot.

But in the end, he just blurted out, "You cannot marry Colonel Kent if you're carrying my child," and was mildly relieved the words came out firm rather than desperate.

She turned to him with wide eyes. "What an odd thing to say."

He opened his mouth to respond, to tell her that, no, it was *not* odd to claim one's child as one's own, and furthermore, she could *not* marry Kent, baby or no baby—although, Nathaniel fully intended there to be a baby. As soon as possible.

But just then, she halted and looked about. They had almost reached the lake.

"Yes, right here," she said, more to herself than him. "This is the place."

He looked at the daffodils bobbing their golden heads at his boots, and recognition flooded him.

Ah, yes.

"The place where I tripped over my own feet," he murmured, chagrined that she would pick this particular spot to remind him of his failings as compared with the estimable colonel.

"No. The place where I fell in love with you."

He froze. And stared at her in astonishment.

And joy.

Had he heard correctly?

"You…what?"

His heart magically reappeared in its rightful spot and immediately began beating as fast as humanly possible to make up for lost time.

She pointed to the far side of the lake. "Over there is where I saw you. I did not realize it was you at first, only that there was a half-naked man running madly around the lake. I should have left immediately. It was terribly improper of me to stay, but I couldn't help myself." She gave him a shy little smile. "You were magnificent."

Happiness broke over him like a wave. *She thought he was magnificent?*

"But that wasn't love," she continued. "It was merely lust. Much as was our first kiss."

"Well, I—" His throat closed.

"I have given it a great deal of thought, trying to pinpoint the exact moment I fell in love with you, Nathaniel Eastwood," she said.

"Did you?" he said rather breathlessly. It was all he could manage. He removed his jacket and dropped it to the ground. It was absurdly hot for April.

"Oh, yes. And what I determined was, it wasn't a single moment. Rather, it was a series of moments, starting right here when you sat down next to me, and I realized how happy I was to talk to you."

He removed his cravat. It was choking him. That must be why he couldn't speak more than two syllables at a time.

"It was when I knew I would get you out of that ridiculous hole or die trying. It was when you asked me to marry you and I couldn't say yes, but, oh, how I wanted to! It was when you challenged Nicholas to a duel." She frowned suddenly. "Although, you must never do that again. Never. My nerves couldn't stand it."

God, she was so adorable with her brow puckered up in concern. He removed her bonnet and unbuttoned her pelisse. She distractedly allowed him to slip it from her shoulders. It joined his jacket and cravat on the ground.

"I want more of those moments," she said. "I want to hear all your stories, and tell you all mine. I want to laugh with you and dance with you and…and kiss you. I want to spend the rest of my life falling in love with you over and over again. I want— What are you doing?"

He flicked open the last two buttons on his shirt. "Undressing."

"You can't. We're out of doors! Someone could see." But her eyes were drifting down his chest. She licked her lips.

He put his arms around her and pressed kisses to her collarbone. "Lie with me."

"Nathaniel, pay attention! I am asking you to marry me!"

He smiled against her neck. "Does that mean you are not going to marry Colonel Kent? I heard there was a special license."

She leaned back and looked at him incredulously. "Colonel Kent? Oh, do be serious. The license is for *us*."

Thank God. Sometimes being wrong was the best feeling in the world.

He pulled her back against him. "I'm very serious. Lie with me."

"I— I…"

He could feel the moment she surrendered. She melted against him, and he guided her gently down to her pelisse.

"Alice." His hands dove under her dress, pushing down her undergarments. He found her soft curls and sifted them between his fingers. "Look at me, sweetheart."

She gazed up at him. He watched her eyelids slowly grow hooded while he played with her. When she was wet and swollen, he freed himself and settled between her legs.

"I love you." He held her gaze with his. "Love me."

"I do," she whispered.

He surged into her. She cried out, arching her hips to meet him.

Long moments later, after they had both floated back to earth, he tried to roll off of her, but his strength deserted him. He shifted his weight so he wasn't crushing her and buried his face in her throat. She lazily traced the muscles on his shoulder with her fingertips.

"Nathaniel," she said. "You didn't answer my question."

"Hmm?" he muttered. He was so pleasantly sleepy.

Her nails sank into his shoulder, making him yelp.

Then he remembered.

He smiled.

"God, yes, I'll marry you." He nipped her lightly on her bottom lip. "I thought you would never ask."

Chapter Sixty-Four

"What do you suppose Nicholas did with Manning?" Alice asked Nathaniel later that evening.

"I truly do not care," he said.

He had not let her out of his sight since they'd made love by the lake…and sweetly promised each other to spend their lives together.

After dinner, he had insisted she keep him company in his study while he attended to a few pressing matters. Which was slightly ridiculous, since the danger to both of them was now over…not to mention she was growing dreadfully bored.

"I would like to go now," she said. "I'm sure Eliza is looking for me."

"No."

"But—"

"No, Alice."

Petulant, she sat on his desk, swinging her legs and trying her best to distract him from his work.

"What are you doing now?" she asked a few minutes later, peering over his arm.

"I am writing to your father. It is hard to convey the proper urgency of the matter. I cannot just say, *I must marry your daughter at once to keep her in my bed*." He paused. "Can I?"

She chuckled despite herself. "Probably not the best approach."

Not that her father would need convincing. Nathaniel was in line for an earldom, after all. Alice's prospects couldn't get better than that. Her mother would be over the moon. And Adelaide—

Alice was filled with a newfound peace when she thought about her dear sister. She still missed her terribly, but her pain was slowly turning to acceptance and forgiveness…and hope. When Alice had planned her revenge a year ago, she could never have guessed that it would lead to her life's greatest happiness.

Somehow, she was certain Adelaide was looking down at her from heaven, and smiling.

She leaned up and kissed her beloved's jaw. "You will think of something, I'm sure."

He pursed his lips as he pored over the letter. "I really should present myself in person and ask your father properly."

Good lord. "I believe the special license is only good for a few days," she hastened to say. She had no idea if that was true or not, but she liked the idea of a delay even less than Nathaniel did. She gave him a sly glance. "I suppose that won't matter, though, since my mother will no doubt insist we have a proper engagement. Six months, at least."

He glanced at her. "No."

"Why not?" She gave an exaggerated shrug. "I daresay you'll survive that long without me in your bed."

His chair scraped back, and two strong arms wrapped around her in a vise. "*No*, Alice."

She struggled to free herself, stifling a giggle. He was so easy. "Why *no*? Why do you never say *yes*?"

"I say yes to a great many things. When you say *more tea*, for example. Or *kiss me*. Or, my particular favorite, *please*. To all those things, I say yes. But a long engagement? To that, I say absolutely not."

She smiled. "More tea?" she asked pleasantly.

"Always." He freed her arms, and she refilled his cup, adding milk.

"Kiss me?"

"With pleasure." He leaned in, kissing her sweetly.

"Please?" she whispered.

He stood up, strode to the door, and locked it.

"Someone will discover us," she said, but opened her arms to him.

"No, they won't. I'm in my study, tending to estate business. You are likely taking an evening stroll. Miss Benton is with you."

Alice laughed. His arms went around her, and he nibbled along her jaw to her earlobe.

"We will marry in three days' time, and that's the end of it. Agreed?"

"Yes," she murmured.

"Yes, what?"

"Yes, thank you." She wound her arms around her lover's neck.

"I like 'please' better."

"Please, my love," she whispered.

"God, yes. Always."

She felt it again, then, deep in her chest. It always happened that way when she was with him—that feeling of expanding to fullness. Just when she thought she had reached the end of it, that she couldn't possibly love him any more than she already did, she found she could. Her heart could stretch and grow. Just a little bit. And then a little bit more.

And it would continue to grow and fill with her love for him, and for their children, and for the happiness she would find with him.

For the rest of their lives.

Acknowledgments

It's a strange and wonderful thing to watch a story become a book. I am so grateful to my editor, Nina Bruhns, and the rest of the talented Entangled team for making it possible.

Friendship is an important part of this story, and I am happy to say I have real-life inspiration to draw from. Elizabeth—thank you for giving me the adventure of a cross-country road trip. Lauren—you were my running partner when my life went to hell, and I'll always be grateful. Lori—thank you for making Seneca Rocks happen. Nicole—when this book comes out, I'll be standing at the top of Half Dome, and you put me there. Also, I owe you a blacksmith. It will happen, someday, I promise.

About the Author

Debut author Elizabeth Bright is a writer, attorney, and mother. After spending ten years in New Orleans (yes, she survived Hurricane Katrina), she relocated to Washington, D.C. to be closer to family. When she's not writing, arguing, or mothering, she can be found hiking in the Shenandoah or rock climbing at Great Falls.

Get Scandalous with these historical reads...

THE ROGUE'S CONQUEST
a *Townsends* novel by Lily Maxton

Former prizefighter James MacGregor wants to be a gentleman, like the men he trains in his boxing saloon. A chance encounter with Eleanor Townsend gives him the leverage he needs. She'll gain him entry to high society and help him with his atrocious manners, and in return, he won't reveal her secret. It's the perfect arrangement. At least until the sparks between them become more than just their personalities clashing.

THE WOLF OF KISIMUL CASTLE
a *Highland Isles* novel by Heather McCollum

Mairi Maclean is kidnapped on her wedding day. Taken north to Kisimul Castle, she is held captive. Alec MacNeil, The Wolf of Kisimul Castle, soon learns Mairi is not a docile pawn in this game of war between neighboring Scots. When he finds his enemy dead, he takes his wife to replace the one that was murdered. But Mairi refuses to bend to his will, and the passion that flares between them threatens to tear Alec's strategy apart.

THE GENTLEMAN'S PROMISE
a *Daughters of Amhurst* novel by Frances Fowlkes

A social pariah, Lady Sarah Beauchamp yearns for redemption to marry. The assistance of Mr. Jonathon Annesley gives her hope of success. Offering a gentleman's promise to help his sister's friend regain the favor of the *ton* should be easy. After all, he's well liked and considered a rising star in Parliament. Until he learns Sarah's ultimate goal is a husband. She is not for him—his focus rests on gaining political reforms. Yet, a promise made cannot be broken...

LADY OF INTRIGUE
by Sabrina Darby

Lady Jane Langley's reason and logic gives way to terrible, icy fear when she finds herself in a devastating carriage accident where her companion is murdered. But this was no mere accident. This was an assassination. Spy Gerard Badeau takes Jane hostage. But if he doesn't kill her, he risks a fate that is far, far worse...falling in love with her.

Made in the USA
Coppell, TX
22 November 2022